THE WINGS OF THE DOVE

THE WINGS OF
THE DOVE

BY

HENRY JAMES

IN TWO VOLUMES
VOL I

УДК 82-31
ББК 84(4Cое)6-44

H. James

The Wings Of The Dove / Henry James. – M.: T8RUGRAM, 2017. – 292 стр.

ISBN 978-5-519-50510-9

«Крылья голубки» — знаменитый роман американского писателя Генри Джеймса. Представительница некогда знатного рода, Кейт, влюблена в простого журналиста Мёртона, но традиции и устои XIX века запрещают подобные альянсы: аристократка и бедный писака — плохая пара с любой точки зрения. Но заметив интерес своей богатой подруги к Мёртону, у Кейт возникает план… Однако любовный треугольник существует только по своим собственным законам.
     Читайте зарубежную литературу в оригинале!

УДК 82-31
ББК 84(4Cое)6-44
BIC FC
BISAC FIC004000

ISBN 978-5-519-50510-9

PREFACE

The Wings of the Dove, published in 1902, represents
to my memory a very old—if I shouldn't perhaps
rather say a very young—motive ; I can scarce
remember the time when the situation on which this
long-drawn fiction mainly rests was not vividly
present to me. The idea, reduced to its essence, is
that of a young person conscious of a great capacity
for life, but early stricken and doomed, condemned
to die under short respite, while also enamoured of
the world ; aware moreover of the condemnation and
passionately desiring to " put in " before extinction
as many of the finer vibrations as possible, and so
achieve, however briefly and brokenly, the sense of
having lived. Long had I turned it over, standing
off from it, yet coming back to it ; convinced of what
might be done with it, yet seeing the theme as for-
midable. The image so figured would be, at best, but
half the matter ; the rest would be all the picture of
the struggle involved, the adventure brought about,
the gain recorded or the loss incurred, the precious
experience somehow compassed. These things, I had
from the first felt, would require much working-out ;
that indeed was the case with most things worth
working at all ; yet there are subjects and subjects,
and this one seemed particularly to bristle. It was
formed, I judged, to make the wary adventurer walk
round and round it—it had in fact a charm that

invited and mystified alike that attention ; not being somehow what one thought of as a " frank " subject, after the fashion of some, with its elements well in view and its whole character in its face. It stood there with secrets and compartments, with possible treacheries and traps ; it might have a great deal to give, but would probably ask for equal services in return, and would collect this debt to the last shilling. It involved, to begin with, the placing in the strongest light a person infirm and ill—a case sure to prove difficult and to require much handling ; though giving perhaps, with other matters, one of those chances for good taste, possibly even for the play of the very best in the world, that are not only always to be invoked and cultivated, but that are absolutely to be jumped at from the moment they make a sign.

Yes then, the case prescribed for its central figure a sick young woman, at the whole course of whose disintegration and the whole ordeal of whose consciousness one would have quite honestly to assist. The expression of her state and that of one's intimate relation to it might therefore well need to be discreet and ingenious ; a reflexion that fortunately grew and grew, however, in proportion as I focussed my image —roundabout which, as it persisted, I repeat, the interesting possibilities and the attaching wonderments, not to say the insoluble mysteries, thickened apace. Why had one to look so straight in the face and so closely to cross-question that idea of making one's protagonist " sick " ?—as if to be menaced with death or danger hadn't been from time immemorial, for heroine or hero, the very shortest of all cuts to the interesting state. Why should a figure be disqualified for a central position by the particular circumstance that might most quicken, that might crown with a fine intensity, its liability to many accidents, its consciousness of all relations ? This circumstance, true

enough, might disqualify it for many activities—
even though we should have imputed to it the unsur-
passable activity of passionate, of inspired resistance.
This last fact was the real issue, for the way grew
straight from the moment one recognised that the
poet essentially *can't* be concerned with the act of
dying. Let him deal with the sickest of the sick, it is
still by the act of living that they appeal to him, and
appeal the more as the conditions plot against them
and prescribe the battle. The process of life gives
way fighting, and often may so shine out on the lost
ground as in no other connexion. One had had
moreover, as a various chronicler, one's secondary
physical weaklings and failures, one's accessory
invalids—introduced with a complacency that made
light of criticism. To Ralph Touchett in *The Portrait
of a Lady*, for instance, his deplorable state of health
was not only no drawback ; I had clearly been right
in counting it, for any happy effect he should produce,
a positive good mark, a direct aid to pleasantness and
vividness. The reason of this moreover could never
in the world have been his fact of sex ; since men,
among the mortally afflicted, suffer on the whole more
overtly and more grossly than women, and resist with
a ruder, an inferior strategy. I had thus to take
that anomaly for what it was worth, and I give it here
but as one of the ambiguities amid which my subject
ended by making itself at home and seating itself
quite in confidence.

With the clearness I have just noted, accordingly,
the last thing in the world it proposed to itself was
to be the record predominantly of a collapse. I don't
mean to say that my offered victim was not present
to my imagination, constantly, as dragged by a greater
force than any she herself could exert ; she had been
given me from far back as contesting every inch of
the road, as catching at every object the grasp of

which might make for delay, as clutching these things to the last moment of her strength. Such an attitude and such movements, the passion they expressed and the success they in fact represented, what were they in truth but the soul of drama?—which is the portrayal, as we know, of a catastrophe determined in spite of oppositions. My young woman would *herself* be the opposition—to the catastrophe announced by the associated Fates, powers conspiring to a sinister end and, with their command of means, finally achieving it, yet in such straits really to *stifle* the sacred spark that, obviously, a creature so animated, an adversary so subtle, couldn't but be felt worthy, under whatever weaknesses, of the foreground and the limelight. She would meanwhile wish, moreover, all along, to live for particular things, she would found her struggle on particular human interests, which would inevitably determine, in respect to her, the attitude of other persons, persons affected in such a manner as to make them part of the action. If her impulse to wrest from her shrinking hour still as much of the fruit of life as possible, if this longing can take effect only by the aid of others, their participation (appealed to, entangled and coerced as they find themselves) becomes their drama too—that of their promoting her illusion, under her importunity, for reasons, for interests and advantages, from motives and points of view, of their own. Some of these promptings, evidently, would be of the highest order—others doubtless mightn't; but they would make up together, for her, contributively, her sum of experience, represent to her somehow, in good faith or in bad, what she should have *known*. Somehow, too, at such a rate, one would see the persons subject to them drawn in as by some pool of a Lorelei—see them terrified and tempted and charmed; bribed away, it may even be, from more prescribed and natural orbits, inheriting from their connexion with her strange difficulties and still stranger opportunities, confronted with rare questions and called upon for new discriminations. Thus the scheme of her situation would, in a comprehensive way, see itself constituted ; the rest of the interest would be in the number and nature of the particulars. Strong among these, naturally, the need that life should, apart from her infirmity, present itself to our young woman as quite dazzlingly liveable, and that if the great pang for her is in what she must give up we shall appreciate it the more from the sight of all she has.

One would see her then as possessed of all things, all but the single most precious assurance ; freedom and money and a mobile mind and personal charm, the power to interest and attach ; attributes, each one, enhancing the value of a future. From the moment his imagination began to deal with her at close quarters, in fact, nothing could more engage her designer than to work out the detail of her perfect rightness for her part ; nothing above all more solicit him than to recognise fifty reasons for her national and social status. She should be the last fine flower—blooming alone, for the fullest attestation of her freedom—of an " old " New York stem ; the happy congruities thus preserved for her being matters, however, that I may not now go into, and this even though the fine association that shall yet elsewhere await me is of a sort, at the best, rather to defy than to encourage exact expression. There goes with it, for the heroine of *The Wings of the Dove*, a strong and special implication of liberty, liberty of action, of choice, of appreciation, of contact—proceeding from sources that provide better for large independence, I think, than any other conditions in the world—and this would be in particular what we should feel ourselves deeply concerned with. I had from far back mentally projected a certain sort of young American as more the " heir of all the ages " than any other young person whatever (and precisely on those grounds I have just glanced at but to pass them by for the moment) ; so that here was a chance to confer on some such figure a supremely touching value. To be the heir of all the ages only to know yourself, as that consciousness should deepen, balked of your' inheritance, would be to play the part, it struck me, or at least to arrive at the type, in the light on the whole the most becoming. Otherwise, truly, what a perilous part to play *out*—what a suspicion of " swagger " in positively attempting it ! So at least I could reason—so I even think I *had* to—to keep my subject to a decent compactness. For already, from an early stage, it had begun richly to people itself : the difficulty was to see whom the situation I had primarily projected might, by this, that or the other turn, *not* draw in. My business was to watch its turns as the fond parent watches a child perched, for its first riding-lesson, in the saddle ; yet its interest, I had all the while to recall, was just in its making, on such a scale, for developments.

What one had discerned, at all events, from an early stage, was that a young person so devoted and exposed, a creature with her security hanging so by a hair, couldn't but fall somehow into some abysmal trap—this being, dramatically speaking, what such a situation most naturally implied and imposed. Didn't the truth and a great part of the interest also reside in the appearance that she would constitute for others (given her passionate yearning to live while she might) a complication as great as any they might constitute for herself ?—which is what I mean when I speak of such matters as " natural." They would be as natural, these tragic, pathetic, ironic, these indeed for the most part sinister, liabilities, to her

living associates, as they could be to herself as prime
subject. If her story was to consist, as it could so
little help doing, of her being let in, as we say, for
this, that and the other irreducible anxiety, how
could she not have put a premium on the acquisition,
by any close sharer of her life, of a consciousness
similarly embarrassed ? I have named the Rhine-
maiden, but our young friend's existence would
create rather, all round her, very much that whirlpool
movement of the waters produced by the sinking of
a big vessel or the failure of a great business ; when
we figure to ourselves the strong narrowing eddies,
the immense force of suction, the general engulfment
that, for any neighbouring object, makes immersion
inevitable. I need scarce say, however, that in spite
of these communities of doom I saw the main dramatic
complication much more prepared *for* my vessel of
sensibility than by her—the work of other hands
(though with her own imbrued too, after all, in the
measure of their never not being, in some direction,
generous and extravagant, and thereby provoking).

The great point was, at all events, that if in a predicament she was to be, accordingly, it would be of
the essence to create the predicament promptly and
build it up solidly, so that it should have for us as
much as possible its ominous air of awaiting her.
That reflexion I found, betimes, not less inspiring than
urgent ; one begins so, in such a business, by looking
about for one's compositional key, unable as one can
only be to move till one has found it. To start
without it is to pretend to enter the train and, still
more, to remain in one's seat, without a ticket. Well
—in the steady light and for the continued charm of
these verifications—I had secured my ticket over the
tolerably long line laid down for *The Wings of the
Dove* from the moment I had noted that there could
be no full presentation of Milly Theale as *engaged*

I   xi   b

with elements amid which she was to draw her breath in such pain, should not the elements have been, with all solicitude, duly prefigured. If one had seen that her stricken state was but half her case, the correlative half being the state of others as affected by her (they too should have a " case," bless them, quite as much as she !) then I was free to choose, as it were, the half with which I should begin. If, as I had fondly noted, the little world determined for her was to " bristle "—I delighted in the term !—with meanings, so, by the same token, could I but make my medal hang free, its obverse and its reverse, its face and its back, would beautifully become optional for the spectator. I somehow wanted them correspondingly embossed, wanted them inscribed and figured with an equal salience ; yet it was none the less visibly my " key," as I have said, that though my regenerate young New Yorker, and what might depend on her, should form my centre, my circumference was every whit as treatable. Therefore I must trust myself to know when to proceed from the one and when from the other. Preparatively and, as it were, yearningly—given the whole ground—one began, in the event, with the outer ring, approaching the centre thus by narrowing circumvallations. There, full-blown, accordingly, from one hour to the other, rose one's process—for which there remained all the while so many amusing formulae. •

The medal *did* hang free—I felt this perfectly, I remember, from the moment I had comfortably laid the ground provided in my first Book, ground from which Milly is superficially so absent. I scarce remember perhaps a case—I like even with this public grossness to insist on it—in which the curiosity of " beginning far back," as far back as possible, and even of going, to the same tune, far " behind," that is behind the face of the subject, was to assert itself with less scruple. The free hand, in this connexion, was above all agreeable—the hand the freedom of which I owed to the fact that the work had ignominiously failed, in advance, of all power to see itself "serialised." This failure had repeatedly waited, for me, upon shorter fictions ; but the considerable production we here discuss was (as *The Golden Bowl* was to be, two or three years later) born, not otherwise than a little bewilderedly, into a world of periodicals and editors, of roaring "successes" in fine, amid which it was wellnigh unnotedly to lose itself. There is fortunately something bracing, ever, in the alpine chill, that of some high icy *arête*, shed by the cold editorial shoulder ; sour grapes may at moments fairly intoxicate and the story-teller worth his salt rejoice to feel again how many accommodations he can practise. Those addressed to "conditions of publication" have in a degree their interesting, or at least their provoking, side ; but their charm is qualified by the fact that the prescriptions here spring from a soil often wholly alien to the ground of the work itself. They are almost always the fruit of another air altogether and conceived in a light liable to represent *within* the circle of the work itself little else than darkness. Still, when not too blighting, they often operate as a tax on ingenuity—that ingenuity of the expert craftsman which likes to be taxed very much to the same tune to which a well-bred horse likes to be saddled. The best and finest ingenuities, nevertheless, with all respect to that truth, are apt to be, not one's compromises, but one's fullest conformities, and I well remember, in the case before us, the pleasure of feeling my divisions, my proportions and general rhythm, rest all on permanent rather than in any degree on momentary proprieties. It was enough for my alternations, thus, that they were good in themselves ; it was in fact so much for them

that I really think any further account of the con-
stitution of the book reduces itself to a just notation
of the law they followed.

There was the " fun," to begin with, of establishing
one's successive centres—of fixing them so exactly
that the portions of the subject commanded by them
as by happy points of view, and accordingly treated
from them, would constitute, so to speak, sufficiently
solid *blocks* of wrought material, squared to the sharp
edge, as to have weight and mass and carrying power ;
to make for construction, that is, to conduce to effect
and to provide for beauty. Such a block, obviously,
is the whole preliminary presentation of Kate Croy,
which, from the first, I recall, absolutely declined to
enact itself save in terms of amplitude. Terms of
amplitude, terms of atmosphere, those terms, and
those terms only, in which images assert their fullness
and roundness, their power to revolve, so that they
have sides and backs, parts in the shade as true as
parts in the sun—these were plainly to be my conditions, right and left, and I was so far from overrating
the amount of expression the whole thing, as I saw
and felt it, would require, that to retrace the way at
present is, alas, more than anything else, but to mark
the gaps and the lapses, to miss, one by one, the
intentions that, with the best will in the world, were
not to fructify. I have just said that the process of
the general attempt is described from the moment
the " blocks " are numbered, and that would be a
true enough picture of my plan. Yet one's plan, alas,
is one thing and one's result another ; so that I am
perhaps nearer the point in saying that this last
strikes me at present as most characterised by the
happy features that *were*, under my first and most
blest illusion, to have contributed to it. I meet them
all, as I renew acquaintance, I mourn for them all as
I remount the stream, the absent values, the palpable

voids, the missing links, the mocking shadows, that reflect, taken together, the early bloom of one's good faith. Such cases are of course far from abnormal—so far from it that some acute mind ought surely to have worked out by this time the "law" of the degree in which the artist's energy fairly depends on his fallibility. How much and how often, and in what connexions and with what almost infinite variety, must he be a dupe, that of his prime object, to be at all measurably a master, that of his actual substitute for it—or in other words at all appreciably to exist ? He places, after an earnest survey, the piers of his bridge—he has at least sounded deep enough, heaven knows, for their brave position ; yet the bridge spans the stream, after the fact, in apparently complete independence of these properties, the principal grace of the original design. *They* were an illusion, for their necessary hour ; but the span itself, whether of a single arch or of many, seems by the oddest chance in the world to be a reality ; since, actually, the rueful builder, passing under it, sees figures and hears sounds above : he makes out, with his heart in his throat, that it bears and is positively being " used."

The building-up of Kate Croy's consciousness to the capacity for the load little by little to be laid on it was, by way of example, to have been a matter of as many hundred close-packed bricks as there are actually poor dozens. The image of her so compromised and compromising father was all effectively to have pervaded her life, was in a certain particular way to have tampered with her spring ; by which I mean that the shame and the irritation and the depression, the general poisonous influence of him, were to have been *shown*, with a truth beyond the compass even of one's most emphasised " word of honour " for it, to do these things. But where do we find him, at this time of day, save in a beggarly scene or two which scarce arrives at the dignity of functional reference ? He but " looks in," poor beautiful dazzling, damning apparition that he was to have been ; he sees his place so taken, his company so little missed, that, cocking again that fine form of hat which has yielded him for so long his one effective cover, he turns away with a whistle of indifference that nobly misrepresents the deepest disappointment of his life. One's poor word of honour has *had* to pass muster for the show. Every one, in short, was to have enjoyed so much better a chance that, like stars of the theatre condescending to oblige, they have had to take small parts, to content themselves with minor identities, in order to come on at all. I haven't the heart now, I confess, to adduce the detail of so many lapsed importances ; the explanation of most of which, after all, I take to have been in the crudity of a truth beating full upon me through these recon- siderations, the odd inveteracy with which picture, at almost any turn, is jealous of drama, and drama (though on the whole with a greater patience, I think) suspicious of picture. Between them, no doubt, they do much for the theme ; yet each baffles insidiously the other's ideal and eats round the edges of its position ; 'each is too ready to say " I can take the thing for ' done ' only when done in *my* way." The residuum of comfort for the witness of these broils is of course meanwhile in the convenient reflexion, invented for him in the twilight of time and the infancy of art by the Angel, not to say by the Demon, of Compromise, that nothing is so easy to " do " as not to be thankful for almost any stray help in its getting done. It wasn't, after this fashion, by making good one's dream of Lionel Croy that my structure was to stand on its feet—any more than it was by letting him go that I was to be left irretrievably lamenting. The who and the what, the how and the why, the whence and the whither of Merton Densher, these, no less, were quantities and attributes that should have danced about him with the antique grace of nymphs and fauns circling round a bland Hermes and crowning him with flowers. One's main anxiety, for each one's agents, is that the air of each shall be *given* ; but what does the whole thing become, after all, as one goes, but a series of sad places at which the hand of generosity has been cautioned and stayed ? The young man's situation, personal, professional, social, was to have been so decanted for us that we should get all the taste ; we were to have been penetrated with Mrs. Lowder, by the same token, saturated with her presence, her "personality," and felt all her weight in the scale. We were to have revelled in Mrs. Stringham, my heroine's attendant friend, her fairly choral Bostonian, a subject for innumerable touches, and in an extended and above all an *animated* reflexion of Milly Theale's experience of English society ; just as the strength and sense of the situation in Venice, for our gathered friends, was to have come to us in a deeper draught out of a larger cup, and just as the pattern of Densher's final position and fullest consciousness there was to have been marked in fine stitches, all silk and gold, all pink and silver, that have had to remain, alas, but entwined upon the reel.

It isn't, no doubt, however—to recover, after all, our critical balance—that the pattern didn't, for each compartment, get itself somehow wrought, and that we mightn't thus, piece by piece, opportunity offering, trace it over and study it. The thing has doubtless, as a whole, the advantage that each piece is true to its pattern, and that while it pretends to make no simple statement it yet never lets go its scheme of clearness. Applications of this scheme are continuous and exemplary enough, though I scarce leave myself room to glance at them. The clearness is obtained in Book

PREFACE

First—or otherwise, as I have said, in the first " piece,"
each Book having its subordinate and contributive
pattern—through the associated consciousness of my
two prime young persons, for whom I early recognised
that I should have to consent, under stress, to a
practical *fusion* of consciousness. It is into the young
woman's " ken " that Merton Densher is represented
as swimming ; but her mind is not here, rigorously,
the one reflector. There are occasions when it plays
this part, just as there are others when his plays it,
and an intelligible plan consists naturally not a little
in fixing such occasions and making them, on one
side and the other, sufficient to themselves. Do I
sometimes in fact forfeit the advantage of that distinctness ? Do I ever abandon one centre for another
after the former has been postulated ? From the
moment we proceed by " centres "—and I have never,
I confess, embraced the logic of any superior process
—they must *be*, each, as a basis, selected and fixed ;
after which it is that, in the high interest of economy
of treatment, they determine and rule. There is no
economy of treatment without an adopted, a related
point of view, and though I understand, under certain
degrees of pressure, a represented community of
vision between several parties to the action when it
makes for concentration, I understand no breaking-up
of the register, no sacrifice of the recording consistency, that doesn't rather scatter and weaken. In
this truth resides the secret of the discriminated
occasion—that aspect of the subject which we have
our noted choice of treating either as picture or
scenically, but which is apt, I think, to show its fullest
worth in the Scene. Beautiful exceedingly, for that
matter, those occasions or parts of an occasion when
the boundary line between picture and scene bears a
little the weight of the double pressure.

Such would be the case, I can't but surmise, for

xviii

the long passage that forms here before us the opening
of Book Fourth, where all the offered life centres, to
intensity, in the disclosure of Milly's single throbbing
consciousness, but where, for a due rendering, everything has to be brought to a head. This passage,
the view of her introduction to Mrs. Lowder's circle,
has its mate, for illustration, later on in the book and
at a crisis for which the occasion submits to another
rule. My registers or " reflectors," as I so conveniently name them (burnished indeed as they generally
are by the intelligence, the curiosity, the passion, the
force of the moment, whatever it be, directing them),
work, as we have seen, in arranged alternation ; so
that in the second connexion I here glance at it is
Kate Croy who is, " for all she is worth," turned on.
She is turned on largely at Venice, where the appearances, rich and obscure and portentous (another word
I rejoice in) as they have by that time become and
altogether exquisite as they remain, are treated almost
wholly through her vision of them and Densher's
(as to the lucid interplay of which conspiring and
conflicting agents there would be a great deal to say).
It is in Kate's consciousness that at the stage in
question the drama is brought to a head, and the
occasion on which, in the splendid saloon of poor
Milly's hired palace, she takes the measure of her
friend's festal evening, squares itself to the same
synthetic firmness as the compact constructional
block inserted by the scene at Lancaster Gate. Milly's
situation ceases at a given moment to be " render-
able " in terms closer than those supplied by Kate's
intelligence, or, in a richer degree, by Densher's, or,
for one fond hour, by poor Mrs. Stringham's (since
to that sole brief futility is this last participant,
crowned by my original plan with the quaintest
functions, in fact reduced) ; just as Kate's relation
with Densher and Densher's with Kate have ceased

previously, and are then to cease again, to be projected for us, so far as Milly is concerned with them,
on any more responsible plate than that of the latter's
admirable anxiety. It is as if, for these aspects, the
impersonal plate—in other words the poor author's
comparatively cold affirmation or thin guarantee—
had felt itself a figure of attestation at once too gross
and too bloodless, likely to affect us as an abuse of
privilege when not as an abuse of knowledge.

Heaven forbid, we say to ourselves during almost
the whole Venetian climax, heaven forbid we should
" know " anything more of our ravaged sister than
what Densher darkly pieces together, or than what
Kate Croy pays, heroically, it must be owned, at the
hour of her visit alone to Densher's lodging, for her
superior handling and her dire profanation of. For
we have time, while this passage lasts, to turn round
critically ; we have time to recognise intentions and
proprieties ; we have time to catch glimpses of an
economy of composition, as I put it, interesting in
itself : all in spite of the author's scarce more than
half-dissimulated despair at the inveterate displace-
ment of his general centre. *The Wings of the Dove*
happens to offer perhaps the most striking example
I may cite (though with public penance for it already
performed) of my regular failure to keep the appointed
halves of my whole equal. Here the makeshift
middle—for which the best I can say is that it's
always rueful and never impudent—reigns with even
more than its customary contrition, though passing
itself off perhaps too with more than its usual craft.
Nowhere, I seem to recall, had the need of dissimula-
tion been felt so as anguish ; nowhere had I condemned a luckless theme to complete its revolution,
burdened with the accumulation of its difficulties, the
difficulties that grow with a theme's development,
in quarters so cramped. Of course, as every novelist

knows, it is difficulty that inspires ; only, for that
perfection of charm, it must have been difficulty
inherent and congenital, and not difficulty " caught "
by the wrong frequentations. The latter half, that
is the false and deformed half, of *The Wings* would
verily, I think, form a signal object-lesson for a literary
critic bent on improving his occasion to the profit of
the budding artist. This whole corner of the picture
bristles with " dodges "—such as he should feel
himself all committed to recognise and denounce—
for disguising the reduced scale of the exhibition, for
foreshortening at any cost, for imparting to patches
the value of presences, for dressing objects in an *air*
as of the dimensions they can't possibly have. Thus
he would have his free hand for pointing out what a
tangled web we weave when—well, when, through
our mislaying or otherwise trifling with our blest pair
of compasses, we have to produce the illusion of mass
without the illusion of extent. *There* is a job quite
to the measure of most of our monitors—and with
the interest for them well enhanced by the preliminary
cunning quest for the spot where deformity has begun.

I recognise meanwhile, throughout the long earlier
reach of the book, not only no deformities but, I
think, a positively close and felicitous application of
method, the preserved consistencies of which, often
illusive, but never really lapsing, it would be of a
certain diversion, and might be of some profit, to
follow. The author's accepted task at the outset has
been to suggest with force the nature of the tie
formed between the two young persons first introduced—to give the full impression of its peculiar
worried and baffled, yet clinging and confident,
ardour. The picture constituted, so far as may be,
is that of a pair of natures wellnigh consumed by a
sense of their intimate affinity and congruity, the
reciprocity of their desire, and thus passionately

impatient of barriers and delays, yet with qualities of intelligence and character that they are meanwhile extraordinarily able to draw upon for the enrichment of their relation, the extension of their prospect and the support of their " game." They are far from a common couple, Merton Densher and Kate Croy, as befits the remarkable fashion in which fortune was to waylay and opportunity was to distinguish them —the whole strange truth of their response to which opening involves also, in its order, no vulgar art of exhibition ; but what they have most to tell us is that, all unconsciously and with the best faith in the world, all by mere force of the terms of their superior passion combined with their superior diplomacy, they are laying a trap for the great innocence to come. If I like, as I have confessed, the " portentous " look, I was perhaps never to set so high a value on it as for all this prompt provision of forces unwittingly waiting to close round my eager heroine (to the eventual deep chill of her eagerness) as the result of her mere lifting of a latch. Infinitely interesting to have built up the relation of the others to the point at which its aching restlessness, its need to affirm itself otherwise than by an exasperated patience, meets as with instinctive relief and recognition the possibilities shining out of Milly Theale. Infinitely interesting to have prepared and organised, correspondingly, that young woman's precipitations and liabilities, to have constructed, for Drama essentially to take possession, the whole bright house of her exposure.

These references, however, reflect too little of the detail of the treatment imposed ; such a detail as I for instance get hold of in the fact of Densher's interview with Mrs. Lowder before he goes to America. It forms, in this preliminary picture, the one patch not strictly seen over Kate Croy's shoulder ; though it's notable that immediately after, at the first

possible moment, we surrender again to our major
convenience, as it happens to be at the time, that of
our drawing breath through the young woman's lungs.
Once more, in other words, before we know it,
Densher's direct vision of the scene at Lancaster Gate
is replaced by her apprehension, her contributive
assimilation, of his experience : it melts back into
that accumulation, which we have been, as it were,
saving up. Does my apparent deviation here count
accordingly as a muddle ?—one of the muddles ever
blooming so thick in any soil that fails to grow
reasons and determinants. No, distinctly not ; for
I had definitely opened the door, as attention of
perusal of the first two Books will show, to the sub-
jective community of my young pair. (Attention of
perusal, I thus confess by the way, is what I at every
point, as well as here, absolutely invoke and take for
granted ; a truth I avail myself of this occasion to
note once for all—in the interest of that variety of
ideal reigning, I gather, in the connexion. The
enjoyment of a work of art, the acceptance of an
irresistible illusion, constituting, to my sense, our
highest experience of " luxury," the luxury is not
greatest, by my consequent measure, when the work
asks for as little attention as possible. It is greatest,
it is delightfully, divinely great, when we feel the
surface, like the thick ice of the skater's pond, bear
without cracking the strongest pressure we throw on
it. The sound of the crack one may recognise, but
never surely to call it a luxury) That I had scarce
availed myself of the privilege of seeing with Densher's
eyes is another matter ; the point is that I had
intelligently marked my possible, my occasional need
of it. So, at all events, the constructional " block "
of the first two Books compactly forms itself. A
new block, all of the squarest and not a little of the
smoothest, begins with the Third—by which I mean

of course a new mass of interest governed from a new centre. Here again I make prudent *provision*—to be sure to keep my centre strong. It dwells mainly, we at once see, in the depths of Milly Theale's " case," where, close beside it, however, we meet a supplementary reflector, that of the lucid even though so quivering spirit of her dedicated friend.

The more or less associated consciousness of the two women deals thus, unequally, with the next presented face of the subject—deals with it to the exclusion of the dealing of others ; and if, for a highly particular moment, I allot to Mrs. Stringham the responsibility of the direct appeal to us, it is again, charming to relate, on behalf of that play of the portentous which I cherish so as a " value " and am accordingly for ever setting in motion. There is an hour of evening, on the alpine height, at which it becomes of the last importance that our young woman should testify eminently in this direction. But as I was to find it long since of a blest wisdom that no expense should be incurred or met, in any corner of picture of mine, without some concrete image of the account kept of it, that is of its being organically re-economised, so under that dispensation Mrs. Stringham has to register the transaction. Book Fifth is a new block mainly in its provision of a new set of occasions, which readopt, for their order, the previous centre, Milly's now almost full-blown consciousness. At my game, with renewed zest, of driving portents home, I have by this time all the choice of those that are to brush that surface with a dark wing. They are used, to our profit, on an elastic but a definite system ; by which I mean that having to sound here and there a little deep, as a test, for my basis of method, I find it everywhere obstinately present. It draws the " occasion " into tune and keeps it so, to repeat my tiresome term ; my nearest approach to muddlement is to have sometimes—but not too often—to break my occasions small. Some of them succeed in remaining ample and in really aspiring then to the higher, the sustained lucidity. The whole actual centre of the work, resting on a misplaced pivot and lodged in Book Fifth, pretends to a long reach, or at any rate to the larger fore-shortening — though bringing home to me, on re-perusal, what I find striking, charming and curious, the author's instinct everywhere for the *indirect* presenta-tion of his main image. I note how, again and again, I go but a little way with the direct—that is with the straight exhibition of Milly ; it resorts for relief, this process, whenever it can, to some kinder, some merciful indirection : all as if to approach her circuit-ously, deal with her at second hand, as an unspotted princess is ever dealt with ; the pressure all round her kept easy for her, the sounds, the movements regulated, the forms and ambiguities made charming. All of which proceeds, obviously, from her painter's tenderness of imagination about her, which reduces him to watching her, as it were, through the successive windows of other people's interest in her. So, if we talk of princesses, do the balconies opposite the palace gates, do the coigns of vantage and respect enjoyed for a fee, rake from afar the mystic figure in the gilded coach as it comes forth into the great *place*. But my use of windows and balconies is doubtless at best an extravagance by itself, and as to what there may be to note, of this and other supersubtleties, other arch-refinements, of tact and taste, of design and instinct, in *The Wings of the Dove*, I become conscious of overstepping my space without having brought the full quantity to light. The failure leaves me with a burden of residuary comment of which I yet boldly hope elsewhere to discharge myself.

HENRY JAMES.

BOOK FIRST

I

SHE waited, Kate Croy, for her father to come in, but he kept her unconscionably, and there were moments at which she showed herself, in the glass over the mantel, a face positively pale with the irritation that had brought her to the point of going away without sight of him. It was at this point, however, that she remained ; changing her place, moving from the shabby sofa to the armchair upholstered in a glazed cloth that gave at once—she had tried it—the sense of the slippery and of the sticky. She had looked at the sallow prints on the walls and at the lonely magazine, a year old, that combined, with a small lamp in coloured glass and a knitted white centre-piece wanting in freshness, to enhance the effect of the purplish cloth on the principal table ; she had above all from time to time taken a brief stand on the small balcony to which the pair of long windows gave access. The vulgar little street, in this view, offered scant relief from the vulgar little room ; its main office was to suggest to her that the narrow black house-fronts, adjusted to a standard that would have been low even for backs, constituted quite the publicity implied by such privacies. One felt them in the room exactly as one felt the room—the hundred like it or worse—in the street. Each time she turned in again, each time, in her impatience, she gave him up, it was to sound to a deeper depth, while she tasted the

3

faint flat emanation of things, the failure of fortune and of honour. If she continued to wait it was really in a manner that she mightn't add the shame of fear, of individual, of personal collapse, to all the other shames. To feel the street, to feel the room, to feel the table-cloth and the centre-piece and the lamp, gave her a small salutary sense at least of neither shirking nor lying. This whole vision was the worst thing yet—as including in particular the interview to which she had braced herself ; and for what had she come but for the worst ? She tried to be sad so as not to be angry, but it made her angry that she couldn't be sad. And yet where was misery, misery too beaten for blame and chalk-marked by fate like a " lot " at a common auction, if not in these merciless signs of mere mean stale feelings ?

Her father's life, her sister's, her own, that of her two lost brothers—the whole history of their house had the effect of some fine florid voluminous phrase, say even a musical, that dropped first into words and notes without sense and then, hanging unfinished, into no words nor any notes at all, Why should a set of people have been put in motion, on such a scale and with such an air of being equipped for a profitable journey, only to break down without an accident, to stretch themselves in the wayside dust without a reason ? The answer to these questions was not in Chirk Street, but the questions themselves bristled there, and the girl's repeated pause before the mirror and the chimney-place might have represented her nearest approach to an escape from them. Wasn't it in fact the partial escape from this " worst " in which she was steeped to be able to make herself out again as agreeable to see ? She stared into the tarnished glass too hard indeed to be staring at her beauty alone. She readjusted the poise of her black closely-feathered hat ; retouched, beneath it, the thick fall of her dusky

4

hair ; kept her eyes aslant no less on her beautiful averted than on her beautiful presented oval. She was dressed altogether in black, which gave an even tone, by contrast, to her clear face and made her hair more harmoniously dark. Outside, on the balcony, her eyes showed as blue ; within, at the mirror, they showed almost as black, She was handsome, but the degree of it was not sustained by items and aids ; a circumstance moreover playing its part at almost any time in the impression she produced. The impression was one that remained, but as regards the sources of it no sum in addition would have made up the total. She had stature without height, grace without motion, presence without mass. Slender and simple, frequently soundless, she was somehow always in the line of the eye—she counted singularly for its pleasure. More "dressed," often, with fewer accessories, than other women, or less dressed, should occasion require, with more, she probably couldn't have given the key to these felicities. They were mysteries of which her friends were conscious—those friends whose general explanation was to say that she was clever, whether or no it were taken by the world as the cause or as the effect of her charm. If she saw more things than her fine face in the dull glass of her father's lodgings she might have seen that after all she was not herself a fact in the collapse. She didn't hold herself cheap, she didn't make for misery. Personally, no, she wasn't chalk-marked for auction. She hadn't given up yet, and the broken sentence, if she was the last word, *would* end with a sort of meaning. There was a minute during which, though her eyes were fixed, she quite visibly lost herself in the thought of the way she might still pull things round had she only been a man. It was the name, above all, she would take in hand—the precious name she so liked and that, in spite of the harm her wretched

5

father had done it, wasn't yet past praying for. She loved it in fact the more tenderly for that bleeding wound. But what could a penniless girl do with it but let it go ?

When her father at last appeared she became, as usual, instantly aware of the futility of any effort to hold him to anything. He had written her he was ill, too ill to leave his room, and that he must see her without delay ; and if this had been, as was probable, the sketch of a design he was indifferent even to the moderate finish required for deception. He had clearly wanted, for the perversities he called his reasons, to see her, just as she herself had sharpened for a talk ; but she now again felt, in the inevitability of the freedom he used with her, all the old ache, her poor mother's very own, that he couldn't touch you ever so lightly without setting up. No relation with him could be so short or so superficial as not to be somehow to your hurt ; and this, in the strangest way in the world, not because he desired it to be—feeling often, as he surely must, the profit for him of its not being—but because there was never a mistake for you that he could leave unmade, nor a conviction of his impossibility in you that he could approach you without strengthening. He might have awaited her on the sofa in his sitting-room, or might have stayed in bed and received her in that situation. She was glad to be spared the sight of such penetralia, but it would have reminded her a little less that there was no truth in him. This was the weariness of every fresh meeting ; he dealt out lies as he might the cards from the greasy old pack for the game of diplomacy to which you were to sit down with him. The inconvenience— as always happens in such cases—was not that you minded what was false, but that you missed what was true. He might be ill and it might suit you to know it, but no contact with him, for this, could ever be

6

straight enough. Just so he even might die, but Kate
fairly wondered on what evidence of his own she would
some day have to believe it.

He had not at present come down from his room,
which she knew to be above the one they were in :
he had already been out of the house, though he
would either, should she challenge him, deny it or
present it as a proof of his extremity. She had, however, by this time, quite ceased to challenge him ; not
only, face to face with him, vain irritation dropped,
but he breathed upon the tragic consciousness in such
a way that after a moment nothing of it was left. The
difficulty was not less that he breathed in the same
way upon the comic : she almost believed that with
this latter she might still have found a foothold for
clinging to him. He had ceased to be amusing—he
was really too inhuman. His perfect look, which had
floated him so long, was practically perfect still ; but
one had long since for every occasion taken it for
granted. Nothing could have better shown than the
actual how right one had been. He looked exactly as
much as usual—all pink and silver as to skin and
hair, all straightness and starch as to figure and dress ;
the man in the world least connected with anything
unpleasant. He was so particularly the English
gentleman and the fortunate settled normal person.
Seen at a foreign table d'hôte he suggested but one
thing : " In what perfection England produces them ! "
He had kind safe eyes, and a voice which, for all its
clean fulness, told the quiet tale of its having never
had once to raise itself. Life had met him so, halfway, and had turned round so to walk with him,
placing a hand in his arm and fondly leaving him to
choose the pace. Those who knew him a little said
" How he does dress ! "—those who knew him better
said " How *does* he ? " The one stray gleam of
comedy just now in his daughter's eyes was the absurd

feeling he momentarily made her have of being herself
"looked up" by him in sordid lodgings. For a
minute after he came in it was as if the place were her
own and he the visitor with susceptibilities. He gave
you absurd feelings, he had indescribable arts, that
quite turned the tables : this had been always how he
came to see her mother so long as her mother would
see him. He came from places they had often not
known about, but he patronised Lexham Gardens.
Kate's only actual expression of impatience, however,
was " I'm glad you're so much better ! "

" I'm not so much better, my dear—I'm exceedingly unwell ; the proof of which is precisely that I've
been out to the chemist's—that beastly fellow at the
corner." So Mr. Croy showed he could qualify the
humble hand that assuaged him. " I'm taking something he has made up for me. It's just why I've sent
for you—that you may see me as I really am."

" Oh papa, it's long since I've ceased to see you
otherwise than as you really are ! I think we've all
arrived by this time at the right word for that :
' You're beautiful—*n'en parlons plus.*' You're as
beautiful as ever—you look lovely." He judged
meanwhile her own appearance, as she knew she could
always trust him to do ; recognising, estimating,
sometimes disapproving, what she wore, showing her
the interest he continued to take in her. He might
really take none at all, yet she virtually knew herself
the creature in the world to whom he was least indifferent. She had often enough wondered what on
earth, at the pass he had reached, could give him
pleasure, and had come back on these occasions to
that. It gave him pleasure that she was handsome,
that she was in her way a tangible value. It was at
least as marked, nevertheless, that he derived none
from similar conditions, so far as they *were* similar, in
his other child. Poor Marian might be handsome,

8

but he certainly didn't care. The hitch here of course was that, with whatever beauty, her sister, widowed and almost in want, with four bouncing children, had no such measure. She asked him the next thing how long he had been in his actual quarters, though aware of how little it mattered, how little any answer he might make would probably have in common with the truth She failed in fact to notice his answer, truthful or not, already occupied as she was with what she had on her own side to say to him. This was really what had made her wait—what superseded the small remainder of her resentment at his constant practical impertinence ; the result of all of which was that within a minute she had brought it out. " Yes—even now I'm willing to go with you. I don't know what you may have wished to say to me, and even if you hadn't written you would within a day or two have heard from me. Things have happened, and I've only waited, for seeing you, till I should be quite sure. I *am* quite sure. I'll go with you."

It produced an effect. " Go with me where ? "

" Anywhere. I'll stay with you. Even here." She had taken off her gloves and, as if she had arrived with her plan, she sat down.

Lionel Croy hung about in his disengaged way— hovered there as if looking, in consequence of her words, for a pretext to back out easily : on which she immediately saw she had discounted, as it might be called, what he had himself been preparing. He wished her not to come to him, still less to settle with him, and had sent for her to give her up with some style and state ; a part of the beauty of which, however, was to have been his sacrifice to her own detachment. There was no style, no state, unless she wished to forsake him. His idea had accordingly been to surrender her to her wish with all nobleness ; it had by

9

no means been to have positively to keep her off. She
cared, however, not a straw for his embarrassment—
feeling how little, on her own part, she was moved by
charity. She had seen him, first and last, in so many
attitudes that she could now deprive him quite without compunction of the luxury of a new one. Yet she
felt the disconcerted gasp in his tone as he said : " Oh
my child, I can never consent to that ! "

" What then are you going to do ? "

" I'm turning it over," said Lionel Croy. " You
may imagine if I'm not thinking."

" Haven't you thought then," his daughter asked,
" of what I speak of ? I mean of my being ready."

Standing before her with his hands behind him
and his legs a little apart, he swayed slightly to and
fro, inclined toward her as if rising on his toes. It
had an effect of conscientious deliberation. " No—
I haven't. I couldn't. I wouldn't." It was so re-
spectable a show that she felt afresh, and with the
memory of their old despair, the despair at home,
how little his appearance ever by any chance told
about him. His plausibility had been the heaviest
of her mother's crosses ; inevitably so much more
present to the world than whatever it was that was
horrid—thank God they didn't really know !—that
he had done. He had positively been, in his way,
by the force of his particular type, a terrible husband
not to live with ; his type reflecting so invidiously on
the woman who had found him distasteful. Had
this thereby not kept directly present to Kate herself
that it might, on some sides, prove no light thing for
her to leave uncompanion'd a parent with such a face
and such a manner ? Yet if there was much she
neither knew nor dreamed of it passed between them
at this very moment that he was quite familiar with
himself as the subject of such quandaries. If he
recognised his younger daughter's happy aspect as

a tangible value, he had from the first still more exactly appraised every point of his own. The great wonder was not that in spite of everything these points had helped him ; the great wonder was that they hadn't helped him more. However, it was, to its eternal recurrent tune, helping him all the while ; her drop into patience with him showed how it was helping him at this moment. She saw the next instant precisely the line he would take. " Do you really ask me to believe you've been making up your mind to that ? "

She had to consider her own line. " I don't think I care, papa, what you believe. I never, for that matter, think of you as believing anything ; hardly more," she permitted herself to add, " than I ever think of you as yourself believed. I don't know you, father, you see."

" And it's your idea that you may make that up ? "

" Oh dear, no ; not at all. That's no part of the question. If I haven't understood you by this time I never shall, and it doesn't matter. It has seemed to me you may be lived with, but not that you may be understood. Of course I've not the least idea how you get on."

" I don't get on," Mr. Croy almost gaily replied.

His daughter took the place in again, and it might well have seemed odd that with so little to meet the eye there should be so much to show. What showed was the ugliness—so positive and palpable that it was somehow sustaining. It was a medium, a setting, and to that extent, after all, a dreadful sign of life ; so that it fairly gave point to her answer. " Oh I beg your pardon. You flourish."

" Do you throw it up at me again," he pleasantly put to her, " that I've not made away with myself ? "

She treated the question as needing no reply ; she sat there for real things. " You know how all our anxieties, under mamma's will, have come out. She had still less to leave than she feared. We don't know how we lived. It all makes up about two hundred a year for Marian, and two for me, but I give up a hundred to Marian."

" Oh you weak thing ! " her father sighed as from depths of enlightened experience.

" For you and me together," she went on, " the other hundred would do something."

" And what would do the rest ? "

" Can you yourself do nothing ? "

He gave her a look ; then, slipping his hands into his pockets and turning away, stood for a little at the window she had left open. She said nothing more —she had placed him there with that question, and the silence lasted a minute, broken by the call of an appealing costermonger, which came in with the mild March air, with the shabby sunshine, fearfully unbecoming to the room, and with the small homely hum of Chirk Street. Presently he moved nearer, but as if her question had quite dropped. " I don't see what has so suddenly wound you up."

" I should have thought you might perhaps guess. Let me at any rate tell you. Aunt Maud has made me a proposal. But she has also made me a con- dition. She wants to keep me."

" And what in the world else *could* she possibly want ? "

" Oh I don't know—many things. I'm not so precious a capture," the girl a little dryly explained. " No one has ever wanted to keep me before."

Looking always what was proper, her father looked now still more surprised than interested. " You've not had proposals ? " He spoke as if that were in- credible of Lionel Croy's daughter ; as if indeed such an admission scarce consorted, even in filial intimacy, with her high spirit and general form.

" Not from rich relations. She's extremely kind
to me, but it's time she says, that we should understand each other."

Mr. Croy fully assented. " Of course it is—high
time ; and I can quite imagine what she means
by it."

" Are you very sure ? "

" Oh perfectly. She means that she'll ' do ' for
you handsomely if you'll break off all relations with
me. You speak of her condition. Her condition's of
course that."

" Well then," said Kate, " it's what has wound me
up. Here I am."

He showed with a gesture how thoroughly he had
taken it in ; after which, within a few seconds, he had
quite congruously turned the situation about. " Do
you really suppose me in a position to justify your
throwing yourself upon me ? "

She waited a little, but when she spoke it was clear.
" Yes."

" Well then, you're of feebler intelligence than I
should have ventured to suppose you."

" Why so ? You live. You flourish. You
bloom."

" Ah how you've all always hated me ! " he murmured with a pensive gaze again at the window.

" No one could be less of a mere cherished memory,"
she declared as if she had not heard him. " You're
an actual person, if there ever was one. We agreed
just now that you're beautiful. You strike me, you
know, as—in your own way—much more firm on
your feet than I. Don't put it to me therefore as
monstrous that the fact that we're after all parent
and child should at present in some manner count
for us. My idea has been that it should have some
effect for each of us. I don't at all, as I told you
just now," she pursued, " make out your life ; but

whatever it is I hereby offer to accept it. And, on my
side, I'll do everything I can for you."

" I see," said Lionel Croy. Then with the sound
of extreme relevance : " And what *can* you ? " She
only, at this, hesitated, and he took up her silence.
" You can describe yourself—*to* yourself—as, in a
fine flight, giving up your aunt for me ; but what
good, I should like to know, would your fine flight
do me ? " As she still said nothing he developed a
little. " We're not possessed of so much, at this
charming pass, please to remember, as that we can
afford not to take hold of any perch held out to us.
I like the way you talk, my dear, about ' giving up ' !
One doesn't give up the use of a spoon because one's
reduced to living on broth. And your spoon, that is
your aunt, please consider, is partly mine as well."
She rose now, as if in sight of the term of her effort,
in sight of the futility and the weariness of many
things, and moved back to the poor little glass with
which she had communed before. She retouched here
again the poise of her hat, and this brought to her
father's lips another remark—in which impatience,
however, had already been replaced by a free flare
of appreciation. " Oh you're all right ! Don't
muddle yourself up with *me* ! "

His daughter turned round to him. " The condition Aunt Maud makes is that I shall have absolutely nothing to do with you ; never see you, nor
speak nor write to you, never go near you nor make
you a sign, nor hold any sort of communication with
you. What she requires is that you shall simply
cease to exist for me."

He had always seemed—it was one of the marks
of what they called the " unspeakable " in him—to
walk a little more on his toes, as if for jauntiness,
under the touch of offence. Nothing, however, was
more wonderful than what he sometimes would take

14

for offence, unless it might be what he sometimes
wouldn't. He walked at any rate on his toes now.
" A very proper requirement of your Aunt Maud, my
dear—I don't hesitate to say it ! " Yet as this, much
as she had seen, left her silent at first from what
might have been a sense of sickness, he had time to
go on : " That's her condition then. But what are
her promises ? Just what does she engage to do ?
You must work it, you know."

" You mean make her feel," Kate asked after a
moment, " how much I'm attached to you ? "

" Well, what a cruel invidious treaty it is for you
to sign. I'm a poor ruin of an old dad to make a
stand about giving up—I quite agree. But I'm not,
after all, quite the old ruin not to get something *for*
giving up."

" Oh I think her idea," said Kate almost gaily
now, " is that I shall get a great deal."

He met her with his inimitable amenity. " But
does she give you the items ? "

The girl went through the show. " More or less,
I think. But many of them are things I daresay I
may take for granted—things women can do for each
other and that you wouldn't understand."

" There's nothing I understand so well, always, as
the things I needn't ! But what I want to do, you
see," he went on, " is to put it to your conscience that
you've an admirable opportunity ; and that it's moreover one for which, after all, damn you, you've really
to thank *me*."

" I confess I don't see," Kate observed, " what my
' conscience ' has to do with it."

" Then, my dear girl, you ought simply to be
ashamed of yourself. Do you know what you're a
proof of, all you hard hollow people together ? " He
put the question with a charming air of sudden
spiritual heat. " Of the deplorably superficial morality

of the age. The family sentiment, in our vulgar-
ised brutalised life, has gone utterly to pot. There
was a day when a man like me—by which I mean a
parent like me—would have been for a daughter like
you quite a distinct value ; what's called in the business world, I believe, an ' asset.' " He continued
sociably to make it out. " I'm not talking only of
what you might, with the right feeling, do *for* me, but
of what you might—it's what I call your opportunity
—do *with* me. Unless indeed," he the next moment
imperturbably threw off, " they come a good deal to
the same thing. Your duty as well as your chance,
if you're capable of seeing it, is to use me. Show
family feeling by seeing what I'm good for. If you
had it as *I* have it you'd see I'm still good—well,
for a lot of things. There's in fact, my dear," Mr.
Croy wound up, " a coach-and-four to be got out of
me." His lapse, or rather his climax, failed a little
of effect indeed through an undue precipitation of
memory. Something his daughter had said came
back to him. " You've settled to give away half your
little inheritance ? "

Her hesitation broke into laughter. " No — I
haven't ' settled ' anything."

" But you mean practically to let Marian collar
it ? " They stood there face to face, but she so denied
herself to his challenge that he could only go on.
" You've a view of three hundred a year for her in
addition to what her husband left her with ? Is *that*,"
the remote progenitor of such wantonness audibly
wondered, " your morality ? "

Kate found her answer without trouble. " Is it
your idea that I should give you everything ? "

The " everything " clearly struck him—to the
point even of determining the tone of his reply. " Far
from it. How can you ask that when I refuse what
you tell me you came to offer ? Make of my idea what

you can ; I think I've sufficiently expressed it, and it's at any rate to take or to leave. It's the only one, I may nevertheless add ; it's the basket with all my eggs. It's my conception, in short, of your duty."

The girl's tired smile watched the word as if it had taken on a small grotesque visibility. " You're wonderful on such subjects ! I think I should leave you in no doubt," she pursued, " that if I were to sign my aunt's agreement I should carry it out, in honour, to the letter."

" Rather, my own love ! It's just your honour that I appeal to. The only way to play the game *is* to play it. There's no limit to what your aunt can do for you."

" Do you mean in the way of marrying me ? "

" What else should I mean ? Marry properly——"

" And then ? " Kate asked as he hung fire.

" And then—well, I *will* talk with you. I'll resume relations."

She looked about her and picked up her parasol. " Because you're not so afraid of any one else in the world as you are of *her*? My husband, if I should marry, would be at the worst less of a terror ? If that's what you mean there may be something in it. But doesn't it depend a little also on what you mean by my getting a proper one ? However," Kate added as she picked out the frill of her little umbrella, " I don't suppose your idea of him is *quite* that he should persuade you to live with us."

" Dear no—not a bit." He spoke as not resenting either the fear or the hope she imputed ; met both imputations in fact with a sort of intellectual relief. " I place the case for you wholly in your aunt's hands. I take her view with my eyes shut ; I accept in all confidence any man she selects. If he's good enough for *her*—elephantine snob as she is—he's good enough for me ; and quite in spite of the fact that she'll be sure to select one who can be trusted to be nasty to me. My only interest is in your doing what she wants. You shan't be so beastly poor, my darling," Mr. Croy declared, " if I can help it."

" Well then good-bye, papa," the girl said after a reflexion on this that had perceptibly ended for her in a renunciation of further debate. " Of course you understand that it may be for long."

Her companion had hereupon one of his finest in-spirations. " Why not frankly for ever ? You must do me the justice to see that I don't do things, that I've never done them, by halves—that if I offer you to efface myself it's for the final fatal sponge I ask, well saturated and well applied."

She turned her handsome quiet face upon him at such length that it might indeed have been for the last time. " I don't know what you're like."

" No more do I, my dear. I've spent my life in trying in vain to discover. Like nothing—more's the pity. If there had been many of us and we could have found each other out there's no knowing what we mightn't have done. But it doesn't matter now. Good-bye, love." He looked even not sure of what she would wish him to suppose on the subject of a kiss, yet also not embarrassed by his uncertainty.

She forbore in fact for a moment longer to clear it up. " I wish there were some one here who might serve—for any contingency—as a witness that I *have* put it to you that I'm ready to come."

" Would you like me," her father asked, " to call the landlady ? "

" You may not believe me," she pursued, " but I came really hoping you might have found some way. I'm very sorry at all events to leave you unwell." He turned away from her on this and, as he had done before, took refuge, by the window, in a stare at the street. " Let me put it—unfortunately without a

18

witness," she added after a moment, " that there's only one word you really need speak."

When he took these words up it was still with his back to her " If I don't strike you as having already spoken it our time has been singularly wasted."

" I'll engage with you in respect to my aunt exactly to what she wants of me in respect to you. She wants me to choose. Very well, I *will* choose. I'll wash my hands of her for you to just that tune."

He at last brought himself round. " Do you know, dear, you make me sick ? I've tried to be clear and it isn't fair."

But she passed this over ; she was too visibly sincere. " Father ! "

" I don't quite see what's the matter with you," he said, " and if you can't pull yourself together I'll —upon my honour—take you in hand. Put you into a cab and deliver you again safe at Lancaster Gate."

She was really absent, distant. " Father."

It was too much, and he met it sharply. " Well ? "

" Strange as it may be to you to hear me say it, there's a good you can do me and a help you can render."

" Isn't it then exactly what I've been trying to make you feel ? "

" Yes," she answered patiently, " but so in the wrong way. I'm perfectly honest in what I say, and I know what I'm talking about. It isn't that I'll pretend I could have believed a month ago in any-thing to call aid or support from you. The case is changed—that's what has happened ; my difficulty is a new one. But even now it's not a question of any-thing I should ask you in a way to ' do.' It's simply a question of your not turning me away—taking yourself out of my life. It's simply a question of your saying : ' Yes then, since you will, we'll stand together. We won't worry in advance about how or where ; we'll have a faith and find a way.' That's all —*that* would be the good you'd do me. I should *have* you, and it would be for my benefit. Do you see ? "

If he didn't it wasn't for want of looking at her hard. " The matter with you is that you're in love, and that your aunt knows and—for reasons, I'm sure, perfect—hates and opposes it. Well she may ! It's a matter in which I trust her with my eyes shut. Go, please." Though he spoke not in anger—rather in infinite sadness—he fairly turned her out. Before she took it up he had, as the fullest expression of what he felt, opened the door of the room. He had fairly, in his deep disapproval, a generous compassion to spare. " I'm sorry for her, deluded woman, if she builds on you."

Kate stood a moment in the draught. " She's not the person *I* pity most, for, deluded in many ways though she may be, she's not the person who's most so. I mean," she explained, " if it's a question of what you call building on me."

He took it as if what she meant might be other than her description of it. " You're deceiving *two* persons then, Mrs. Lowder and somebody else ? "

She shook her head with detachment. " I've no intention of that sort with respect to any one now— to Mrs. Lowder least of all. If you fail me "—she seemed to make it out for herself—" that has the merit at least that it simplifies. I shall go my way— as I see my way."

" Your way, you mean then, will be to marry some blackguard without a penny ? "

" You demand a great deal of satisfaction," she observed, " for the little you give."

It brought him up again before her as with a sense that she was not to be hustled, and though he glared at her a little this had long been the practical limit

20

to his general power of objection. "If you're base enough to incur your aunt's reprobation you're base enough for my argument. What, if you're not thinking of an utterly improper person, do your speeches to me signify ? Who *is* the beggarly sneak ? " he went on as her response failed.

Her response, when it came, was cold but distinct. "He has every disposition to make the best of you. He only wants in fact to be kind to you."

"Then he *must* be an ass ! And how in the world can you consider it to improve him for me," her father pursued, "that he's also destitute and impossible ? There are boobies and boobies even—the right and the wrong—and you appear to have carefully picked out one of the wrong. Your aunt knows *them*, by good fortune ; I perfectly trust, as I tell you, her judgement for them ; and you may take it from me once for all that I won't hear of any one of whom *she* won't." Which led up to his last word. "If you should really defy us both—— ! "

"Well, papa ? "

"Well, my sweet child, I think that—reduced to insignificance as you may fondly believe me—I should still not be quite without some way of making you regret it."

She had a pause, a grave one, but not, as appeared, that she might measure this danger. "If I shouldn't do it, you know, it wouldn't be because I'm afraid of you."

"Oh, if you don't do it," he retorted, "you may be as bold as you like ! "

"Then you can do nothing at all for me ? "

He showed her, this time unmistakably—it was before her there on the landing, at the top of the tortuous stairs and in the midst of the strange smell that seemed to cling to them—how vain her appeal remained. "I've never pretended to do more than

my duty; I've given you the best and the clearest
advice." And then came up the spring that moved
him. "If it only displeases you, you can go to
Marian to be consoled." What he couldn't forgive
was her dividing with Marian her scant share of the
provision their mother had been able to leave them.
She should have divided it with *him*.

II

SHE had gone to Mrs. Lowder on her mother's death —gone with an effort the strain and pain of which made her at present, as she recalled them, reflect on the long way she had travelled since then. There had been nothing else to do—not a penny in the other house, nothing but unpaid bills that had gathered thick while its mistress lay mortally ill, and the admonition that there was nothing she must attempt to raise money on, since everything belonged to the " estate." How the estate would turn out at best presented itself as a mystery altogether gruesome ; it had proved in fact since then a residuum a trifle less scant than, with her sister, she had for some weeks feared ; but the girl had had at the beginning rather a wounded sense of its being watched on behalf of Marian and her children. What on earth was it supposed that *she* wanted to do to it ? She wanted in truth only to give up—to abandon her own interest, which she doubtless would already have done hadn't the point been subject to Aunt Maud's sharp intervention. Aunt Maud's intervention was all sharp now, and the other point, the great one, was that it was to be, in this light, either all put up with or all declined. Yet at the winter's end, nevertheless, she could scarce have said what stand she conceived she had taken. It wouldn't be the first time she had seen herself obliged to accept with smothered irony other

23

people's interpretation of her conduct. She often ended by giving up to them—it seemed really the way to live—the version that met their convenience. The tall rich heavy house at Lancaster Gate, on the other side of the Park and the long South Kensington stretches, had figured to her, through childhood, through girlhood, as the remotest limit of her vague young world. It was further off and more occasional than anything else in the comparatively compact circle in which she revolved, and seemed, by a rigour early marked, to be reached through long, straight, discouraging vistas, perfect telescopes of streets, and which kept lengthening and straightening, whereas almost everything else in life was either at the worst roundabout Cromwell Road or at the furthest in the nearer parts of Kensington Gardens. Mrs. Lowder was her only " real " aunt, not the wife of an uncle, and had been thereby, both in ancient days and when the greater trouble came, the person, of all persons, properly to make some sign ; in accord with which our young woman's feeling was founded on the impression, quite cherished for years, that the signs made across the interval just mentioned had never been really in the note of the situation. The main office of this relative for the young Croys—apart from giving them their fixed measure of social greatness—had struck them as being to form them to a conception of what they were not to expect. When Kate came to think matters over with wider knowledge, she failed quite to see how Aunt Maud could have been different—she had rather perceived by this time how many other things might have been ; yet she also made out that if they had all consciously lived under a liability to the chill breath of *ultima Thule* they couldn't, either, on the facts, very well have done less. What in the event appeared established was that if Mrs. Lowder had disliked them she

24

yet hadn't disliked them so much as they supposed. It had at any rate been for the purpose of showing how she struggled with her aversion that she sometimes came to see them, that she at regular periods invited them to her house and in short, as it now looked, kept them along on the terms that would best give her sister the perennial luxury of a grievance. This sister, poor Mrs. Croy, the girl knew, had always judged her resentfully, and had brought them up, Marian, the boys and herself, to the idea of a particular attitude, for signs of the practice of which they watched each other with awe. The attitude was to make plain to Aunt Maud, with the same regularity as her invitations, that they sufficed—thanks awfully—to themselves. But the ground of it, Kate lived to discern, was that this was only because *she* didn't suffice to them. The little she offered was to be accepted under protest, yet not really because it was excessive. It wounded them—there was the rub!—because it fell short.

The number of new things our young lady looked out on from the high south window that hung over the Park—this number was so great (though some of the things were only old ones altered and, as the phrase was of other matters, done up) that life at present turned to her view from week to week more and more the face of a striking and distinguished stranger. She had reached a great age—for it quite seemed to her that at twenty-five it was late to reconsider, and her most general sense was a shade of regret that she hadn't known earlier. The world was different—whether for worse or for better—from her rudimentary readings, and it gave her the feeling of a wasted past. If she had only known sooner she might have arranged herself more to meet it. She made at all events discoveries every day, some of which were about herself and others about other persons. Two of

these—one under each head—more particularly engaged, in alternation, her anxiety. She saw as she
had never seen before how material things spoke to
her. She saw, and she blushed to see, that if in contrast with some of its old aspects life now affected her
as a dress successfully " done up," this was exactly by
reason of the trimmings and lace, was a matter of
ribbons and silk and velvet. She had a dire access-
ibility to pleasure from such sources. She liked the
charming quarters her aunt had assigned her—liked
them literally more than she had in all her other
days liked anything ; and nothing could have been
more uneasy than her suspicion of her relative's view
of this truth. Her relative was prodigious—she had
never done her relative justice. These larger conditions all tasted of her, from morning till night ; but
she was a person in respect to whom the growth of
acquaintance could only—strange as it might seem
—keep your heart in your mouth.

The girl's second great discovery was that, so far
from having been for Mrs. Lowder a subject of superficial consideration, the blighted home in Lexham
Gardens had haunted her nights and her days. Kate
had spent, all winter, hours of observation that were
not less pointed for being spent alone ; recent events,
which her mourning explained, assured her a measure
of isolation, and it was in the isolation above all that
her neighbour's influence worked. Sitting far down-
stairs Aunt Maud was yet a presence from which a
sensitive niece could feel herself extremely under
pressure. She knew herself now, the sensitive niece,
as having been marked from far back. · She knew more
than she could have told you, by the upstairs fire, in a
whole dark December afternoon. She knew so much
that her knowledge was what fairly kept her there,
making her at times circulate more endlessly between
the small silk-covered sofa that stood for her in the

THE WINGS OF THE DOVE

firelight and the great grey map of Middlesex spread beneath her lookout. To go down, to forsake her refuge, was to meet some of her discoveries halfway, to have to face them or fly before them ; whereas they were at such a height only like the rumble of a far-off siege heard in the provisioned citadel. She had almost liked, in these weeks, what had created her suspense and her stress : the loss of her mother, the submersion of her father, the discomfort of her sister, the confirmation of their shrunken prospects, the certainty, in especial, of her having to recognise that should she behave, as she called it, decently—that is still do something for others—she would be herself wholly without supplies. She held that she had a right to sadness and stillness ; she nursed them for their postponing power. What they mainly post-poned was the question of a surrender, though she couldn't yet have said exactly of what : a general sur-render of everything—that was at moments the way it presented itself—to Aunt Maud's looming " per-sonality." It was by her personality that Aunt Maud was prodigious, and the great mass of it loomed because, in the thick, the foglike air of her arranged existence, there were parts doubtless magnified and parts certainly vague. They represented at all events alike, the dim and the distinct, a strong will and a high hand. It was perfectly present to Kate that she might be devoured, and she compared herself to a trembling kid, kept apart a day or two till her turn should come, but sure sooner or later to be introduced into the cage of the lioness.

The cage was Aunt Maud's own room, her office, her counting-house, her battlefield, her especial scene, in fine, of action, situated on the ground-floor, opening from the main hall and figuring rather to our young woman on exit and entrance as a guard-house or a toll-gate. The lioness waited—the kid had at

least that consciousness ; was aware of the neigh-
bourhood of a morsel she had reason to suppose
tender. She would have been meanwhile a wonderful
lioness for a show, an extraordinary figure in a cage or
anywhere ; majestic, magnificent, high-coloured, all
brilliant gloss, perpetual satin, twinkling bugles and
flashing gems, with a lustre of agate eyes, a sheen of
raven hair, a polish of complexion that was like that
of well-kept china and that—as if the skin were too
tight—told especially at curves and corners. Her
niece had a quiet name for her—she kept it quiet :
thinking of her, with a free fancy, as somehow typic-
ally insular, she talked to herself of Britannia of the
Market Place—Britannia unmistakable but with a
pen on her ear—and felt she should not be happy till
she might on some occasion add to the rest of the
panoply a helmet, a shield, a trident, and a ledger. It
wasn't in truth, however, that the forces with which,
as Kate felt, she would have to deal were those most
suggested by an image simple and broad ; she was
learning after all each day to know her companion,
and what she had already most perceived was the
mistake of trusting to easy analogies. There was a
whole side of Britannia, the side of her florid philistin-
ism, her plumes and her train, her fantastic furniture
and heaving bosom, the false gods of her taste and
false notes of her talk, the sole contemplation of which
would be dangerously misleading. She was a com-
plex and subtle Britannia, as passionate as she was
practical, with a reticule for her prejudices as deep as
that other pocket, the pocket full of coins stamped in
her image, that the world best knew her by. She
carried on in short, behind her aggressive and defensive front, operations determined by her wisdom. It
was in fact as a besieger, we have hinted, that our
young lady, in the provisioned citadel, had for the
present most to think of her, and what made her for-

midable in this character was that she was unscrupu-
lous and immoral. So at all events in silent sessions
and a youthful off-hand way Kate conveniently
pictured her : what this sufficiently represented being
that her weight was in the scale of certain dangers—
those dangers that, by our showing, made the younger
woman linger and lurk above, while the elder, below,
both militant and diplomatic, covered as much of the
ground as possible. Yet what were the dangers, after
all, but just the dangers of life and of London ? Mrs.
Lowder *was* London, *was* life—the roar of the siege
and the thick of the fray. ˙ There were some things,
after all, of which Britannia was afraid ; but Aunt
Maud was afraid of nothing—not even, it would
appear, of arduous thought.

These impressions, none the less, Kate kept so
much to herself that she scarce shared them with
poor Marian, the ostensible purpose of her frequent
visits to whom yet continued to be to talk over every-
.thing. One of her reasons for holding off from the
last concession to Aunt Maud was that she might
be the more free to commit herself to this so much
nearer and so much less fortunate relative, with whom
Aunt Maud would have almost nothing direct to do.
The sharpest pinch of her state, meanwhile, was
exactly that all intercourse with her sister had the
effect of casting down her courage and tying her
hands, adding daily to her sense of the part, not
always either uplifting or sweetening, that the bond
of blood might play in one's life. She was face to face
with it now, with the bond of blood ; the consciousness of it was what she seemed most clearly to have
" come into " by the death of her mother, much of
that consciousness as her mother had absorbed and
carried away. Her haunting harassing father, her
menacing uncompromising aunt, her portionless little
nephews and nieces, were figures that caused the

chord of natural piety superabundantly to vibrate. Her manner of putting it to herself — but more especially in respect to Marian—was that she saw what you might be brought to by the cultivation of consanguinity. She had taken, in the old days, as she supposed, the measure of this liability ; those being the days when, as the second-born, she had thought no one in the world so pretty as Marian, no one so charming, so clever, so assured in advance of happiness and success. The view was different now, but her attitude had been obliged, for many reasons, to show as the same. The subject of this estimate was no longer pretty, as the reason for thinking her clever was no longer plain ; yet, bereaved, disappointed, demoralised, querulous, she was all the more sharply and insistently Kate's elder and Kate's own. Kate's most constant feeling about her was that she would make her, Kate, do things ; and always, in comfortless Chelsea, at the door of the small house the small rent of which she couldn't help having on her mind, · she fatalistically asked herself, before going in, which thing it would probably be this time. She noticed with profundity that disappointment made people selfish ; she marvelled at the serenity—it was the poor woman's only one—of what Marian took for granted : her own state of abasement as the second-born, her life reduced to mere inexhaustible sisterhood. She existed in that view wholly for the small house in Chelsea ; the moral of which moreover, of course, was that the more you gave yourself the less of you was left. There were always people to snatch at you, and it would never occur to *them* that they were eating you up. They did that without tasting.

There was no such misfortune, or at any rate no such discomfort, she further reasoned, as to be formed at once for being and for seeing. You always saw, in this case, something else than what you were, and you got in consequence none of the peace of your condition. However, as she never really let Marian see what she was Marian might well not have been aware that she herself saw. Kate was accordingly to her own vision not a hypocrite of virtue, for she gave herself up ; but she was a hypocrite of stupidity, for she kept to herself everything that was not herself. What she most kept was the particular sentiment with which she watched her sister instinctively neglect nothing that would make for her submission to their aunt ; a state of the spirit that perhaps marked most sharply how poor you might become when you minded so much the absence of wealth. It was through Kate that Aunt Maud should be worked, and nothing mattered less than what might become of Kate in the process. Kate was to burn her ships in short, so that Marian should profit ; and Marian's desire to profit was quite oblivious of a dignity that had after all its reasons—if it had only understood them—for keeping itself a little stiff. Kate, to be properly stiff for both of them, would therefore have had to be selfish, have had to prefer an ideal of behaviour—than which nothing ever was more selfish—to the possibility of stray crumbs for the four small creatures. The tale of Mrs. Lowder's disgust at her elder niece's marriage to Mr. Condrip had lost little of its point ; the incredibly fatuous behaviour of Mr. Condrip, the parson of a dull suburban parish, with a saintly profile which was always in evidence, being so distinctly on record to keep criticism consistent. He had presented his profile on system, having, goodness knew, nothing else to present—nothing at all to full-face the world with, no imagination of the propriety of living and minding his business. Criticism had remained on Aunt Maud's part consistent enough ; she was not a person to regard such proceedings as less of a mistake for having acquired more of the privilege of pathos. She hadn't been forgiving, and the only approach she made to overlooking them was by overlooking—with the surviving delinquent—the solid little phalanx that now represented them. Of the two sinister ceremonies that she lumped together, the marriage and the interment, she had been present at the former, just as she had sent Marian before it a liberal cheque ; but this had not been for her more than the shadow of an admitted link with Mrs. Condrip's course. She disapproved of clamorous children for whom there was no prospect ; she disapproved of weeping widows who couldn't make their errors good ; and she had thus put within Marian's reach one of the few luxuries left when so much else had gone, an easy pretext for a constant grievance. Kate Croy remembered well what their mother, in a different quarter, had made of it ; and it was Marian's marked failure to pluck the fruit of resentment that committed them as sisters to an almost equal fellowship in abjection. If the theory was that, yes, alas, one of the pair had ceased to be noticed, but that the other was noticed enough to make up for it, who would fail to see that Kate couldn't separate herself without a cruel pride ? That lesson became sharp for our young lady the day after her interview with her father.

" I can't imagine," Marian on this occasion said to her, " how you can think of anything else in the world but the horrid way we're situated."

" And, pray, how do you know," Kate inquired in reply, " anything about my thoughts ? It seems to me I give you sufficient proof of how much I think of *you*. I don't really, my dear, know what else you've to do with ! "

Marian's retort on this was a stroke as to which she had supplied herself with several kinds of preparation, but there was none the less something of an

32

unexpected note in its promptitude. She had foreseen her sister's general fear ; but here, ominously,
was the special one. " Well, your own business is of
course your own business, and you may say there's no
one less in a position than I to preach to you. But,
all the same, if you wash your hands of me for ever in
consequence, I won't, for this once, keep back that I
don't consider you've a right, as we all stand, to throw
yourself away."

It was after the children's dinner, which was also
their mother's, but which their aunt mostly con-
trived to keep from ever becoming her own luncheon ;
and the two young women were still in the presence of
the crumpled table-cloth, the dispersed pinafores, the
scraped dishes, the lingering odour of boiled food.
Kate had asked with ceremony if she might put up a
window a little, and Mrs. Condrip had replied without
it that she might do as she liked. She often received
such inquiries as if they reflected in a manner on the
pure essence of her little ones. The four had retired,
with much movement and noise, under imperfect
control of the small Irish governess whom their aunt
had hunted up for them and whose brooding resolve
not to prolong so uncrowned a martyrdom she already
more than suspected. Their mother had become for
Kate—who took it just for the effect of being their
mother—quite a different thing from the mild Marian
of the past : Mr. Condrip's widow expansively
obscured that image. She was little more than a
ragged relic, a plain prosaic result of him—as if she
had somehow been pulled through him as through an
obstinate funnel, only to be left crumpled and useless
and with nothing in her but what he accounted for.
She had grown red and almost fat, which were not
happy signs of mourning ; less and less like any Croy,
particularly a Croy in trouble, and sensibly like her
husband's two unmarried sisters, who came to see

her, in Kate's view, much too often and stayed too long, with the consequence of inroads upon the tea and bread-and-butter—matters as to which Kate, not unconcerned with the tradesmen's books, had feelings. About them moreover Marian *was* touchy, and her nearer relative, who observed and weighed things, noted as an oddity that she would have taken any reflexion on them as a reflexion on herself. If that was what marriage necessarily did to you Kate Croy would have questioned marriage. It was at any rate a grave example of what a man—and such a man !—might make of a woman. She could see how the Condrip pair pressed their brother's widow on the subject of Aunt Maud—who wasn't, after all, *their* aunt; made her, over their interminable cups, chatter and even swagger about Lancaster Gate, made her more vulgar than it had seemed written that any Croy could possibly become on such a subject. They laid it down, they rubbed it in, that Lancaster Gate was to be kept in sight, and that she, Kate, was to keep it ; so that, curiously, or at all events sadly, our young woman was sure of being in her own person more permitted to them as an object of comment than they would in turn ever be permitted to herself. The beauty of which too was that Marian didn't love them. But they were Condrips—they had grown near the rose ; they were almost like Bertie and Maudie, like Kitty and Guy. They talked of the dead to her, which Kate never did ; it being a relation in which Kate could but mutely listen. She couldn't indeed too often say to herself that if that was what marriage did to you—— ! It may easily be guessed therefore that the ironic light of such reserves fell straight across the field of Marian's warning. " I don't quite see," she answered, " where in particular it strikes you that my danger lies. I'm not conscious, I assure you, of the least disposition to ' throw '

34

myself anywhere. I feel that for the present I've
been quite sufficiently thrown."

" You don't feel "—Marian brought it all out—
" that you'd like to marry Merton Densher ? "

Kate took a moment to meet this inquiry. " Is it
your idea that if I should feel so I would be bound to
give you notice, so that you might step in and head
me off ? Is that your idea ? " the girl asked. Then
as her sister also had a pause, " I don't know what
makes you talk of Mr. Densher," she observed.

" I talk of him just because you don't. That you
never do, in spite of what I know—that's what
makes me think of him. Or rather perhaps it's what
makes me think of *you*. If you don't know by this
time what I hope for you, what I dream of—my
attachment being what it is—it's no use my attempting to tell you." But Marian had in fact warmed to
her work, and Kate was sure she had discussed Mr.
Densher with the Miss Condrips. " If I name that
person I suppose it's because I'm so afraid of him.
If you want really to know, he fills me with terror. If
you want really to know, in fact, I dislike him as
much as I dread him."

" And yet don't think it dangerous to abuse him
to me ? "

" Yes," Mrs. Condrip confessed, " I do think it
dangerous ; but how can I speak of him otherwise ?
I dare say, I admit, that I shouldn't speak of him at
all. Only I do want you for once, as I said just now,
to know."

" To know what, my dear ? "

" That I should regard it," Marian promptly
returned, " as far and away the worst thing that has
happened to us yet."

" Do you mean because he hasn't money ? "

" Yes, for one thing. And because I don't believe
in him."

Kate was civil but mechanical. "What do you mean by not believing in him ? "

"Well, being sure he'll never get it. And you *must* have it. You *shall* have it."

"To give it to you ? "

Marian met her with a readiness that was practically pert. "To *have* it, first. Not at any rate to go on not having it. Then we should see."

"We should indeed ! " said Kate Croy. It was talk of a kind she loathed, but if Marian chose to be vulgar what was one to do ? It made her think of the Miss Condrips with renewed aversion. "I like the way you arrange things—I like what you take for granted. If it's so easy for us to marry men who want us to scatter gold, I wonder we any of us do anything else. I don't see so many of them about, nor what interest I might ever have for them. You live, my dear," she presently added, "in a world of vain thoughts."

"Not so much as you, Kate ; for I see what I see and you can't turn it off that way." The elder sister paused long enough for the younger's face to show, in spite of superiority, an apprehension. "I'm not talking of any man but Aunt Maud's man, nor of any money even, if you like, but Aunt Maud's money. I'm not talking of anything but your doing what *she* wants. You're wrong if you speak of anything that I want of you ; I want nothing but what she does. That's good enough for me ! "—and Marian's tone struck her companion as of the lowest. "If I don't believe in Merton Densher I do at least in Mrs. Lowder."

"Your ideas are the more striking," Kate returned, "that they're the same as papa's. I had them from him, you'll be interested to know—and with all the brilliancy you may imagine—yesterday."

THE WINGS OF THE DOVE

Marian clearly was interested to know. " He has been to see you ? "

" No, I went to him."

" Really ? " Marian wondered. " For what purpose ? "

" To tell him I'm ready to go to him."

Marian stared. " To leave Aunt Maud—— ? "

" For my father, yes."

She had fairly flushed, poor Mrs. Condrip, with horror. " You're ready—— ? "

" So I told him. I couldn't tell him less."

" And pray could you tell him more ? " Marian gasped in her distress. " What in the world is he *to* us ? You bring out such a thing as that this way ? "

They faced each other—the tears were in Marian's eyes. Kate watched them there a moment and then said : " I had thought it well over—over and over. But you needn't feel injured. I'm not going. He won't have me."

Her companion still panted—it took time to subside. " Well, *I* wouldn't have you—wouldn't receive you at all, I can assure you—if he had made you any other answer. I do feel injured—at your having been willing. If you were to go to papa, my dear, you'd have to stop coming to me." Marian put it thus, indefinably, as a picture of privation from which her companion might shrink. Such were the threats she could complacently make, could think herself masterful for making. " But if he won't take you," she continued, " he shows at least his sharpness."

Marian had always her views of sharpness ; she was, as her sister privately commented, great on that resource. But Kate had her refuge from irritation. " He won't take me," she simply repeated. " But he believes, like you, in Aunt Maud. He threatens me with his curse if I leave her."

"So you *won't*?" As the girl at first said nothing her companion caught at it. "You won't, of course? I see you won't. But I don't see why, conveniently, I shouldn't insist to you once for all on the plain truth of the whole matter. The truth, my dear, of your duty. Do you ever think about *that*? It's the greatest duty of all."

"There you are again," Kate laughed. "Papa's also immense on my duty."

"Oh I don't pretend to be immense, but I pretend to know more than you do of life ; more even perhaps than papa." Marian seemed to see that personage at this moment, nevertheless, in the light of a kinder irony. "Poor old papa!"

She sighed it with as many condonations as her sister's ear had more than once caught in her "Dear old Aunt Maud!" These were things that made Kate turn for the time sharply away, and she gathered herself now to go. They were the note again of the abject ; it was hard to say which of the persons in question had most shown how little they liked her. The younger woman proposed at any rate to let discussion rest, and she believed that, for herself, she had done so during the ten minutes elapsing, thanks to her wish not to break off short, before she could gracefully withdraw. It then appeared, however, that Marian had been discussing still, and there was something that at the last Kate had to take up. "Whom do you mean by Aunt Maud's young man?"

"Whom should I mean but Lord Mark?"

"And where do you pick up such vulgar twaddle?" Kate demanded with her clear face. "How does such stuff, in this hole, get to you?"

She had no sooner spoken than she asked herself what had become of the grace to which she had sacrificed. Marian certainly did little to save it, and nothing indeed was so inconsequent as her ground of

38

complaint. She desired her to " work " Lancaster
Gate as she believed that scene of abundance could
be worked ; but she now didn't see why advantage
should be taken of the bloated connexion to put an
affront on her own poor home. She appeared in fact
for the moment to take the position that Kate kept
her in her " hole " and then heartlessly reflected on
her being in it. Yet she didn't explain how she had
picked up the report on which her sister had challenged
her—so that it was thus left to her sister to see in it
once more a sign of the creeping curiosity of the Miss
Condrips. They lived in a deeper hole than Marian,
but they kept their ear to the ground, they spent
their days in prowling, whereas Marian, in garments
and shoes that seemed steadily to grow looser and
larger, never prowled. There were times when Kate
wondered if the Miss Condrips were offered her by
fate as a warning for her own future—to be taken as
showing her what she herself might become at forty
if she let things too recklessly go. What was expected
of her by others—and by so many of them—could,
all the same, on occasion, present itself as beyond a
joke ; and this was just now the aspect it particularly
wore. She was not only to quarrel with Merton
Densher for the pleasure of her five spectators—with
the Miss Condrips there were five ; she was to set
forth in pursuit of Lord Mark on some preposterous
theory of the premium attached to success. Mrs.
Lowder's hand had hung out the premium, and it
figured at the end of the course as a bell that would
ring, break out into public clamour, as soon as touched.
Kate reflected sharply enough on the weak points of
this fond fiction, with the result at last of a certain
chill for her sister's confidence ; though Mrs. Condrip
still took refuge in the plea—which was after all the
great point—that their aunt would be munificent
when their aunt should be content. The exact

identity of her candidate was a detail ; what was of the essence was her conception of the kind of match it was open to her niece to make with her aid. Marian always spoke of marriages as " matches," but that was again a detail. Mrs. Lowder's " aid " meanwhile awaited them—if not to light the way to Lord Mark, then to somebody better. Marian would put up, in fine, with somebody better ; she only wouldn't put up with somebody so much worse. Kate had once more to go through all this before a graceful issue was reached. It was reached by her paying with the sacrifice of Mr. Densher for her reduction of Lord Mark to the absurd. So they separated softly enough. She was to be let off hearing about Lord Mark so long as she made it good that she wasn't underhand about any one else. She had denied everything and every one, she reflected as she went away—and that was a relief ; but it also made rather a clean sweep of ·the future. The prospect put on a bareness that already gave her something in common with the Miss Condrips.

BOOK SECOND

I

MERTON DENSHER, who passed the best hours of each
night at the office of his newspaper, had at times,
during the day, to make up for it, a sense, or at least
an appearance, of leisure, in accordance with which
he was not infrequently to be met in different parts
of the town at moments when men of business are
hidden from the public eye. More than once during
the present winter's end he had deviated toward three
o'clock, or toward four, into Kensington Gardens,
where he might for a while, on each occasion, have
been observed to demean himself as a person with
nothing to do. He made his way indeed, for the most
part, with a certain directness over to the north side ;
but once that ground was reached his behaviour was
noticeably wanting in point. He moved, seemingly
at random, from alley to alley ; he stopped for no
reason and remained idly agaze ; he sat down in a
chair and then changed to a bench ; after which he
walked about again, only again to repeat both the
vagueness and the vivacity. Distinctly he was a man
either with nothing at all to do or with ever so much
to think about ; and it was not to be denied that
the impression he might often thus easily make had
the effect of causing the burden of proof in certain
directions to rest on him. It was a little the fault of
his aspect, his personal marks, which made it almost
impossible to name his profession.

43

He was a longish, leanish, fairish young Englishman, not unamenable, on certain sides, to classification
—as for instance by being a gentleman, by being
rather specifically one of the educated, one of the
generally sound and generally civil ; yet, though to
that degree neither extraordinary nor abnormal, he
would have failed to play straight into an observer's
hands. He was young for the House of Commons,
he was loose for the Army. He was refined, as might
have been said, for the City and, quite apart from
the cut of his cloth, sceptical, it might have been felt,
for the Church. On the other hand he was credulous
for diplomacy, or perhaps even for science, while he
was perhaps at the same time too much in his mere
senses for poetry and yet too little in them for art.
You would have got fairly near him by making out
in his eyes the potential recognition of ideas ; but
you would have quite fallen away again on the question
of the ideas themselves. The difficulty with Densher
was that he looked vague without looking weak—idle
without looking empty. It was the accident, possibly,
of his long legs, which were apt to stretch themselves ;
of his straight hair and his well-shaped head, never,
the latter, neatly smooth, and apt into the bargain,
at the time of quite other calls upon it, to throw itself
suddenly back and, supported behind by his uplifted
arms and interlocked hands, place him for uncon-
scionable periods in communion with the ceiling, the
tree-tops, the sky. He was in short visibly absent-
minded, irregularly clever, liable to drop what was
near and to take up what was far ; he was more a
prompt critic than a prompt follower of custom. He
suggested above all, however, that wondrous state of
youth in which the elements, the metals more or less
precious, are so in fusion and fermentation that the
question of the final stamp, the pressure that fixes
the value, must wait for comparative coolness. And

it was a mark of his interesting mixture that if he was irritable it was by a law of considerable subtlety—a law that in intercourse with him it might be of profit, though not easy, to master. One of the effects of it was that he had for you surprises of tolerance as well as of temper.

He loitered, on the best of the relenting days, the several occasions we speak of, along the part of the Gardens nearest to Lancaster Gate, and when, always, in due time, Kate Croy came out of her aunt's house, crossed the road and arrived by the nearest entrance, there was a general publicity in the proceeding which made it slightly anomalous. If their meeting was to be bold and free it might have taken place within-doors ; if it was to be shy or secret it might have taken place almost anywhere better than under Mrs. Lowder's windows. They failed indeed to remain attached to that spot ; they wandered and strolled, taking in the course of more than one of these interviews a considerable walk, or else picked out a couple of chairs under one of the great trees and sat as much apart—apart from every one else—as possible. But Kate had each time, at first, the air of wishing to expose herself to pursuit and capture if those things were in question. She made the point that she wasn't underhand, any more than she was vulgar ; that the Gardens were charming in themselves and this use of them a matter of taste ; and that, if her aunt chose to glare at her from the drawing-room or to cause her to be tracked and overtaken, she could at least make it convenient that this should be easily done. The fact was that the relation between these young persons abounded in such oddities as were not inaptly symbolised by assignations that had a good deal more appearance than motive. Of the strength of the tie that held them we shall sufficiently take the measure ; but it was meanwhile almost obvious that if the great possibility had come up for them it had done so, to an exceptional degree, under the protection of the famous law of contraries. Any deep harmony that might eventually govern them would not be the result of their having much in common—having anything in fact but their affection ; and would really find its explanation in some sense, on the part of each, of being poor where the other was rich. It is nothing new indeed that generous young persons often admire most what nature hasn't given them—from which it would appear, after all, that our friends were both generous.

Merton Densher had repeatedly said to himself— and from far back—that he should be a fool not to marry a woman whose value would be in her differences ; and Kate Croy, though without having quite so philosophised, had quickly recognised in the young man a precious unlikeness. He represented what her life had never given her and certainly, without some such aid as his, never would give her ; all the high dim things she lumped together as of the mind. It was on the side of the mind that Densher was rich for her and mysterious and strong ; and he had rendered her in especial the sovereign service of making that element real. She had had all her days to take it terribly on trust, no creature she had ever encountered having been able to testify for it directly. Vague rumours of its existence had made their precarious way to her ; but nothing had, on the whole, struck her as more likely than that she should live and die without the chance to verify them. The chance had come—it was an extraordinary one—on the day she first met Densher ; and it was to the girl's lasting honour that she knew on the spot what she was in presence of. That occasion indeed, for everything that straightway flowered in it, would be worthy of high commemoration ; Densher's perception went out

46

to meet the young woman's and quite kept pace with her own recognition. Having so often concluded on the fact of his weakness, as he called it, for life—his strength merely for thought—life, he logically opined, was what he must somehow arrange to annex and possess. This was so much a necessity that thought by itself only went on in the void ; it was from the immediate air of life that it must draw its breath. So the young man, ingenious but large, critical but ardent too, made out both his case and Kate Croy's. They had originally met before her mother's death—an occasion marked for her as the last pleasure permitted by the approach of that event ; after which the dark months had interposed a screen and, for all Kate knew, made the end one with the beginning.

The beginning—to which she often went back— had been a scene, for our young woman, of supreme brilliancy ; a party given at a " gallery " hired by a hostess who fished with big nets. A Spanish dancer, understood to be at that moment the delight of the town, an American reciter, the joy of a kindred people, an Hungarian fiddler, the wonder of the world at large—in the name of these and other attractions the company in which Kate, by a rare privilege, found herself had been freely convoked. She lived under her mother's roof, as she considered, obscurely, and was acquainted with few persons who entertained on that scale ; but she had had dealings with two or three connected, as appeared, with such—two or three through whom the stream of hospitality, filtered or diffused, could thus now and then spread to outlying receptacles. A good-natured lady in fine, a friend of her mother and a relative of the lady of the gallery, had offered to take her to the party in question and had there fortified her, further, with two or three of those introductions that, at large parties, lead to other things—that had at any rate on this occasion culminated for her in conversation with a tall fair, a slightly unbrushed and rather awkward, but on the whole a not dreary, young man. The young man had affected her as detached, as—it was indeed what he called himself—awfully at sea, as much more distinct from what surrounded them than any one else appeared to be, and even as probably quite disposed to be making his escape when pulled up to be placed in relation with her. He gave her his word for it indeed, this same evening, that only their meeting had prevented his flight, but that now he saw how sorry he should have been to miss it. This point they had reached by midnight, and though for the value of such remarks everything was in the tone, by midnight the tone was there too. She had had originally her full apprehension of his coerced, certainly of his vague, condition—full apprehensions often being with her immediate ; then she had had her equal consciousness that within five minutes something between them had—well, she couldn't call it anything but *come*. It was nothing to look at or to handle, but was somehow everything to feel and to know ; it was that something for each of them had happened.

They had found themselves regarding each other straight, and for a longer time on end than was usual even at parties in galleries ; but that in itself after all would have been a small affair for two such handsome persons. It wasn't, in a word, simply that their eyes had met ; other conscious organs, faculties, feelers had met as well, and when Kate afterwards imaged to herself the sharp deep fact she saw it, in the oddest way, as a particular performance. She had observed a ladder against a garden-wall and had trusted herself so to climb it as to be able to see over into the probable garden on the other side. On reaching the top she had found herself face to face with a gentleman engaged in a like calculation at the same

48

moment, and the two inquirers had remained confronted on their ladders. The great point was that for the rest of that evening they had been perched— they had not climbed down ; and indeed during the time that followed Kate at least had had the perched feeling—it was as if she were there aloft without a retreat. A simpler expression of all this is doubtless but that they had taken each other in with interest ; and without a happy hazard six months later the incident would have closed in that account of it. The accident meanwhile had been as natural as anything in London ever is : Kate had one afternoon found herself opposite Mr. Densher on the Underground Railway. She had entered the train at Sloane Square to go to Queen's Road, and the carriage in which she took her place was all but full. Densher was already in it—on the other bench and at the furthest angle ; she was sure of him before they had again started. The day and the hour were darkness, there were six other persons and she had been busy seating herself ; but her consciousness had gone to him as straight as if they had come together in some bright stretch of a desert. They had on neither part a second's hesitation ; they looked across the choked compartment exactly as if she had known he would be there and he had expected her to come in ; so that, though in the conditions they could only exchange the greeting of movements, smiles, abstentions, it would have been quite in the key of these passages that they should have alighted for ease at the very next station. Kate was in fact sure the very next station was the young man's true goal—which made it clear he was going on only from the wish to speak to her. He had to go on, for this purpose, to High Street Kensington, as it was not till then that the exit of a passenger gave him his chance.

His chance put him however in quick possession of

the seat facing her, the alertness of his capture of
which seemed to show her his impatience. It helped
them moreover, with strangers on either side, little to
talk ; though this very restriction perhaps made such
a mark for them as nothing else could have done. If
the fact that their opportunity had again come round
for them could be so intensely expressed without a
word, they might very well feel on the spot that it had
not come round for nothing. The extraordinary part
of the matter was that they were not in the least
meeting where they had left off, but ever so much
further on, and that these added links added still
another between High Street and Notting Hill Gate,
and then worked between the latter station and
Queen's Road an extension really inordinate. At
Notting Hill Gate Kate's right-hand neighbour
descended, whereupon Densher popped straight into
that seat ; only there was not much gained when a
lady the next instant popped into Densher's. He
could say almost nothing—Kate scarce knew, at
least, what he said ; she was so occupied with a
certainty that one of the persons opposite, a youngish
man with a single eye-glass which he kept constantly
in position, had made her out from the first as
visibly, as strangely affected. If such a person made
her out what then did Densher do ?—a question in
truth sufficiently answered when, on their reaching
her station, he instantly followed her out of the train.
That had been the real beginning—the beginning of
everything else ; the other time, the time at the
party, had been but the beginning of *that*. Never
in life before had she so let herself go ; for always
before—so far as small adventures could have been
in question for her—there had been, by the vulgar
measure, more to go upon. He had walked with
her to Lancaster Gate, and then she had walked
with him away from it — for all the world, she

50

said to herself, like the housemaid giggling to the baker.

This appearance, she was afterwards to feel, had been all in order for a relation that might precisely best be described in the terms of the baker and the housemaid. She could say to herself that from that hour they had kept company : that had come to represent, technically speaking, alike the range and the limit of their tie. He had on the spot, naturally, asked leave to call upon her—which, as a young person who wasn't really young, who didn't pretend to be a sheltered flower, she as rationally gave. That —she was promptly clear about it—was now her only possible basis ; she was just the contemporary London female, highly modern, inevitably battered, honourably free. She had of course taken her aunt straight into her confidence—had gone through the form of asking her leave ; and she subsequently remembered that though on this occasion she had left the history of her new alliance as scant as the facts themselves, Mrs. Lowder had struck her at the time as surprisingly mild. The occasion had been in every way full of the reminder that her hostess was deep : it was definitely then that she had begun to ask herself what Aunt Maud was, in vulgar parlance, " up to." " You may receive, my dear, whom you like "—that was what Aunt Maud, who in general objected to people's doing as they liked, had replied ; and it bore, this unexpectedness, a good deal of looking into. There were many explanations, and they were all amusing— amusing, that is, in the line of the sombre and brooding amusement cultivated by Kate in her actual high retreat. Merton Densher came the very next Sunday ; but Mrs. Lowder was so consistently magnanimous as to make it possible to her niece to see him alone. She saw him, however, on the Sunday following, in order to invite him to dinner ; and when, after dining, he came again—which he did three times, she found means to treat his visit as preponderantly to herself. Kate's conviction that she didn't like him made that remarkable ; it added to the evidence, by this time voluminous, that she was remarkable all round. If she had been, in the way of energy, merely usual she would have kept her dislike direct ; whereas it was now as if she were seeking to know him in order to see best where to "have" him. That was one of the reflexions made in our young woman's high retreat ; she smiled from her lookout, in the silence that was only the fact of hearing irrelevant sounds, as she caught the truth that you could easily accept people when you wanted them so to be delivered to you. When Aunt Maud wished them despatched it was not to be done by deputy ; it was clearly always a matter reserved for her own hand.

But what made the girl wonder most was the implication of so much diplomacy in respect to her own value. What view might she take of her position in the light of this appearance that her companion feared so as yet to upset her ? It was as if Densher were accepted partly under the dread that if he hadn't been she would act in resentment. Hadn't her aunt considered the danger that she would in that case have broken off, have seceded ? The danger was exaggerated—she would have done nothing so gross ; but that, it would seem, was the way Mrs. Lowder saw her and believed her to be reckoned with. What importance therefore did she really attach to her, what strange interest could she take in their keeping on terms ? Her father and her sister had their answer to this—even without knowing how the question struck her : they saw the lady of Lancaster Gate as panting to make her fortune, and the explanation of that appetite was that, on the accident of a nearer view than she had before enjoyed, she had been charmed, been dazzled. They approved, they admired in her one of the belated fancies of rich capricious violent old women — the more marked moreover because the result of no plot ; and they piled up the possible fruits for the person concerned. Kate knew what to think of her own power thus to carry by storm ; she saw herself as handsome, no doubt, but as hard, and felt herself as clever but as cold ; and as so much too imperfectly ambitious, furthermore, that it was a pity, for a quiet life, she couldn't decide to be either finely or stupidly indifferent. Her intelligence sometimes kept her still—too still—but her want of it was restless ; so that she got the good, it seemed to her, of neither extreme. She saw herself at present, none the less, in a situation, and even her sad disillusioned mother, dying, but with Aunt Maud interviewing the nurse on the stairs, had not failed to remind her that it was of the essence of situations to be, under Providence, worked. The dear woman had died in the belief that she was actually working the one then recognised.

Kate took one of her walks with Densher just after her visit to Mr. Croy ; but most of it went, as usual, to their sitting in talk. They had under the trees by the lake the air of old friends—particular phases of apparent earnestness in which they might have been settling every question in their vast young world ; and periods of silence, side by side, perhaps even more, when " A long engagement ! " would have been the final reading of the signs on the part of a passer struck with them, as it was so easy to be. They would have presented themselves thus as very old friends rather than as young persons who had met for the first time but a year before and had spent most of the interval without contact. It was indeed for each, already, as if they were older friends ; and though the succession of their meetings might, between them, have been

straightened out, they only had a confused sense of
a good many, very much alike, and a confused intention of a good many more, as little different as possible.
The desire to keep them just as they were had perhaps
to do with the fact that in spite of the presumed
diagnosis of the stranger there had been for them
as yet no formal, no final understanding. Densher
had at the very first pressed the question, but that,
it had been easy to reply, was too soon ; so that a
singular thing had afterwards happened. They had
accepted their acquaintance as too short for an
engagement, but they had treated it as long enough
for almost anything else, and marriage was somehow
before them like a temple without an avenue. They
belonged to the temple and they met in the grounds ;
they were in the stage at which grounds in general
offered much scattered refreshment. But Kate had
meanwhile had so few confidants that she wondered
at the source of her father's suspicions. The diffusion
of rumour was of course always remarkable in London,
and for Marian not less — as Aunt Maud touched
neither directly — the mystery had worked. No
doubt she had been seen. Of course she had been
seen. She had taken no trouble not to be seen, and
it was a thing she was clearly incapable of taking.
But she had been seen how ?—and what *was* there to
see ? She was in love—she knew that : but it was
wholly her own business, and she had the sense of
having conducted herself, of still so doing, with almost
violent conformity.

"I've an idea—in fact I feel sure—that Aunt
Maud means to write to you ; and I think you had
better know it." So much as this she said to him as
soon as they met, but immediately adding to it :
" So as to make up your mind how to take her. I
know pretty well what she'll say to you."

" Then will you kindly tell me ? "

54

She thought a little. " I can't do that. I should spoil it. She'll do the best for her own idea."

" Her idea, you mean, that I'm a sort of a scoundrel ; or, at the best, not good enough for you ? "

They were side by side again in their penny chairs, and Kate had another pause. " Not good enough for *her.*"

" Oh I see. And that's necessary."

He put it as a truth rather more than as a question ; but there had been plenty of truths between them that each had contradicted. Kate, however, let this one sufficiently pass, only saying the next moment : " She has behaved extraordinarily."

" And so have we," Densher declared. " I think, you know, we've been awfully decent."

" For ourselves, for each other, for people in general, yes. But not for *her* For her," said Kate, " we've been monstrous. She has been giving us rope. So if she does send for you," the girl repeated, " you must know where you are."

" That I always know. It's where *you* are that concerns me."

" Well," said Kate after an instant, " her idea of that is what you'll have from her." He gave her a long look, and whatever else people who wouldn't let her alone might have wished, for her advancement, his long looks were the thing in the world she could never have enough of. What she felt was that, whatever might happen, she must keep them, must make them most completely her possession ; and it was already strange enough that she reasoned, or at all events began to act, as if she might work them in with other and alien things, privately cherish them and yet, as regards the rigour of it, pay no price. She looked it well in the face, she took it intensely home, that they were lovers ; she rejoiced to herself and, frankly, to him, in their wearing of the name ; but, distinguished

55

creature that, in her way, she was, she took a view of this character that scarce squared with the conventional. The character itself she insisted on as their right, taking that so for granted that it didn't seem even bold ; but Densher, though he agreed with her, found himself moved to wonder at her simplifications, her values. Life might prove difficult—was evidently going to ; but meanwhile they had each other, and that was everything. This was her reasoning, but meanwhile, for *him*, each other was what they didn't have, and it was just the point. Repeatedly, however, it was a point that, in the face of strange and special things, he judged it rather awkwardly gross to urge. It was impossible to keep Mrs. Lowder out of their scheme. She stood there too close to it and too solidly ; it had to open a gate, at a given point, do what they would, to take her in. And she came in, always, while they sat together rather helplessly watching her, as in a coach-and-four ; she drove round their prospect as the principal lady at the circus drives round the ring, and she stopped the coach in the middle to alight with majesty. It was our young man's sense that she was magnificently vulgar, but yet quite that this wasn't all. It wasn't with her vulgarity that she felt his want of means, though that might have helped her richly to embroider it ; nor was it with the same infirmity that she was strong original dangerous.

His want of means—of means sufficient for any one but himself—was really the great ugliness, and was moreover at no time more ugly for him than when it rose there, as it did seem to rise, all shameless, face to face with the elements in Kate's life colloquially and conveniently classed by both of them as funny. He sometimes indeed, for that matter, asked himself if these elements were as funny as the innermost fact, so often vivid to him, of his own consciousness—his

56

private inability to believe he should ever be rich. His conviction on this head was in truth quite positive and a thing by itself ; he failed, after analysis, to understand it, though he had naturally more lights on it than any one else. He knew how it subsisted in spite of an equal consciousness of his being neither mentally nor physically quite helpless, neither a dunce nor a cripple ; he knew it to be absolute, though secret, and also, strange to say, about common undertakings, not discouraging, not prohibitive. Only now was he having to think if it were prohibitive in respect to marriage ; only now, for the first time, had he to weigh his case in scales. The scales, as he sat with Kate, often dangled in the line of his vision ; he saw them, large and black, while he talked or listened, take, in the bright air, singular positions. Sometimes the right was down and sometimes the left ; never a happy equipoise—one or the other always kicking the beam. Thus was kept before him the question of whether it were more ignoble to ask a woman to take her chance with you, or to accept it from your conscience that her chance could be at the best but one of the degrees of privation ; whether too, otherwise, marrying for money mightn't after all be a smaller cause of shame than the mere dread of marrying without. Through these variations of mood and view, nevertheless, the mark on his forehead stood clear ; he saw himself remain without whether he married or not. It was a line on which his fancy could be admirably active ; the innumerable ways of making money were beautifully present to him ; he could have handled them for his newspaper as easily as he handled everything. He was quite aware how he handled everything ; it was another mark on his forehead : the pair of smudges from the thumb of fortune, the brand on the passive fleece, dated from the primal hour and kept each other

company. He wrote, as for print, with deplorable
ease; since there had been nothing to stop him even
at the age of ten, so there was as little at twenty; it
was part of his fate in the first place and part of the
wretched public's in the second. The innumerable
ways of making money were, no doubt, at all events,
what his imagination often was busy with after he
had tilted his chair and thrown back his head with his
hands clasped behind it. What would most have prolonged that attitude, moreover, was the reflexion that
the ways were ways only for others. Within the
minute now—however this might be—he was aware
of a nearer view than he had yet quite had of those
circumstances on his companion's part that made
least for simplicity of relation. He saw above all how
she saw them herself, for she spoke of them at present
with the last frankness, telling him of her visit to her
father and giving him, in an account of her subsequent
scene with her sister, an instance of how she was
perpetually reduced to patching-up, in one way or
another, that unfortunate woman's hopes.

"The tune," she exclaimed, "to which we're a
failure as a family!" With which he had it all again
from her—and this time, as it seemed to him, more
than all : the dishonour her father had brought them,
his folly and cruelty and wickedness ; the wounded
state of her mother, abandoned despoiled and helpless, yet, for the management of such a home as
remained to them, dreadfully unreasonable too ; the
extinction of her two young brothers—one, at nine-
teen, the eldest of the house, by typhoid fever con-
tracted at a poisonous little place, as they had afterwards found out, that they had taken for a summer ;
the other, the flower of the flock, a middy on the
Britannia, dreadfully drowned, and not even by an
accident at sea, but by cramp, unrescued, while bath-
ing, too late in the autumn, in a wretched little river

58

during a holiday visit to the home of a shipmate. Then Marian's unnatural marriage, in itself a kind of spiritless turning of the other cheek to fortune : her actual wretchedness and plaintiveness, her greasy children, her impossible claims, her odious visitors—these things completed the proof of the heaviness, for them all, of the hand of fate. Kate confessedly described them with an excess of impatience ; it was much of her charm for Densher that she gave in general that turn to her descriptions, partly as if to amuse him by free and humorous colour, partly—and that charm was the greatest—as if to work off, for her own relief, her constant perception of the incongruity of things. She had seen the general show too early and too sharply, and was so intelligent that she knew it and allowed for that misfortune ; therefore when, in talk with him, she was violent and almost un-feminine, it was quite as if they had settled, for inter-course, on the short cut of the fantastic and the happy language of exaggeration. It had come to be definite between them at a primary stage that, if they could have no other straight way, the realm of thought at least was open to them. They could think whatever they liked about whatever they would—in other words they could say it. Saying it for each other, for each other alone, only of course added to the taste. The implication was thereby constant that what they said when not together had no taste for them at all, and nothing could have served more to launch them, at special hours, on their small floating island than such an assumption that they were only making believe everywhere else. Our young man, it must be added, was conscious enough that it was Kate who profited most by this particular play of the fact of intimacy. It always struck him she had more life than he to react from, and when she recounted the dark disasters of her house and glanced at the hard odd offset of her

present exaltation—since as exaltation it was apparently to be considered—he felt his own grey domestic
annals make little show.   It was naturally, in all such
reference, the question of her father's character that
engaged him most, but her picture of her adventure in
Chirk Street gave him a sense of how little as yet that
character was clear to him.   What was it, to speak
plainly, that Mr. Croy had originally done ?

"I don't know—and I don't want to.   I only know
that years and years ago—when I was about fifteen
—something or other happened that made him impossible.   I mean impossible for the world at large
first, and then, little by little, for mother.   We of
course didn't know it at the time," Kate explained,
"but we knew it later ; and it was, oddly enough, my
sister who first made out that he had done something.
I can hear her now—the way, one cold black Sunday
morning when, on account of an extraordinary fog,
we hadn't gone to church, she broke it to me by the
school-room fire.   I was reading a history-book by the
lamp—when we didn't go to church we had to read
history-books—and I suddenly heard her say, out of
the fog, which was in the room, and apropos of
nothing : ' Papa has done something wicked.'   And
the curious thing was that I believed it on the spot
and have believed it ever since, though she could tell
me nothing more—neither what was the wickedness,
nor how she knew, nor what would happen to him, nor
anything else about it.   We had our sense always that
all sorts of things *had* happened, were all the while
happening, to him ; so that when Marian only said
she was sure, tremendously sure, that she had made
it out for herself, but that that was enough, I took
her word for it—it seemed somehow so natural.   We
were not, however, to ask mother—which made it
more natural still, and I said never a word.   But
mother, strangely enough, spoke of it to me, in time,

of her own accord—this was very much later on. He
hadn't been with us for ever so long, but we were used
to that. She must have had some fear, some conviction that I had an idea, some idea of her own that
it was the best thing to do. She came out as abruptly
as Marian had done : ' If you hear anything against
your father—anything I mean except that he's odious
and vile—remember it's perfectly false.' That was
the way I knew it was true, though I recall my saying
to her then that I of course knew it wasn't. She
might have told me it was true, and yet have trusted
me to contradict fiercely enough any accusation of
him that I should meet—to contradict it much more
fiercely and effectively, I think, than she would have
done herself. As it happens, however," the girl went
on, " I've never had occasion, and I've been conscious
of it with a sort of surprise. It has made the world
seem at times more decent. No one has so much as
breathed to me. That has been a part of the silence,
the silence that surrounds him, the silence that, for
the world, has washed him out. He doesn't exist for
people. And yet I'm as sure as ever. In fact,
though I know no more than I did then, I'm more
sure. And that," she wound up, " is what I sit here
and tell you about my own father. If you don't call
it a proof of confidence I don't know what will satisfy
you."

"It satisfies me beautifully," Densher returned,
" but it doesn't, my dear child, very greatly enlighten
me. You don't, you know, really tell me anything.
It's so vague that what am I to think but that you
may very well be mistaken ? What has he done, if
no one can name it ? "

" He has done everything."

" Oh—everything ! Everything's nothing."

" Well then," said Kate, " he has done some particular thing. It's known—only, thank God, not to

us. But it has been the end of him. *You* could doubtless find out with a little trouble. You can ask about."

Densher for a moment said nothing ; but the next moment he made it up. " I wouldn't find out for the world, and I'd rather lose my tongue than put a question."

" And yet it's a part of me," said Kate.

" A part of you ? "

" My father's dishonour." Then she sounded for him, but more deeply than ever yet, her note of proud still pessimism. " How can such a thing as that not be the great thing in one's life ? "

She had to take from him again, on this, one of his long looks, and she took it to its deepest, its headiest dregs. " I shall ask you, for the great thing in your life," he said, " to depend on *me* a little more." After which, just debating, " Doesn't he belong to some club ? " he asked.

She had a grave headshake. " He used to—to many."

" But he has dropped them ? "

" They've dropped *him*. Of that I'm sure. It ought to do for you. I offered him," the girl immediately continued—" and it was for that I went to him—to come and be with him, make a home for him so far as is possible. But he won't hear of it."

Densher took this in with marked but generous wonder. " You offered him—' impossible ' as you describe him to me—to live with him and share his disadvantages ? " The young man saw for the moment only the high beauty of it. " You *are* gallant ! "

" Because it strikes you as being brave for him ? " She wouldn't in the least have this. " It wasn't courage—it was the opposite. I did it to save myself —to escape."

He had his air, so constant at this stage, as of her giving him finer things than any one to think about. " Escape from what ? "

" From everything."

" Do you by any chance mean from me ? "

" No ; I spoke to him of you, told him—or what amounted to it—that I would bring you, if he would allow it, with me."

" But he won't allow it," said Densher.

" Won't hear of it on any terms. He won't help me, won't save me, won't hold out a finger to me," Kate went on. " He simply wriggles away, in his inimitable manner, and throws me back."

" Back then, after all, thank goodness," Densher concurred, " on me."

But she spoke again as with the sole vision of the whole scene she had evoked. " It's a pity, because you'd like him. He's wonderful—he's charming." Her companion gave one of the laughs that showed again how inveterately he felt in her tone something that banished the talk of other women, so far as he knew other women, to the dull desert of the conventional, and she had already continued. " He would make himself delightful to you."

" Even while objecting to me ? "

" Well, he likes to please," the girl explained— " personally. I've seen it make him wonderful. He would appreciate you and be clever with you. It's to *me* he objects—that is as to my liking you."

" Heaven be praised then," cried Densher, " that you like me enough for the objection ! "

But she met it after an instant with some inconsequence. " I don't. I offered to give you up, if necessary, to go to him. But it made no difference, and that's what I mean," she pursued, " by his declining me on any terms. The point is, you see, that I don't escape."

Densher wondered. " But if you didn't wish to escape *me* ? "

" I wished to escape Aunt Maud. But he insists that it's through her and through her only that I may help him ; just as Marian insists that it's through her, and through her only, that I can help *her*. That's what I mean," she again explained, " by their turning me back."

The young man thought. " Your sister turns you back too ? "

" Oh with a push ! "

" But have you offered to live with your sister ? "

" I would in a moment if she'd have me. That's all my virtue—a narrow little family feeling. I've a small stupid piety—I don't know what to call it." Kate bravely stuck to that ; she made it out. " Sometimes, alone, I've to smother my shrieks when I think of my poor mother. She went through things—they pulled her down ; I know what they were now—I didn't then, for I was a pig ; and my position, compared with hers, is an insolence of success. That's what Marian keeps before me ; that's what papa himself, as I say, so inimitably does. My position's a value, a great value, for them both "—she followed and followed. Lucid and ironic, she knew no merciful muddle. " It's *the* value—the only one they have."

Everything between our young couple moved to-day, in spite of their pauses, their margin, to a quicker measure—the quickness and anxiety playing lightning-like in the sultriness. Densher watched, decidedly, as he had never done before. " And the fact you speak of holds you ! "

" Of course it holds me. It's a perpetual sound in my ears. It makes me ask myself if I've any right to personal happiness, any right to anything but to be as rich and overflowing, as smart and shining, as I can be made."

64

Densher had a pause. " Oh you might by good
luck have the personal happiness too."

Her immediate answer to this was a silence like his
own ; after which she gave him straight in the face,
but quite simply and quietly : " Darling ! "

It took him another moment ; then he was also
quiet and simple. " Will you settle it by our being
married to-morrow—as we can, with perfect ease,
civilly ? "

" Let us wait to arrange it," Kate presently replied,
" till after you've seen her."

" Do you call that adoring me ? " Densher demanded.

They were talking, for the time, with the strangest
mixture of deliberation and directness, and nothing
could have been more in the tone of it than the way
she at last said : " You're afraid of her yourself."

He gave rather a glazed smile. " For young
persons of a great distinction and a very high spirit
we're a caution ! "

" Yes," she took it straight up ; " we're hideously
intelligent. But there's fun in it too. We must get
our fun where we can. I think," she added, and for
that matter not without courage, " our relation's
quite beautiful. It's not a bit vulgar. I cling to
some saving romance in things."

It made him break into a laugh that had more
freedom than his smile. " How you must be afraid
you'll chuck me ! "

" No, no, *that* would be vulgar. But of course,"
she admitted, " I do see my danger of doing something
base."

" Then what can be so base as sacrificing me ? "

" I *shan't* sacrifice you. Don't cry out till you're
hurt. I shall sacrifice nobody and nothing, and that's
just my situation, that I want and that I shall try
for everything. That," she wound up, " is how I see

myself (and how I see you quite as much) acting for them."

" For ' them ' ? "—and the young man extravagantly marked his coldness. " Thank you ! "

" Don't you care for them ? "

" Why should I ? What are they to me but a serious nuisance ? "

As soon as he had permitted himself this qualification of the unfortunate persons she so perversely cherished he repented of his roughness—and partly because he expected a flash from her. But it was one of her finest sides that she sometimes flashed with a mere mild glow. " I don't see why you don't make out a little more that if we avoid stupidity we may do *all*. We may keep her."

He stared. " Make her pension us ? "

" Well, wait at least till we've seen."

He thought. " Seen what can be got out of her ? "

Kate for a moment said nothing. " After all I never asked her ; never, when our troubles were at the worst, appealed to her nor went near her. She fixed upon me herself, settled on me with her wonderful gilded claws."

" You speak," Densher observed, " as if she were a vulture."

" Call it an eagle—with a gilded beak as well, and with wings for great flights. If she's a thing of the air, in short—say at once a great seamed silk balloon —I never myself got into her car. I was her choice."

It had really, her sketch of the affair, a high colour and a great style ; at all of which he gazed a minute as at a picture by a master. " What she must see in you ! "

" Wonders ! " . And, speaking it loud, she stood straight up. " Everything. There it is."

Yes, there it was, and as she remained before him

he continued to face it. " So that what you mean is that I'm to do my part in somehow squaring her ? "

" See her, see her," Kate said with impatience.

" And grovel to her ? "

" Ah do what you like ! " And she walked in her impatience away.

II

His eyes had followed her at this time quite long enough, before he overtook her, to make out more than ever in the poise of her head, the pride of her step—he didn't know what best to call it—a part at least of Mrs. Lowder's reasons. He consciously winced while he figured his presenting himself as a reason opposed to these ; though at the same moment, with the source of Aunt Maud's inspiration thus before him, he was prepared to conform, by almost any abject attitude or profitable compromise, to his companion's easy injunction. He would do as *she* liked—his own liking might come off as it would. He would help her to the utmost of his power ; for, all the rest of this day and the next, her easy injunction, tossed off that way as she turned her beautiful back, was like the crack of a great whip in the blue air, the high element in which Mrs. Lowder hung. He wouldn't grovel perhaps—he wasn't quite ready for that ; but he would be patient, ridiculous, reasonable, unreasonable, and above all deeply diplomatic. He would be clever with all his cleverness—which he now shook hard, as he sometimes shook his poor dear shabby old watch, to start it up again. It wasn't, thank goodness, as if there weren't plenty of that " factor " (to use one of his great newspaper-words), and with what they could muster between them it would be little to the credit of their star, however pale, that

defeat and surrender—surrender so early, so immediate—should have to ensue. It was not indeed that
he thought of that disaster as at the worst a direct
sacrifice of their possibilities : he imagined it—which
was enough—as some proved vanity, some exposed
fatuity in the idea of bringing Mrs. Lowder round.
When shortly afterwards, in this lady's vast drawing-
room—the apartments at Lancaster Gate had struck
him from the first as of prodigious extent—he awaited
her, at her request, conveyed in a " reply-paid " tele-
gram, his theory was that of their still clinging to their
idea, though with a sense of the difficulty of it really
enlarged to the scale of the place.

He had the place for a long time—it seemed to him
a quarter of an hour—to himself ; and while Aunt
Maud kept him and kept him, while observation and
reflexion crowded on him, he asked himself what was
to be expected of a person who could treat one like
that. The visit, the hour were of her own proposing,
so that her delay, no doubt, was but part of a general
plan of putting him to inconvenience. As he walked
to and fro, however, taking in the message of her
massive florid furniture, the immense expression of
her signs and symbols, he had as little doubt of the
inconvenience he was prepared to suffer. He found
himself even facing the thought that he had nothing
to fall back on, and that that was as great an humilia-
tion in a good cause as a proud man could desire. It
hadn't yet been so distinct to him that he made no
show—literally not the smallest ; so complete a show
seemed made there all about him ; so almost abnor-
mally affirmative, so aggressively erect, were the huge
heavy objects that syllabled his hostess's story.
" When all's said and done, you know, she's colossally
vulgar "—he had once all but noted that of her to her
niece ; only just keeping it back at the last, keeping it
to himself with all its danger about it. It mattered

69

because it bore so directly, and he at all events quite felt it a thing that Kate herself would some day bring out to him. It bore directly at present, and really all the more that somehow, strangely, it didn't in the least characterise the poor woman as dull or stale. She was vulgar with freshness, almost with beauty, since there was beauty, to a degree, in the play of so big and bold a temperament. She was in fine quite the largest possible quantity to deal with ; and he was in the cage of the lioness without his whip—the whip, in a word, of a supply of proper retorts. He had no retort but that he loved the girl—which in such a house as that was painfully cheap. Kate had mentioned to him more than once that her aunt was Passionate, speaking of it as a kind of offset and uttering it as with a capital P, marking it as something that he might, that he in fact ought to, turn about in some way to their advantage. He wondered at this hour to what advantage he could turn it ; but the case grew less simple the longer he waited. Decidedly there was something he hadn't enough of.

His slow march to and fro seemed to give him the very measure ; as he paced and paced the distance it became the desert of his poverty ; at the sight of which expanse moreover he could pretend to himself as little as before that the desert looked redeemable. Lancaster Gate looked rich—that was all the effect ; which it was unthinkable that any state of his own should ever remotely resemble. He read more vividly, more critically, as has been hinted, the appearances about him ; and they did nothing so much as make him wonder at his esthetic reaction. He hadn't known—and in spite of Kate's repeated reference to her own rebellions of taste—that he should " mind " so much how an independent lady might decorate her house. It was the language of the house itself that spoke to him, writing out for him with sur-

passing breadth and freedom the associations and con-
ceptions, the ideals and possibilities of the mistress.
Never, he felt sure, had he seen so many things so
unanimously ugly—operatively, ominously so cruel.
He was glad to have found this last name for the
whole character; "cruel" somehow played into the
subject for an article—an article that his impression
put straight into his mind. He would write about
the heavy horrors that could still flourish, that lifted
their undiminished heads, in an age so proud of its
short way with false gods; and it would be funny if
what he should have got from Mrs. Lowder were to
prove after all but a small amount of copy. Yet the
great thing, really the dark thing, was that, even while
he thought of the quick column he might add up, he
felt it less easy to laugh at the heavy horrors than to
quail before them. He couldn't describe and dismiss
them collectively, call them either Mid-Victorian or
Early—not being certain they were rangeable under
one rubric. It was only manifest they were splendid
and were furthermore conclusively British. They
constituted an order and abounded in rare material—
precious woods, metals, stuffs, stones. He had never
dreamed of anything so fringed and scalloped, so
buttoned and corded, drawn everywhere so tight and
curled everywhere so thick. He had never dreamed
of so much gilt and glass, so much satin and plush, so
much rosewood and marble and malachite. But it
was above all the solid forms, the wasted finish, the
misguided cost, the general attestation of morality
and money, a good conscience and a big balance.
These things finally represented for him a portentous
negation of his own world of thought—of which, for
that matter, in presence of them, he became as for the
first time hopelessly aware. They revealed it to him
by their merciless difference.

His interview with Aunt Maud, none the less, took

by no means the turn he had expected. Passionate though her nature, no doubt, Mrs. Lowder on this occasion neither threatened nor appealed. Her arms of aggression, her weapons of defence, were presumably close at hand, but she left them untouched and unmentioned, and was in fact so bland that he properly perceived only afterwards how adroit she had been. He properly perceived something else as well, which complicated his case ; he shouldn't have known what to call it if he hadn't called it her really imprudent good nature. Her blandness, in other words, wasn't mere policy—he wasn't dangerous enough for policy : it was the result, he could see, of her fairly liking him a little. From the moment she did that she herself became more interesting, and who knew what might happen should he take to liking *her* ? Well, it was a risk he naturally must face. She fought him at any rate but with one hand, with a few loose grains of stray powder. He recognised at the end of ten minutes, and even without her explaining it, that if she had made him wait it hadn't been to wound him ; they had by that time almost directly met on the fact of her intention. She had wanted him to think for himself of what she proposed to say to him—not having otherwise announced it ; wanted to let it come home to him on the spot, as she had shrewdly believed it would. Her first question, on appearing, had practically been as to whether he hadn't taken her hint, and this inquiry assumed so many things that it immediately made discussion frank and large. He knew, with the question put, that the hint was just what he *had* taken ; knew that she had made him quickly forgive her the display of her power ; knew that if he didn't take care he should understand her, and the strength of her purpose, to say nothing of that of her imagination, nothing of the length of her purse, only too well. Yet he pulled himself up with

the thought too that he wasn't going to be afraid of
understanding her ; he was just going to understand
and understand without detriment to the feeblest,
even, of his passions. The play of one's mind gave
one away, at the best, dreadfully, in action, in the
need for action, where simplicity was all ; but when
one couldn't prevent it the thing was to make it
complete. There would never be mistakes but for
the original fun of mistakes. What he must *use* his
fatal intelligence for was to resist. Mrs. Lowder
meanwhile might use it for whatever she liked.

It was after she had begun her statement of her
own idea about Kate that he began on his side to
reflect that—with her manner of offering it as really
sufficient if he would take the trouble to embrace it
—she couldn't half hate him. That was all, positively,
she seemed to show herself for the time as attempting ;
clearly, if she did her intention justice she would have
nothing more disagreeable to do. " If I hadn't been
ready to go very much further, you understand, I
wouldn't have gone so far. I don't care what you
repeat to her—the more you repeat to her perhaps
the better ; and at any rate there's nothing she doesn't
already know. I don't say it for her ; I say it for
you—when I want to reach my niece I know how to
do it straight." So Aunt Maud delivered herself—
as with homely benevolence, in the simplest but the
clearest terms ; virtually conveying that, though a
word to the wise was doubtless, in spite of the adage,
not always enough, a word to the good could never
fail to be. The sense our young man read into her
words was that she liked him because he was good—
was really by her measure good enough : good enough
that is to give up her niece for her and go his way
in peace. But *was* he good enough—by his own
measure ? He fairly wondered, while she more fully
expressed herself, if it might be his doom to prove so.

" She's the finest possible creature—of course you flatter yourself you know it. But I know it quite as well as you possibly can—by which I mean a good deal better yet ; and the tune to which I'm ready to prove my faith compares favourably enough, I think, with anything you can do. I don't say it because she's my niece—that's nothing to me : I might have had fifty nieces, and I wouldn't have brought one of them to this place if I hadn't found her to my taste. I don't say I wouldn't have done something else, but I wouldn't have put up with her presence. Kate's presence, by good fortune, I marked early. Kate's presence—unluckily for *you*—is everything I could possibly wish. Kate's presence is, in short, as fine as you know, and I've been keeping it for the comfort of my declining years. I've watched it long ; I've been saving it up and letting it, as you say of investments, appreciate ; and you may judge whether, now it has begun to pay so, I'm likely to consent to treat for it with any but a high bidder. I can do the best with her, and I've my idea of the best."

" Oh I quite conceive," said Densher, " that your idea of the best isn't me."

It was an oddity of Mrs. Lowder's that her face in speech was like a lighted window at night, but that silence immediately drew the curtain. The occasion for reply allowed by her silence was never easy to take, yet she was still less easy to interrupt. The great glaze of her surface, at all events, gave her visitor no present help. " I didn't ask you to come to hear what it isn't—I asked you to come to hear what it *is*."

" Of course," Densher laughed, " that's very great indeed."

His hostess went on as if his contribution to the subject were barely relevant. " I want to see her high, high up—high up and in the light."

74

" Ah you naturally want to marry her to a duke and are eager to smooth away any hitch."

She gave him so, on this, the mere effect of the drawn blind that it quite forced him at first into the sense, possibly just, of his having shown for flippant, perhaps even for low.   He had been looked at so, in blighted moments of presumptuous youth, by big cold public men, but never, so far as he could recall, by any private lady.   More than anything yet it gave him the measure of his companion's subtlety, and thereby of Kate's possible career.   " Don't be *too* impossible ! "—he feared from his friend, for a moment, some such answer as that ; and then felt, as she spoke otherwise, as if she were letting him off easily.   " I want her to marry a great man."   That was all ; but, more and more, it was enough ; and if it hadn't been her next words would have made it so. " And I think of her what I think.   There you are."

They sat for a little face to face upon it, and he was conscious of something deeper still, of something she wished him to understand if he only would.   To that extent she did appeal—appealed to the intelligence she desired to show she believed him to possess.   He was meanwhile, at all events, not the man wholly to fail of comprehension.   " Of course I'm aware how little I can answer to any fond proud dream.   You've a view—a grand one ; into which I perfectly enter. I thoroughly understand what I'm not, and I'm much obliged to you for not reminding me of it in any rougher way."   She said nothing—she kept that up ; it might even have been to let him go further, if he was capable of it, in the way of poorness of spirit.   It was one of those cases in which a man couldn't show, if he showed at all, save for poor ; unless indeed he preferred to show for asinine.   It was the plain truth : he *was*—on Mrs. Lowder's basis, the only one in question—a very small quantity, and he did know,

damnably, what made quantities large. He desired
to be perfectly simple, yet in the midst of that effort
a deeper apprehension throbbed. Aunt Maud clearly
conveyed it, though he couldn't later on have said
how. "You don't really matter, I believe, so much
as you think, and I'm not going to make you a martyr
by banishing you. Your performances with Kate in
the Park are ridiculous so far as they're meant as
consideration for me; and I had much rather see
you myself—since you're, in your way, my dear
young man, delightful—and arrange with you, count
with you, as I easily, as I perfectly should. Do you
suppose me so stupid as to quarrel with you if it's not
really necessary ? It won't—it would be too absurd !
—be necessary. I can bite your head off any day,
any day I really open my mouth ; and I'm dealing
with you now, see—and successfully judge—without
opening it. I do things handsomely all round—I
place you in the presence of the plan with which,
from the moment it's a case of taking you seriously,
you're incompatible. Come then as near it as you
like, walk all round it—don't be afraid you'll hurt it !
—and live on with it before you."

He afterwards felt that if she hadn't absolutely
phrased all this it was because she so soon made him
out as going with her far enough. He was so pleasantly affected by her asking no promise of him, her
not proposing he should pay for her indulgence by his
word of honour not to interfere, that he gave her a
kind of general assurance of esteem. Immediately
afterwards then he was to speak of these things to
Kate, and what by that time came back to him first of
all was the way he had said to her—he mentioned it
to the girl—very much as one of a pair of lovers says
in a rupture by mutual consent : " I hope immensely
of course that you'll always regard me as a friend."
This had perhaps been going far—he submitted it

all to Kate ; but really there had been so much in it
that it was to be looked at, as they might say, wholly
in its own light.   Other things than those we have
presented had come up before the close of his scene
with Aunt Maud, but this matter of her not treating
him as a peril of the first order easily predominated.
There was moreover plenty to talk about on the
occasion of his subsequent passage with our young
woman, it having been put to him abruptly, the night
before, that he might give himself a lift and do his
newspaper a service—so flatteringly was the case
expressed—by going for fifteen or twenty weeks to
America.   The idea of a series of letters from the
United States from the strictly social point of view
had for some time been nursed in the inner sanctuary
at whose door he sat, and the moment was now
deemed happy for letting it loose.   The imprisoned
thought had, in a word, on the opening of the door,
flown straight out into Densher's face, or perched at
least on his shoulder, making him look up in surprise
from his mere inky office-table.   His account of the
matter to Kate was that he couldn't refuse—not
being in a position as yet to refuse anything ; but
that his being chosen for such an errand confounded
his sense of proportion.   He was definite as to his
scarce knowing how to measure the honour, which
struck him as equivocal ; he hadn't quite supposed
himself the man for the class of job.   This confused
consciousness, he intimated, he had promptly enough
betrayed to his manager ; with the effect, however,
of seeing the question surprisingly clear up.   What
it came to was that the sort of twaddle that wasn't in
his chords was, unexpectedly, just what they happened
this time not to want.   They wanted his letters, for
queer reasons, about as good as he could let them
come ; he was to play his own little tune and not be
afraid : that was the whole point.

It would have been the whole, that is, had there not been a sharper one still in the circumstance that he was to start at once. His mission, as they called it at the office, would probably be over by the end of June, which was desirable ; but to bring that about he must now not lose a week ; his inquiries, he understood, were to cover the whole ground, and there were reasons of state—reasons operating at the seat of empire in Fleet Street—why the nail should be struck on the head. Densher made no secret to Kate of his having asked for a day to decide ; and his account of that matter was that he felt he owed it to her to speak to her first. She assured him on this that nothing so much as that scruple had yet shown her how they were bound together : she was clearly proud of his letting a thing of such importance depend on her, but she was clearer still as to his instant duty. She rejoiced in his prospect and urged him to his task ; she should miss him too dreadfully—of course she should miss him ; but she made so little of it that she spoke with jubilation of what he would see and would do. She made so much of this last quantity that he laughed at her innocence, though also with scarce the heart to give her the real size of his drop in the daily bucket. He was struck at the same time with her happy grasp of what had really occurred in Fleet Street—all the more that it was his own final reading. He was to pull the subject up—that was just what they wanted ; and it would take more than all the United States together, visit them each as he might, to let *him* down. It was just because he didn't nose about and babble, because he wasn't the usual gossip-monger, that they had picked him out. It was a branch of their correspondence with which they evidently wished a new tone associated, such a tone as, from now on, it would have always to take from his example.

" How you ought indeed, when you understand so well, to be a journalist's wife ! " Densher exclaimed in admiration even while she struck him as fairly hurrying him off.

But she was almost impatient of the praise. " What do you expect one *not* to understand when one cares for you ? "

" Ah then I'll put it otherwise and say ' How much you care for me ! ' "

" Yes," she assented ; " it fairly redeems my stupidity. I *shall*, with a chance to show it," she added, " have some imagination for you."

She spoke of the future this time as so little contingent that he felt a queerness of conscience in making her the report that he presently arrived at on what had passed for him with the real arbiter of their destiny. The way for that had been blocked a little by his news from Fleet Street ; but in the crucible of their happy discussion this element soon melted into the other, and in the mixture that ensued the parts were not to be distinguished. The young man moreover, before taking his leave, was to see why Kate had spoken with a wisdom indifferent to that, and was to come to the vision by a devious way that deepened the final cheer. Their faces were turned to the illumined quarter as soon as he had answered her question on the score of their being to appearance able to play patience, a prodigious game of patience, with success. It was for the possibility of the appearance that she had a few days before so earnestly pressed him to see her aunt ; and if after his hour with that lady it had not struck Densher that he had seen her to the happiest purpose the poor facts flushed with a better meaning as Kate, one by one, took them up.

" If she consents to your coming why isn't that everything ? "

" It *is* everything ; everything *she* thinks it. It's

the probability—I mean as Mrs. Lowder measures probability—that I may be prevented from becoming a complication for her by some arrangement, *any* arrangement, through which you shall see me often and easily. She's sure of my want of money, and that gives her time. She believes in my having a certain amount of delicacy, in my wishing to better my state before I put the pistol to your head in respect to sharing it. The time this will take figures for her as the time that will help her if she doesn't spoil her chance by treating me badly. She doesn't at all wish moreover," Densher went on, " to treat me badly, for I believe, upon my honour, odd as it may sound to you, that she personally rather likes me and that if you weren't in question I might almost become her pet young man. She doesn't disparage intellect and culture—quite the contrary ; she wants them to adorn her board and be associated with her name ; and I'm sure it has sometimes cost her a real pang that I should be so desirable, at once, and so impossible." He paused a moment, and his companion then saw how strange a smile was in his face—a smile as strange even as the adjunct in her own of this informing vision. " I quite suspect her of believing that, if the truth were known, she likes me literally better than—deep down—you yourself do : wherefore she does me the honour to think I may be safely left to kill my own cause. There, as I say, comes in her margin. I'm not the sort of stuff of romance that wears, that washes, that survives use, that resists familiarity. Once in any degree admit that, and your pride and prejudice will take care of the rest !—the pride fed full, meanwhile, by the system she means to practise with you, and the prejudice excited by the comparisons she'll enable you to make, from which I shall come off badly. She likes me, but she'll never like me so much as when she has succeeded a little better in making me look wretched. For then *you'll* like me less."

Kate showed for this evocation a due interest, but no alarm ; and it was a little as if to pay his tender cynicism back in kind that she after an instant replied : " I see, I see—what an immense affair she must think me ! One was aware, but you deepen the impression."

" I think you'll make no mistake," said Densher, " in letting it go as deep as it will."

He had given her indeed, she made no scruple of showing, plenty to amuse herself with. " Her facing the music, her making you boldly as welcome as you say—that's an awfully big theory, you know, and worthy of all the other big things that in one's acquaintance with people give her a place so apart."

" Oh she's grand," the young man allowed ; " she's on the scale altogether of the car of Juggernaut —which was a kind of image that came to me yesterday while I waited for her at Lancaster Gate. The things in your drawing-room there were like the forms of the strange idols, the mystic excrescences, with which one may suppose the front of the car to bristle."

" Yes, aren't they ? " the girl returned ; and they had, over all that aspect of their wonderful lady, one of those deep and free interchanges that made everything but confidence a false note for them. There were complications, there were questions ; but they were so much more together than they were anything else. Kate uttered for a while no word of refutation of Aunt Maud's " big " diplomacy, and they left it there, as they would have left any other fine product, for a monument to her powers. But, Densher related further, he had had in other respects too the car of Juggernaut to face ; he omitted nothing from his account of his visit, least of all the way Aunt Maud had frankly at last—though indeed only under artful pressure—fallen foul of his very type, his want of the right marks, his foreign accidents, his queer ante-cedents. She had told him he was but half a Briton, which, he granted Kate, would have been dreadful if he hadn't so let himself in for it.

" I was really curious, you see," he explained, " to find out from her what sort of queer creature, what sort of social anomaly, in the light of such conventions as hers, such an education as mine makes one pass for."

Kate said nothing for a little ; but then, " Why should you care ? " she asked.

" Oh," he laughed, " I like her so much ; and then, for a man of my trade, her views, her spirit, are essentially a thing to get hold of : they belong to the great public mind that we meet at every turn and that we must keep setting up ' codes ' with. Besides," he added, " I want to please her personally."

" Ah yes, we must please her personally ! " his companion echoed ; and the words may represent all their definite recognition, at· the time, of Densher's politic gain. They had in fact between this and his start for New York many matters to handle, and the question he now touched upon came up for Kate above all. She looked at him as if he had really told her aunt more of his immediate personal story than he had ever told herself. This, if it had been so, was an accident, and it perched him there with her for half an hour, like a cicerone and his victim on a tower-top, before as much of the bird's-eye view of his early years abroad, his migratory parents, his Swiss schools, his German university, as she had easy attention for. A man, he intimated, a man of their world, would have spotted him straight as to many of these points ; a man of their world, so far as they had a world, would have been through the English mill. But it was none the less charming to make his confession to

82

a woman ; women had in fact for such differences
blessedly more imagination and blessedly more sympathy.   Kate showed at present as much of both as
his case could require ; when she had had it from
beginning to end she declared that she now made out
more than ever yet what she loved him for.   She had
herself, as a child, lived with some continuity in the
world across the Channel, coming home again still a
child ; and had participated after that, in her teens,
in her mother's brief but repeated retreats to Dresden,
to Florence, to Biarritz, weak and expensive attempts
at economy from which there stuck to her—though
in general coldly expressed, through the instinctive
avoidance of cheap raptures—the religion of foreign
things.   When it was revealed to her how many more
foreign things were in Merton Densher than he had
hitherto taken the trouble to catalogue, she almost
faced him as if he were a map of the continent or a
handsome present of a delightful new " Murray."
He hadn't meant to swagger, he had rather meant to
plead, though with Mrs. Lowder he had meant also
a little to explain.   His father had been, in strange
countries, in twenty settlements of the English,
British chaplain, resident or occasional, and had had
for years the unusual luck of never wanting a billet.
His career abroad had therefore been unbroken, and
as his stipend had never been great he had educated
his children, at the smallest cost, in the schools
nearest ; which was also a saving of railway-fares.
Densher's mother, it further appeared, had practised
on her side a distinguished industry, to the success of
which—so far as success ever crowned it—this period
of exile had much contributed : she copied, patient
lady, famous pictures in great museums, having begun
with a happy natural gift and taking in betimes the
scale of her opportunity.   Copyists abroad of course
swarmed, but Mrs. Densher had had a sense and a

83

hand of her own, had arrived at a perfection that persuaded, that even deceived, and that made the " placing " of her work blissfully usual. Her son, who had lost her, held her image sacred, and the effect of his telling Kate all about her, as well as about other matters until then mixed and dim, was to render his history rich, his sources full, his outline anything but common. He had come round, he had come back, he insisted abundantly, to being a Briton : his Cambridge years, his happy connexion, as it had proved, with his father's college, amply certified to that, to say nothing of his subsequent plunge into London, which filled up the measure. But brave enough though his descent to English earth, he had passed, by the way, through zones of air that had left their ruffle on his wings—he had been exposed to initiations indelible. Something had happened to him that could never be undone.

When Kate Croy said to him as much he besought her not to insist, declaring that this indeed was what was gravely the matter with him, that he had been but too probably spoiled for native, for insular use. On which, not unnaturally, she insisted the more, assuring him, without mitigation, that if he was various and complicated, complicated by wit and taste, she wouldn't for the world have had him more helpless ; so that he was driven in the end to accuse her of putting the dreadful truth to him in the hollow guise of flattery. She was making him out as all abnormal in order that she might eventually find him impossible, and since she could make it out but with his aid she had to bribe him by feigned delight to help her. If her last word for him in the connexion was that the way he saw himself was just a precious proof the more of his having tasted of the tree and being thereby prepared to assist her to eat, this gives the happy tone of their whole talk, the measure of the flight of time in the near presence of his settled departure. Kate showed, however, that she was to be more literally taken when she spoke of the relief Aunt Maud would draw from the prospect of his absence.

" Yet one can scarcely see why," he replied, " when she fears me so little."

His friend weighed his objection. " Your idea is that she likes you so much that she'll even go so far as to regret losing you ? "

Well, he saw it in their constant comprehensive way. " Since what she builds on is the gradual process of your alienation, she may take the view that the process constantly requires me. Mustn't I be there to keep it going ? It's in my exile that it may languish."

He went on with that fantasy, but at this point Kate ceased to attend. He saw after a little that she had been following some thought of her own, and he had been feeling the growth of something determinant even through the extravagance of much of the pleasantry, the warm transparent irony, into which their livelier intimacy kept plunging like a confident swimmer. Suddenly she said to him with extra-ordinary beauty : " I engage myself to you for ever."

The beauty was in everything, and he could have separated nothing—couldn't have thought of her face as distinct from the whole joy. Yet her face had a new light. " And I pledge you—I call God to wit-ness !—every spark of my faith ; I give you every drop of my life." That was all, for the moment, but it was enough, and it was almost as quiet as if it were nothing. They were in the open air, in an alley of the Gardens ; the great space, which seemed to arch just then higher and spread wider for them, threw them back into deep concentration. They moved by a common instinct to a spot, within sight, that struck

85

them as fairly sequestered, and there, before their time together was spent, they had extorted from concentration every advance it could make them. They had exchanged vows and tokens, sealed their rich compact, solemnised, so far as breathed words and murmured sounds and lighted eyes and clasped hands could do it, their agreement to belong only, and to belong tremendously, to each other. They were to leave the place accordingly an affianced couple, but before they left it other things still had passed. Densher had declared his horror of bringing to a premature end her happy relation with her aunt ; and they had worked round together to a high level of discretion. Kate's free profession was that she wished not to deprive *him* of Mrs. Lowder's countenance, which in the long run she was convinced he would continue to enjoy ; and as by a blest turn Aunt Maud had demanded of him no promise that would tie his hands they should be able to propitiate their star in their own way and yet remain loyal. One difficulty alone stood out, which Densher named.

" Of course it will never do—we must remember that—from the moment you allow her to found hopes of you for any one else in particular. So long as her view is content to remain as general as at present appears I don't see that we deceive her. At a given hour, you see, she must be undeceived : the only thing therefore is to be ready for the hour and to face it. Only, after all, in that case," the young man observed, " one doesn't quite make out what we shall have got from her."

" What she'll have got from *us* ? " Kate put it with a smile. " What she'll have got from us," the girl went on, " is her own affair—it's for *her* to measure. I asked her for nothing," she added ; " I never put myself upon her. She must take her risks, and she surely understands them. What we shall

86

have got from her is what we've already spoken of," Kate further explained ; " it's that we shall have gained time. And so, for that matter, will she."

Densher gazed a little at all this clearness ; his gaze was not at the present hour into romantic obscurity. " Yes ; no doubt, in our particular situation, time's everything. And then there's the joy of it."

She hesitated. " Of our secret ? "

" Not so much perhaps of our secret in itself, but of what's represented and, as we must somehow feel, secured to us and made deeper and closer by it." And his fine face, relaxed into happiness, covered her with all his meaning. " Our being as we are."

It was as if for a moment she let the meaning sink into her. " So gone ? "

" So gone. So extremely gone. However," he smiled, " we shall go a good deal further." Her answer to which was only the softness of her silence— a silence that looked out for them both at the far reach of their prospect. This was immense, and they thus took final possession of it. They were practically united and splendidly strong ; but there were other things—things they were precisely strong enough to be able successfully to count with and safely to allow for ; in consequence of which they would for the present, subject to some better reason, keep their understanding to themselves. It was not indeed however till after one more observation of Densher's that they felt the question completely straightened out. " The only thing of course is that she may any day absolutely put it to you."

Kate considered. " Ask me where, on my honour, we are ? She may, naturally ; but I doubt if in fact she will. While you're away she'll make the most of that drop of the tension. She'll leave me alone."

" But there'll be my letters."

The girl faced his letters. " Very, very many ? "

87

" Very, very, very many—more than ever ; and you know what that is ! And then," Densher added, " there'll be yours."

" Oh I shan't leave mine on the hall-table. I shall post them myself."

He looked at her a moment. " Do you think then I had best address you elsewhere ? " After which, before she could quite answer, he added with some emphasis : " I'd rather not, you know. It's straighter."

She might again have just waited. " Of course it's straighter. Don't be afraid I shan't be straight. Address me," she continued, " where you like. I shall be proud enough of its being known you write to me."

He turned it over for the last clearness. " Even at the risk of its really bringing down the inquisition ? "

Well, the last clearness now filled her. " I'm not afraid of the inquisition. If she asks if there's anything definite between us I know perfectly what I shall say."

" That I am of course ' gone ' for you ? "

" That I love you as I shall never in my life love any one else, and that she can make what she likes of that." She said it out so splendidly that it was like a new profession of faith, the fulness of a tide breaking through ; and the effect of that in turn was to make her companion meet her with such eyes that she had time again before he could otherwise speak. " Besides, she's just as likely to ask you."

" Not while I'm away."

" Then when you come back."

" Well then," said Densher, " we shall have had our particular joy. But what I feel is," he candidly added, " that, by an idea of her own, her superior policy, she won't ask me. She'll let me off. I shan't have to lie to her."

" It will be left all to me ? " asked Kate.

" All to you ! " he tenderly laughed.

But it was oddly, the very next moment, as if he had perhaps been a shade too candid. His discrimination seemed to mark a possible, a natural reality, a reality not wholly disallowed by the account the girl had just given of her own intention. There *was* a difference in the air—even if none other than the supposedly usual difference in truth between man and woman ; and it was almost as if the sense of this provoked her. She seemed to cast about an instant, and then she went back a little resentfully to something she had suffered to pass a minute before. She appeared to take up rather more seriously than she need the joke about her freedom to deceive. Yet she did this too in a beautiful way. " Men are too stupid —even you. You didn't understand just now why, if I post my letters myself, it won't be for anything so vulgar as to hide them."

" Oh you named it—for the pleasure."

" Yes ; but you didn't, you don't, understand what the pleasure may be. There are refinements—— ! " she more patiently dropped. ' I mean of consciousness, of sensation, of appreciation," she went on. " No," she sadly insisted—" men *don't* know. They know in such matters almost nothing but what women show them."

This was one of the speeches, frequent in her, that, liberally, joyfully, intensely adopted and, in itself, as might be, embraced, drew him again as close to her, and held him as long, as their conditions permitted. " Then that's exactly why we've such an abysmal need of you ! "

BOOK THIRD

I

THE two ladies who, in advance of the Swiss season,
had been warned that their design was unconsidered,
that the passes wouldn't be clear, nor the air mild,
nor the inns open—the two ladies who, characteristic-
ally, had braved a good deal of possibly interested
remonstrance were finding themselves, as their adventure turned out, wonderfully sustained. It was
the judgement of the head-waiters and other function-
aries on the Italian lakes that approved itself now as
interested ; they themselves had been conscious of
impatiences, of bolder dreams—at least the younger
had ; so that one of the things they made out together
—making out as they did an endless variety—was
that in those operatic palaces of the Villa d'Este, of
Cadenabbia, of Pallanza and Stresa, lone women,
however re-enforced by a travelling-library of instruc-
tive volumes, were apt to be beguiled and undone.
Their flights of fancy moreover had been modest ;
they had for instance risked nothing vital in hoping to
make their way by the Brünig. They were making it
in fact happily enough as we meet them, and were
only wishing that, for the wondrous beauty of the
early high-climbing spring, it might have been longer
and the places to pause and rest more numerous.

Such at least had been the intimated attitude of
Mrs. Stringham, the elder of the companions, who
had her own view of the impatiences of the younger,

to which, however, she offered an opposition but of the most circuitous. She moved, the admirable Mrs. Stringham, in a fine cloud of observation and suspicion ; she was in the position, as she believed, of knowing much more about Milly Theale than Milly herself knew, and yet of having to darken her knowledge as well as make it active. The woman in the world least formed by nature, as she was quite aware, for duplicities and labyrinths, she found herself dedicated to personal subtlety by a new set of circumstances, above all by a new personal relation ; had now in fact to recognise that an education in the occult —she could scarce say what to call it—had begun for her the day she left New York with Mildred. She had come on from Boston for that purpose ; had seen little of the girl—or rather had seen her but briefly, for Mrs. Stringham, when she saw anything at all, saw much, saw everything—before accepting her proposal ; and had accordingly placed herself, by her act, in a boat that she more and more estimated as, humanly speaking, of the biggest, though likewise, no doubt, in many ways, by reason of its size, of the safest. In Boston, the winter before, the young lady in whom we are interested had, on the spot, deeply, yet almost tacitly, appealed to her, dropped into her mind the shy conceit of some assistance, some devotion to render. Mrs. Stringham's little life had often been visited by shy conceits—secret dreams that had fluttered their hour between its narrow walls without, for any great part, so much as mustering courage to look out of its rather dim windows. But this imagination—the fancy of a possible link with the remarkable young thing from New York—*had* mustered courage : had perched, on the instant, at the clearest lookout it could find, and might be said to have remained there till, only a few months later, it had caught, in surprise and joy, the unmistakable flash of a signal.

94

Milly Theale had Boston friends, such as they were, and of recent making ; and it was understood that her visit to them—a visit that was not to be meagre—had been undertaken, after a series of bereavements, in the interest of the particular peace that New York couldn't give. It was recognised, liberally enough, that there were many things—perhaps even too many—New York *could* give ; but this was felt to make no difference in the important truth that what you had most to do, under the discipline of life, or of death, was really to feel your situation as grave. Boston could help you to that as nothing else could, and it had extended to Milly, by every presumption, some such measure of assistance. Mrs. Stringham was never to forget—for the moment had not faded, nor the infinitely fine vibration it set up in any degree ceased—her own first sight of the striking apparition, then unheralded and unexplained : the slim, constantly pale, delicately haggard, anomalously, agreeably angular young person, of not more than two-and-twenty summers, in spite of her marks, whose hair was somehow exceptionally red even for the real thing, which it innocently confessed to being, and whose clothes were remarkably black even for robes of mourning, which was the meaning they expressed. It was New York mourning, it was New York hair, it was a New York history, confused as yet, but multitudinous, of the loss of parents, brothers, sisters, almost every human appendage, all on a scale and with a sweep that had required the greater stage ; it was a New York legend of affecting, of romantic isolation, and, beyond everything, it was by most accounts, in respect to the mass of money so piled on the girl's back, a set of New York possibilities. She was alone, she was stricken, she was rich, and in particular was strange—a combination in itself of a nature to engage Mrs. Stringham's attention. But it was the strangeness that most determined our good lady's sympathy, convinced as she had to be that it was greater than any one else—any one but the sole Susan Stringham—supposed. Susan privately settled it that Boston was not in the least seeing her, was only occupied with her seeing Boston, and that any assumed affinity between the two characters was delusive and vain. *She* was seeing her, and she had quite the finest moment of her life in now obeying the instinct to conceal the vision. She couldn't explain it—no one would understand. They would say clever Boston things—Mrs. Stringham was from Burlington Vermont, which she boldly upheld as the real heart of New England, Boston being " too far south "—but they would only darken counsel.

There could be no better proof (than this quick intellectual split) of the impression made on our friend, who shone herself, she was well aware, with but the reflected light of the admirable city. She too had had her discipline, but it had not made her striking ; it had been prosaically usual, though doubtless a decent dose ; and had only made her usual to match it—usual, that is, as Boston went. She had lost first her husband and then her mother, with whom, on her husband's death, she had lived again ; so that now, childless, she was but more sharply single than before. Yet she sat rather coldly light, having, as she called it, enough to live on—so far, that is, as she lived by bread alone : how little indeed she was regularly content with that diet appeared from the name she had made—Susan Shepherd Stringham—as a contributor to the best magazines. She wrote short stories, and she fondly believed she had her " note," the art of showing New England without showing it wholly in the kitchen. She had not herself been brought up in the kitchen ; she knew others who had not ; and to speak for them had thus become with her

a literary mission. To *be* in truth literary had ever
been her dearest thought, the thought that kept her
bright little nippers perpetually in position. There
were masters, models, celebrities, mainly foreign,
whom she finally accounted so and in whose light she
ingeniously laboured ; there were others whom, however chattered about, she ranked with the inane, for
she bristled with discriminations ; but all categories
failed her—they ceased at least to signify—as soon
as she found herself in presence of the real thing, the
romantic life itself. That was what she saw in Mildred—what positively made her hand a while tremble
too much for the pen. She had had, it seemed to
her, a revelation—such as even New England refined
and grammatical couldn't give ; and, all made up as
she was of small neat memories and ingenuities, little
industries and ambitions, mixed with something
moral, personal, that was still more intensely responsive, she felt her new friend would have done her an
ill turn if their friendship shouldn't develop, and yet
that nothing would be left of anything else if it should.
It was for the surrender of everything else that she
was, however, quite prepared, and while she went
about her usual Boston business with her usual Boston
probity she was really all the while holding herself.
She wore her " handsome " felt hat, so Tyrolese, yet
somehow, though feathered from the eagle's wing,
so truly domestic, with the same straightness and
security ; she attached her fur boa with the same
honest precautions ; she preserved her balance on the
ice-slopes with the same practised skill ; she opened,
each evening, her *Transcript* with the same inter-
fusion of suspense and resignation ; she attended her
almost daily concert with the same expenditure of
patience and the same economy of passion ; she flitted
in and out of the Public Library with the air of con-
scientiously returning or bravely carrying off in her

pocket the key of knowledge itself ; and finally—it was what she most did—she watched the thin trickle of a fictive " love-interest " through that somewhat serpentine channel, in the magazines, which she mainly managed to keep clear for it. But the real thing all the while was elsewhere ; the real thing had gone back to New York, leaving behind it the two unsolved questions, quite distinct, of why it *was* real, and whether she should ever be so near it again.

For the figure to which these questions attached themselves she had found a convenient description—she thought of it for herself always as that of a girl with a background. The great reality was in the fact that, very soon, after but two or three meetings, the girl with the background, the girl with the crown of old gold and the mourning that was not as the mourning of Boston, but at once more rebellious in its gloom and more frivolous in its frills, had told her she had never seen any one like her. They had met thus as opposed curiosities, and that simple remark of Milly's —if simple it was—became the most important thing that had ever happened to her ; it deprived the love-interest, for the time, of actuality and even of pertinence ; it moved her first, in short, in a high degree, to gratitude, and then to no small compassion. Yet in respect to this relation at least it was what did prove the key of knowledge ; it lighted up as nothing else could do the poor young woman's history. That the potential heiress of all the ages should never have seen any one like a mere typical subscriber, after all, to the *Transcript* was a truth that—in especial as announced with modesty, with humility, with regret —described a situation. It laid upon the elder woman, as to the void to be filled, a weight of respons-ibility ; but in particular it led her to ask whom poor Mildred *had* then seen, and what range of contacts it had taken to produce such queer surprises. That was really the inquiry that had ended by clearing the air : the key of knowledge was felt to click in the lock from the moment it flashed upon Mrs. Stringham that her friend had been starved for culture. Culture was what she herself represented for her, and it was living up to that principle that would surely prove the great business. She knew, the clever lady, what the principle itself represented, and the limits of her own store ; and a certain alarm would have grown upon her if something else hadn't grown faster. This was, fortunately for her—and we give it in her own words —the sense of a harrowing pathos. That, primarily, was what appealed to her, what seemed to open the door of romance for her still wider than any, than a still more reckless, connexion with the "picture-papers." For such was essentially the point : it was rich, romantic, abysmal, to have, as was evident, thousands and thousands a year, to have youth and intelligence and, if not beauty, at least in equal measure a high dim charming ambiguous oddity, which was even better, and then on top of all to enjoy boundless freedom, the freedom of the wind in the desert—it was unspeakably touching to be so equipped and yet to have been reduced by fortune to little humble-minded mistakes.

It brought our friend's imagination back again to New York, where aberrations were so possible in the intellectual sphere, and it in fact caused a visit she presently paid there to overflow with interest. As Milly had beautifully invited her, so she would hold out if she could against the strain of so much confidence in her mind ; and the remarkable thing was that even at the end of three weeks she *had* held out. But by this time her mind had grown comparatively bold and free ; it was dealing with new quantities, a different proportion altogether—and that had made for refreshment : she had accordingly gone home in

convenient possession of her subject. New York was
vast, New York was startling, with strange histories,
with wild cosmopolite backward generations that
accounted for anything ; and to have got nearer the
luxuriant tribe of which the rare creature was the final
flower, the immense extravagant unregulated cluster,
with free-living ancestors, handsome dead cousins,
lurid uncles, beautiful vanished aunts, persons all
busts and curls, preserved, though so exposed, in the
marble of famous French chisels—all this, to say
nothing of the effect of closer growths of the stem,
was to have had one's small world-space both crowded
and enlarged. Our couple had at all events effected
an exchange ; the elder friend had been as consciously intellectual as possible, and the younger,
abounding in personal revelation, had been as unconsciously distinguished. This was poetry—it was also
history—Mrs. Stringham thought, to a finer tune
even than Maeterlinck and Pater, than Marbot and
Gregorovius. She appointed occasions for the reading
of these authors with her hostess, rather perhaps
than actually achieved great spans ; but what they
managed and what they missed speedily sank for her
into the dim depths of the merely relative, so quickly,
so strongly had she clutched her central clue. All her
scruples and hesitations, all her anxious enthusiasms,
had reduced themselves to a single alarm—the fear
that she really might act on her companion clumsily
and coarsely. She was positively afraid of what she
might do to her, and to avoid that, to avoid it with
piety and passion, to do, rather, nothing at all, to
leave her untouched because no touch one could apply,
however light, however just, however earnest and
anxious, would be half good enough, would be anything but an ugly smutch upon perfection—this now
imposed itself as a consistent, an inspiring thought.
Less than a month after the event that had so

THE WINGS OF THE DOVE

determined Mrs. Stringham's attitude—close upon
the heels, that is, of her return from New York—she
was reached by a proposal that brought up for her the
kind of question her delicacy might have to contend
with. Would she start for Europe with her young
friend at the earliest possible date, and should she be
willing to do so without making conditions ? The
inquiry was launched by wire ; explanations, in
sufficiency, were promised ; extreme urgency was
suggested and a general surrender invited. It was to
the honour of her sincerity that she made the surrender
on the spot, though it was not perhaps altogether to
that of her logic. She had wanted, very consciously,
from the first, to give something up for her new
acquaintance, but she had now no doubt that she was
practically giving up all. What settled this was the
fullness of a particular impression, the impression
that had throughout more and more supported her
and which she would have uttered so far as she might
by saying that the charm of the creature was positively
in the creature's greatness. She would have been
content so to leave it ; unless indeed she had said,
more familiarly, that Mildred was the biggest impression of her life. That was at all events the biggest
account of her, and none but a big clearly would do.
Her situation, as such things were called, was on the
grand scale ; but it still was not that. It was her
nature, once for all—a nature that reminded Mrs.
Stringham of the term always used in the newspapers
about the great new steamers, the inordinate number
of " feet of water " they drew ; so that if, in your little
boat, you had chosen to hover and approach, you
had but yourself to thank, when once motion was
started, for the way the draught pulled you. Milly
drew the feet of water, and odd though it might seem
that a lonely girl, who was not robust and who hated
sound and show, should stir the stream like a leviathan,

her companion floated off with the sense of rocking violently at her side. More than prepared, however, for that excitement, Mrs. Stringham mainly failed of ease in respect to her own consistency. To attach herself for an indefinite time seemed a roundabout way of holding her hands off. If she wished to be sure of neither touching nor smutching, the straighter plan would doubtless have been not to keep her friend within reach. This in fact she fully recognised, and with it the degree to which she desired that the girl should lead her life, a life certain to be so much finer than that of anybody else. The difficulty, however, by good fortune, cleared away as soon as she had further recognised, as she was speedily able to do, that she Susan Shepherd—the name with which Milly for the most part amused herself—was *not* anybody else. She had renounced that character ; she had now no life to lead ; and she honestly believed that she was thus supremely equipped for leading Milly's own. No other person whatever, she was sure, had to an equal degree this qualification, and it was really to assert it that she fondly embarked.

Many things, though not in many weeks, had come and gone since then, and one of the best of them doubtless had been the voyage itself, by the happy southern course, to the succession of Mediterranean ports, with the dazzled wind-up at Naples. Two or three others had preceded this ; incidents, indeed rather lively marks, of their last fortnight at home, and one of which had determined on Mrs. Stringham's part a rush to New York, forty-eight breathless hours there, previous to her final rally. But the great sustained sea-light had drunk up the rest of the picture, so that for many days other questions and other possibilities sounded with as little effect as a trio of penny whistles might sound in a Wagner overture.

It was the Wagner overture that practically prevailed, up through Italy, where Milly had already been, still further up and across the Alps, which were also partly known to Mrs. Stringham ; only perhaps " taken " to a time not wholly congruous, hurried in fact on account of the girl's high restlessness. She had been expected, she had frankly promised, to be restless— that was partly why she was " great "—or was a consequence, at any rate, if not a cause ; yet she had not perhaps altogether announced herself as straining so hard at the cord. It was familiar, it was beautiful to Mrs. Stringham that she had arrears to make up, the chances that had lapsed for her through the wanton ways of forefathers fond of Paris, but not of its higher sides, and fond almost of nothing else ; but the vagueness, the openness, the eagerness without point and the interest without pause—all a part of the charm of her oddity as at first presented—had become more striking in proportion as they triumphed over movement and change. She had arts and idio-syncrasies of which no great account could have been given, but which were a daily grace if you lived with them ; such as the art of being almost tragically impatient and yet making it as light as air ; of being inexplicably sad and yet making it as clear as noon ; of being unmistakably gay and yet making it as soft as dusk. Mrs. Stringham by this time understood everything, was more than ever confirmed in wonder and admiration, in her view that it was life enough simply to feel her companion's feelings ; but there were special keys she had not yet added to her bunch, impressions that of a sudden were apt to affect her as new.

This particular day on the great Swiss road had been, for some reason, full of them, and they referred themselves, provisionally, to some deeper depth than she had touched—though into two or three such depths, it must be added, she had peeped long enough to find herself suddenly draw back. It was not Milly's unpacified state, in short, that now troubled her—though certainly, as Europe was the great American sedative, the failure was to some extent to be noted : it was the suspected presence of something behind the state—which, however, could scarcely have taken its place there since their departure. What a fresh motive of unrest could suddenly have sprung from was in short not to be divined. It was but half an explanation to say that excitement, for each of them, had naturally dropped, and that what they had left behind, or tried to—the great serious facts of life, as Mrs. Stringham liked to call them—was once more coming into sight as objects loom through smoke when smoke begins to clear ; for these were general appearances from which the girl's own aspect, her really larger vagueness, seemed rather to disconnect itself. The nearest approach to a personal anxiety indulged in as yet by the elder lady was on her taking occasion to wonder if what she had more than anything else got hold of mightn't be one of the finer, one of the finest, one of the rarest—as she called it so that she might call it nothing worse—cases of American intensity. She had just had a moment of alarm—asked herself if her young friend were merely going to treat her to some complicated drama of nerves. At the end of a week, however, with their further progress, her young friend had effectively answered the question and given her the impression, indistinct indeed as yet, of something that had a reality compared with which the nervous explanation would have been coarse. Mrs. Stringham found herself from that hour, in other words, in presence of an explanation that remained a muffled and intangible form, but that assuredly, should it take on sharpness, would explain everything and more than everything,

would become instantly the light in which Milly was
to be read.

Such a matter as this may at all events speak of the
style in which our young woman could affect those
who were near her, may testify to the sort of interest
she could inspire. She worked—and seemingly quite
without design—upon the sympathy, the curiosity,
the fancy of her associates, and we shall really ourselves scarce otherwise come closer to her than by
feeling their impression and sharing, if need be, their
confusion. She reduced them, Mrs. Stringham would
have said, to a consenting bewilderment ; which was
precisely, for that good lady, on a last analysis, what
was most in harmony with her greatness. She
exceeded, escaped measure, was surprising only
because *they* were so far from great. Thus it was that
on this wondrous day by the Brünig the spell of
watching her had grown more than ever irresistible ;
a proof of what—or of a part of what—Mrs. Stringham
had, with all the rest, been reduced to. She had
almost the sense of tracking her young friend as if at
a given moment to pounce. She knew she shouldn't
pounce, she hadn't come out to pounce ; yet she felt
her attention secretive, all the same, and her observation scientific. She struck herself as hovering like
a spy, applying tests, laying traps, concealing signs.
This would last, however, only till she should fairly
know what was the matter ; and to watch was after
all, meanwhile, a way of clinging to the girl, not less
than an occupation, a satisfaction in itself. The
pleasure of watching moreover, if a reason were
needed, came from a sense of her beauty. Her beauty
hadn't at all originally seemed a part of the situation,
and Mrs. Stringham had even in the first flush of
friendship not named it grossly to any one ; having
seen early that for stupid people—and who, she
sometimes secretly asked herself, wasn't stupid ?—it

would take a great deal of explaining. She had learned not to mention it till it was mentioned first —which occasionally happened, but not too often ; and then she was there in force. Then she both warmed to the perception that met her own perception, and disputed it, suspiciously, as to special items ; while, in general, she had learned to refine even to the point of herself employing the word that most people employed. She employed it to pretend she was also stupid and so have done with the matter ; spoke of her friend as plain, as ugly even, in a case of especially dense insistence ; but as, in appearance, so " awfully full of things." This was her own way of describing a face that, thanks doubtless to rather too much forehead, too much nose and too much mouth, together with too little mere conventional colour and conventional line, was expressive, irregular, exquisite, both for speech and for silence. When Milly smiled it was a public event—when she didn't it was a chapter of history. They had stopped on the Brünig for luncheon, and there had come up for them under the charm of the place the question of a longer stay.

Mrs. Stringham was now on the ground of thrilled recognitions, small sharp echoes of a past which she kept in a well-thumbed case, but which, on pressure of a spring and exposure to the air, still showed itself ticking as hard as an honest old watch. The embalmed " Europe " of her younger time had partly stood for three years of Switzerland, a term of continuous school at Vevey, with rewards of merit in the form of silver medals tied by blue ribbons and mild mountain-passes attacked with alpenstocks. It was the good girls who, in the holidays, were taken highest, and our friend could now judge, from what she supposed her familiarity with the minor peaks, that she had been one of the best. These reminiscences, sacred to-day because prepared in the hushed chambers of the past, had been part of the general train laid for the pair of sisters, daughters early fatherless, by their brave Vermont mother, who struck her at present as having apparently, almost like Columbus, worked out, all unassisted, a conception of the other side of the globe. She had focussed Vevey, by the light of nature and with extraordinary completeness, at Burlington ; after which she had embarked, sailed, landed, explored and, above all, made good her presence. She had given her daughters the five years in Switzerland and Germany that were to leave them ever afterwards a standard of comparison for all cycles of Cathay, and to stamp the younger in especial—Susan was the younger—with a character, that, as Mrs. Stringham had often had occasion, through life, to say to herself, made all the difference. It made all the difference for Mrs. Stringham, over and over again and in the most remote connexions, that, thanks to her parent's lonely thrifty hardy faith, she was a woman of the world. There were plenty of women who were all sorts of things that she wasn't, but who, on the other hand, were not that, and who didn't know *she* was (which she liked—it relegated them still further) and didn't know either how it enabled her to judge them. She had never seen herself so much in this light as during the actual phase of her associated, if slightly undirected, pilgrimage ; and the consciousness gave perhaps to her plea for a pause more intensity than she knew. The irrecoverable days had come back to her from far off ; they were part of the sense of the cool upper air and of everything else that hung like an indestructible scent to the torn garment of youth— the taste of honey and the luxury of milk, the sound of cattle-bells and the rush of streams, the fragrance of trodden balms and the dizziness of deep gorges.

Milly clearly felt these things too, but they affected her companion at moments—that was quite the way

Mrs. Stringham would have expressed it—as the princess in a conventional tragedy might have affected the confidant if a personal emotion had ever been permitted to the latter. That a princess could only be a princess was a truth with which, essentially, a confidant, however responsive, had to live. Mrs. Stringham was a woman of the world, but Milly Theale was a princess, the only one she had yet had to deal with, and this, in its way too, made all the difference. It was a perfectly definite doom for the wearer—it was for every one else an office nobly filled. It might have represented possibly, with its involved loneliness and other mysteries, the weight under which she fancied her companion's admirable head occasionally, and ever so submissively, bowed. Milly had quite assented at luncheon to their staying over, and had left her to look at rooms, settle questions, arrange about their keeping on their carriage and horses ; cares that had now moreover fallen to Mrs. Stringham as a matter of course and that yet for some reason, on this occasion particularly, brought home to her—all agreeably, richly, almost grandly—what it was to live with the great. Her young friend had in a sublime degree a sense closed to the general question of difficulty, which she got rid of furthermore not in the least as one had seen many charming persons do, by merely passing it on to others. She kept it completely at a distance : it never entered the circle ; the most plaintive confidant couldn't have dragged it in ; and to tread the path of a confidant was accordingly to live exempt. Service was in other words so easy to render that the whole thing was like court life without the hardships. It came back of course to the question of money, and our observant lady had by this time repeatedly reflected that if one were talking of the " difference," it was just this, this incomparably and nothing else, that when all was said and done most made it. A less vulgarly, a less obviously purchasing or parading person she couldn't have imagined ; but it prevailed even as the truth of truths that the girl couldn't get away from her wealth. She might leave her conscientious companion as freely alone with it as possible and never ask a question, scarce even tolerate a reference ; but it was in the fine folds of the helplessly expensive little black frock that she drew over the grass as she now strolled vaguely off ; it was in the curious and splendid coils of hair, " done " with no eye whatever to the *mode du jour*, that peeped from under the corresponding indifference of her hat, the merely personal tradition that suggested a sort of noble inelegance ; it lurked between the leaves of the uncut but antiquated Tauchnitz volume of which, before going out, she had mechanically possessed herself. She couldn't dress it away, nor walk it away, nor read it away, nor think it away ; she could neither smile it away in any dreamy absence nor blow it away in any softened sigh. She couldn't have lost it if she had tried—that was what it was to be really rich. It had to be *the* thing you were. When at the end of an hour she hadn't returned to the house Mrs. Stringham, though the bright afternoon was yet young, took, with precautions, the same direction, went to join her in case of her caring for a walk. But the purpose of joining her was in truth less distinct than that of a due regard for a possibly preferred detachment : so that, once more, the good lady proceeded with a quietness that made her slightly " underhand " even in her own eyes. She couldn't help that, however, and she didn't care, sure as she was that what she really wanted wasn't to overstep but to stop in time. It was to be able to stop in time that she went softly, but she had on this occasion further to go than ever yet, for she followed in vain, and at last with some anxiety, the footpath she believed Milly to have taken. It wound up a hillside and into the higher Alpine meadows in which, all these last days, they had so often wanted, as they passed above or below, to stray ; and then it obscured itself in a wood, but always going up, up, and with a small cluster of brown old high-perched châlets evidently for its goal. Mrs. Stringham reached in due course the châlets, and there received from a bewildered old woman, a very fearful person to behold, an indication that sufficiently guided her. The young lady had been seen not long before passing further on, over a crest and to a place where the way would drop again, as our unappeased inquirer found it in fact, a quarter of an hour later, markedly and almost alarmingly to do. It led somewhere, yet apparently quite into space, for the great side of the mountain appeared, from where she pulled up, to fall away altogether, though probably but to some issue below and out of sight. Her uncertainty moreover was brief, for she next became aware of the presence on a fragment of rock, twenty yards off, of the Tauchnitz volume the girl had brought out and that therefore pointed to her shortly previous passage. She had rid herself of the book, which was an encumbrance, and meant of course to pick it up on her return ; but as she hadn't yet picked it up what on earth had become of her ? Mrs. Stringham, I hasten to add, was within a few moments to see ; but it was quite an accident that she hadn't, before they were over, betrayed by her deeper agitation the fact of her own nearness.

The whole place, with the descent of the path and as a sequel to a sharp turn that was masked by rocks and shrubs, appeared to fall precipitously and to become a " view " pure and simple, a view of great extent and beauty, but thrown forward and vertiginous. Milly, with the promise of it from just above, had gone straight down to it, not stopping till it was

all before her ; and here, on what struck her friend as
the dizzy edge of it, she was seated at her ease. The
path somehow took care of itself and its final business,
but the girl's seat was a slab of rock at the end of a
short promontory or excrescence that merely pointed
off to the right at gulfs of air and that was so placed
by good fortune, if not by the worst, as to be at last
completely visible. For Mrs Stringham stifled a cry
on taking in what she believed to be the danger of
such a perch for a mere maiden ; her liability to slip,
to slide, to leap, to be precipitated by a single false
movement, by a turn of the head—how could one
tell ?—into whatever was beneath. A thousand
thoughts, for the minute, roared in the poor lady's
ears, but without reaching, as happened, Milly's. It
was a commotion that left our observer intensely still
and holding her breath. What had first been offered
her was the possibility of a latent intention—however
wild the idea—in such a posture ; of some betrayed
accordance of Milly's caprice with a horrible hidden
obsession. But since Mrs. Stringham stood as
motionless as if a sound, a syllable, must have produced the start that would be fatal, so even the lapse
of a few seconds had partly a reassuring effect. It
gave her time to receive the impression which, when
she some minutes later softly retraced her steps, was
to be the sharpest she carried away. This was the
impression that if the girl was deeply and recklessly
meditating there she wasn't meditating a jump ; she
was on the contrary, as she sat, much more in a state
of uplifted and unlimited possession that had nothing
to gain from violence. She was looking down on the
kingdoms of the earth, and though indeed that of
itself might well go to the brain, it wouldn't be with a
view of renouncing them. Was she choosing among
them or did she want them all ? This question,
before Mrs. Stringham had decided what to do, made

others vain ; in accordance with which she saw, or
believed she did, that if it might be dangerous to call
out, to sound in any way a surprise, it would probably
be safe enough to withdraw as she had come. She
watched a while longer, she held her breath, and she
never knew afterwards what time had elapsed.

Not many minutes probably, yet they hadn't
seemed few, and they had given her so much to think
of, not only while creeping home, but while waiting
afterwards at the inn, that she was still busy with
them when, late in the afternoon, Milly reappeared.
She had stopped at the point of the path where the
Tauchnitz lay, had taken it up and, with the pencil
attached to her watch-guard, had scrawled a word—
à bientôt!—across the cover ; after which, even under
the girl's continued delay, she had measured time
without a return of alarm. For she now saw that
the great thing she had brought away was precisely
a conviction that the future wasn't to exist for her
princess in the form of any sharp or simple release
from the human predicament. It wouldn't be for
her a question of a flying leap and thereby of a quick
escape. It would be a question of taking full in the
face the whole assault of life, to the general muster of
which indeed her face might have been directly presented as she sat there on her rock. Mrs. Stringham
was thus able to say to herself during still another
wait of some length that if her young friend still continued absent it wouldn't be because—whatever the
opportunity—she had cut short the thread. She
wouldn't have committed suicide ; she knew herself
unmistakably reserved for some more complicated
passage ; this was the very vision in which she had,
with no little awe, been discovered. The image that
thus remained with the elder lady kept the character
of a revelation. During the breathless minutes of her
watch she had seen her companion afresh ; the latter's

type, aspect, marks, her history, her state, her beauty, her mystery, all unconsciously betrayed themselves to the Alpine air, and all had been gathered in again to feed Mrs. Stringham's flame. They are things that will more distinctly appear for us, and they are meanwhile briefly represented by the enthusiasm that was stronger on our friend's part than any doubt. It was a consciousness she was scarce yet used to carrying, but she had as beneath her feet a mine of something precious. She seemed to herself to stand near the mouth, not yet quite cleared. The mine but needed working and would certainly yield a treasure. She wasn't thinking, either, of Milly's gold.

II

THE girl said nothing, when they met, about the words scrawled on the Tauchnitz, and Mrs. Stringham then noticed that she hadn't the book with her. She had left it lying and probably would never remember it at all. Her comrade's decision was therefore quickly made not to speak of having followed her ; and within five minutes of her return, wonderfully enough, the preoccupation denoted by her forgetfulness further declared itself. " Should you think me quite abominable if I were to say that after all——? "

Mrs. Stringham had already thought, with the first sound of the question, everything she was capable of thinking, and had immediately made such a sign that Milly's words gave place to visible relief at her assent. " You don't care for our stop here—you'd rather go straight on ? We'll start then with the peep of to-morrow's dawn—or as early as you like ; it's only rather late now to take the road again." And she smiled to show how she meant it for a joke that an instant onward rush was what the girl would have wished. " I bullied you into stopping," she added ; " so it serves me right."

Milly made in general the most of her good friend's jokes ; but she humoured this one a little absently. " Oh yes, you do bully me." And it was thus arranged between them, with no discussion at all, that they would resume their journey in the morning. The

younger tourist's interest in the detail of the matter—
in spite of a declaration from the elder that she would
consent to be dragged anywhere—appeared almost
immediately afterwards quite to lose itself; she
promised, however, to think till supper of where,
with the world all before them, they might go—
supper having been ordered for such time as permitted
of lighted candles. It had been agreed between them
that lighted candles at wayside inns, in strange
countries, amid mountain scenery, gave the evening
meal a peculiar poetry—such being the mild adventures, the refinements of impression, that they, as
they would have said, went in for. It was now as if,
before this repast, Milly had designed to " lie down " ;
but at the end of three minutes more she wasn't lying
down, she was saying instead, abruptly, with a transi-
tion that was like a jump of four thousand miles :
" What was it that, in New York, on the ninth, when
you saw him alone, Doctor Finch said to you ? "

It was not till later that Mrs. Stringham fully knew
why the question had startled her still more than its
suddenness explained ; though the effect of it even at
the moment was almost to frighten her into a false
answer. She had to think, to remember the occasion,
the " ninth," in New York, the time she had seen
Doctor Finch alone, and to recall the words he had
then uttered ; and when everything had come back
it was quite, at first, for a moment, as if he had said
something that immensely mattered. He hadn't,
however, in fact ; it was only as if he might perhaps
after all have been going to. It was on the sixth—
within ten days of their sailing—that she had hurried
from Boston under the alarm, a small but a sufficient
shock, of hearing that Mildred had suddenly been
taken ill, had had, from some obscure cause, such an
upset as threatened to stay their journey. The
bearing of the accident had happily soon presented

itself as slight, and there had been in the event but a few hours of anxiety ; the journey had been pronounced again not only possible, but, as representing " change," highly advisable ; and if the zealous guest had had five minutes by herself with the Doctor this was clearly no more at his instance than at her own. Almost nothing had passed between them but an easy exchange of enthusiasms in respect to the remedial properties of " Europe " ; and due assurance, as the facts came back to her, she was now able to give. " Nothing whatever, on my word of honour, that you mayn't know or mightn't then have known. I've no secret with him about you. What makes you suspect it ? I don't quite make out how you know I did see him alone."

" No—you never told me," said Milly. " And I don't mean," she went on, " during the twenty-four hours while I was bad, when your putting your heads together was natural enough. I mean after I was better—the last thing before you went home."

Mrs. Stringham continued to wonder. " Who told you I saw him then ? "

" *He* didn't himself—nor did you write me it afterwards. We speak of it now for the first time. That's exactly why ! " Milly declared—with something in her face and voice that, the next moment, betrayed for her companion that she had really known nothing, had only conjectured and, chancing her charge, made a hit. Yet why had her mind been busy with the question ? " But if you're not, as you now assure me, in his confidence," she smiled, " it's no matter."

" I'm not in his confidence—he had nothing to confide. But are you feeling unwell ? "

The elder woman was earnest for the truth, though the possibility she named was not at all the one that seemed to fit—witness the long climb Milly had just indulged in. The girl showed her constant white face, but this her friends had all learned to discount, and it was often brightest when superficially not bravest. She continued for a little mysteriously to smile. " I don't know—haven't really the least idea. But it might be well to find out."

Mrs. Stringham at this flared into sympathy. " Are you in trouble—in pain ? "

" Not the least little bit. But I sometimes wonder —— ! "

" Yes "—she pressed : " wonder what ? "

" Well, if I shall have much of it."

Mrs. Stringham stared. " Much of what ? Not of pain ? "

" Of everything. Of everything I have."

Anxiously again, tenderly, our friend cast about. " You ' have ' everything ; so that when you say ' much ' of it——"

" I only mean," the girl broke in, " shall I have it for long ? That is if I *have* got it."

She had at present the effect, a little, of confounding, or at least of perplexing her comrade, who was touched, who was always touched, by something helpless in her grace and abrupt in her turns, and yet actually half made out in her a sort of mocking light. " If you've got an ailment ? "

" If I've got everything," Milly laughed.

" Ah *that*—like almost nobody else."

" Then for how long ? "

Mrs. Stringham's eyes entreated her ; she had gone close to her, half-enclosed her with urgent arms. " Do you want to see some one ? " And then as the girl only met it with a slow headshake, though looking perhaps a shade more conscious : " We'll go straight to the best near doctor." This too, however, produced but a gaze of qualified assent and a silence, sweet and vague, that left everything open. Our

friend decidedly lost herself. "Tell me, for God's
sake, if you're in distress."

"I don't think I've really *everything*," Milly said
as if to explain—and as if also to put it pleasantly.
"But what on earth can I do for you?"

The girl debated, then seemed on the point of
being able to say; but suddenly changed and expressed herself otherwise. "Dear, dear thing—I'm
only too happy!"

It brought them closer, but it rather confirmed Mrs.
Stringham's doubt. "Then what's the matter?"

"That's the matter—that I can scarcely bear it."

"But what is it you think you haven't got?"

Milly waited another moment; then she found it,
and found for it a dim show of joy. "The power to
resist the bliss of what I *have*!"

Mrs. Stringham took it in—her sense of being "put
off" with it, the possible, probable irony of it—and
her tenderness renewed itself in the positive grimness
of a long murmur. "Whom will you see?"—for
it was as if they looked down from their height at a
continent of doctors. "Where will you first go?"

Milly had for the third time her air of consideration; but she came back with it to her plea of some
minutes before. "I'll tell you at supper—good-bye
till then." And she left the room with a lightness
that testified for her companion to something that
again particularly pleased her in the renewed promise
of motion. The odd passage just concluded, Mrs.
Stringham mused as she once more sat alone with a
hooked needle and a ball of silk, the "fine" work with
which she was always provided—this mystifying
mood had simply been precipitated, no doubt, by
their prolonged halt, with which the girl hadn't really
been in sympathy. One had only to admit that her
complaint was in fact but the excess of the joy of life,
and everything *did* then fit. She couldn't stop for the

joy, but she could go on for it, and with the pulse of her going on she floated again, was restored to her great spaces. There was no evasion of any truth—so at least Susan Shepherd hoped—in one's sitting there while the twilight deepened and feeling still more finely that the position of this young lady was magnificent. The evening at that height had naturally turned to cold, and the travellers had bespoken a fire with their meal ; the great Alpine road asserted its brave presence through the small panes of the low clean windows, with incidents at the inn-door, the yellow diligence, the great waggons, the hurrying hooded private conveyances, reminders, for our fanciful friend, of old stories, old pictures, historic flights, escapes, pursuits, things that had happened, things indeed that by a sort of strange congruity helped her to read the meanings of the greatest interest into the relation in which she was now so deeply involved. It was natural that this record of the magnificence of her companion's position should strike her as after all the best meaning she could extract ; for she herself was seated in the magnificence as in a court-carriage— she came back to that, and such a method of progression, such a view from crimson cushions, would evidently have a great deal more to give. By the time the candles were lighted for supper and the short white curtains drawn Milly had reappeared, and the little scenic room had then all its romance. That charm, moreover, was far from broken by the words in which she, without further loss of time, satisfied her patient mate. " I want to go straight to London."

It was unexpected, corresponding with no view positively taken at their departure ; when England had appeared, on the contrary, rather relegated and postponed — seen for the moment, as who should say, at the end of an avenue of preparations and introductions. London, in short, might have been supposed to be the crown, and to be achieved, like a siege, by gradual approaches. Milly's actual fine stride was therefore the more exciting, as any simplification almost always was to Mrs. Stringham ; who, besides, was afterwards to recall as a piece of that very " exposition " dear to the dramatist the terms in which, between their smoky candles, the girl had put her preference and in which still other things had come up, come while the clank of waggon-chains in the sharp.air reached their ears, with the stamp of hoofs, the rattle of buckets and the foreign questions, foreign answers, that were all alike a part of the cheery converse of the road. The girl brought it out in truth as she might have brought a huge confession, something she admitted herself shy about and that would seem to show her as frivolous ; it had rolled over her that what she wanted of Europe was " people," so far as they were to be had, and that, if her friend really wished to know, the vision of this same equivocal quantity was what had haunted her during their previous days, in museums and churches, and what was again spoiling for her the pure taste of scenery. She was all for scenery—yes ; but she wanted it human and personal, and all she could say was that there would be in London—wouldn't there ? —more of that kind than anywhere else. She came back to her idea that if it wasn't for long—if nothing should happen to be so for *her*—why the particular thing she spoke of would probably have most to give her in the time, would probably be less than anything else a waste of her remainder. She produced this last consideration indeed with such gaiety that Mrs. Stringham was not again disconcerted by it, was in fact quite ready—if talk of early dying was in order— to match it from her own future. Good, then ; they would eat and drink because of what might happen to-morrow ; and they would direct their course from that moment with a view to such eating and drinking. They ate and drank that night, in truth, as in the spirit of this decision ; whereby the air, before they separated, felt itself the clearer.

It had cleared perhaps to a view only too extensive —extensive, that is, in proportion to the signs of life presented. The idea of " people " was not so entertained on Milly's part as to connect itself with particular persons, and the fact remained for each of the ladies that they would, completely unknown, disembark at Dover amid the completely unknowing. They had no relation already formed ; this plea Mrs. Stringham put forward to see what it would produce. It produced nothing at first but the observation on the girl's side that what she had in mind was no thought of society nor of scraping acquaintance ; nothing was further from her than to desire the opportunities represented for the compatriot in general by a trunkful of " letters." It wasn't a question, in short, of the people the compatriot was after ; it was the human, the English picture itself, as they might see it in their own way—the concrete world inferred so fondly from what one had read and dreamed. Mrs. Stringham did every justice to this concrete world, but when later on an occasion chanced to present itself she made a point of not omitting to remark that it might be a comfort to know in advance one or two of the human particles of its concretion. This still, however, failed, in vulgar parlance, to " fetch " Milly, so that she had presently to go all the way. " Haven't I understood from you, for that matter, that you gave Mr. Densher something of a promise ? "

There was a moment, on this, when Milly's look had to be taken as representing one of two things— either that she was completely vague about the promise or that Mr. Densher's name itself started no train. But she really couldn't be so vague about the promise, the partner of these hours quickly saw, without attaching it to something ; it had to be a promise to somebody in particular to be so repudiated. In the event, accordingly, she acknowledged Mr. Merton Densher, the so unusually " bright " young Englishman who had made his appearance in New York on some special literary business—wasn't it ?— shortly before their departure, and who had been three or four times in her house during the brief period between her visit to Boston and her companion's subsequent stay with her ; but she required much reminding before it came back to her that she had mentioned to this companion just afterwards the confidence expressed by the personage in question in her never doing so dire a thing as to come to London without, as the phrase was, looking a fellow up. She had left him the enjoyment of his confidence, the form of which might have appeared a trifle free—this she now reasserted ; she had done nothing either to impair or to enhance it ; but she had also left Mrs. Stringham, in the connexion and at the time, rather sorry to have missed Mr. Densher. She had thought of him again after that, the elder woman ; she had likewise gone so far as to notice that Milly appeared not to have done so—which the girl might easily have betrayed ; and, interested as she was in everything that concerned her, she had made out for herself, for herself only and rather idly, that, but for interruptions, the young Englishman might have become a better acquaintance. His being an acquaintance at all was one of the signs that in the first days had helped to place Milly, as a young person with the world before her, for sympathy and wonder. Isolated, unmothered, unguarded, but with her other strong marks, her big house, her big fortune, her big freedom, she had lately begun to " receive," for all her few

years, as an older woman might have done—as was
done, precisely, by princesses who had public con-
siderations to observe and who came of age very early.
If it was thus distinct to Mrs. Stringham then that
Mr. Densher had gone off somewhere else in connexion
with his errand before her visit to New York, it had
been also not undiscoverable that he had come back
for a day or two later on, that is after her own second
excursion—that he had in fine reappeared on a single
occasion on his way to the West : his way from
Washington as she believed, though he was out of
sight at the time of her joining her friend for their
departure. It hadn't occurred to her before to
exaggerate—it had not occurred to her that she could;
but she seemed to become aware to-night that there
had been just enough in this relation to meet, to
provoke, the free conception of a little more.

She presently put it that, at any rate, promise or no
promise, Milly would at a pinch be able, in London,
to act on his permission to make him a sign ; to which
Milly replied with readiness that her ability, though
evident, would be none the less quite wasted, inasmuch
as the gentleman would to a certainty be still in
America. He had a great deal to do there—which he
would scarce have begun ; and in fact she might very
well not have thought of London at all if she hadn't
been sure he wasn't yet near coming back. It was
perceptible to her companion that the moment our
young woman had so far committed herself she had a
sense of having overstepped ; which was not quite
patched up by her saying the next minute, possibly
with a certain failure of presence of mind, that the
last thing she desired was the air of running after him.
Mrs. Stringham wondered privately what question
there could be of any such appearance—the danger
of which thus suddenly came up ; but she said for the
time nothing of it—she only said other things : one

of which was, for instance, that if Mr. Densher was
away he was away, and this the end of it : also that of
course they must be discreet at any price. But what
was the measure of discretion, and how was one to be
sure ? So it was that, as they sat there, she produced
her own case : *she* had a possible tie with London,
which she desired as little to disown as she might wish
to risk presuming on it. She treated her companion,
in short, for their evening's end, to the story of Maud
Manningham, the odd but interesting English girl who
had formed her special affinity in the old days at the
Vevey school ; whom she had written to, after their
separation, with a regularity that had at first faltered
and then altogether failed, yet that had been for the
time quite a fine case of crude constancy ; so that it
had in fact flickered up again of itself on the occasion
of the marriage of each. They had then once more
fondly, scrupulously written—Mrs. Lowder first ; and
even another letter or two had afterwards passed.
This, however, had been the end—though with no
rupture, only a gentle drop : Maud Manningham had
made, she believed, a great marriage, while she herself
had made a small ; on top of which, moreover,
distance, difference, diminished community and impossible reunion had done the rest of the work. It
was but after all these years that reunion had begun to
show as possible—if the other party to it, that is,
should be still in existence. That was exactly what
it now appeared to our friend interesting to ascertain,
as, with one aid and another, she believed she might.
It was an experiment she would at all events now make
if Milly didn't object.

Milly in general objected to nothing, and though
she asked a question or two she raised no present plea.
Her questions—or at least her own answers to them
—kindled on Mrs. Stringham's part a backward
train : she hadn't known till to-night how much she

remembered, or how fine it might be to see what had
become of large high-coloured Maud, florid, alien,
exotic—which had been just the spell—even to the
perceptions of youth. There was the danger—she
frankly touched it—that such a temperament mightn't
have matured, with the years, all in the sense of fine-
ness : it was the sort of danger that, in renewing
relations after long breaks, one had always to look in
the face. To gather in strayed threads was to take a
risk—for which, however, she was prepared if Milly
was. The possible " fun," she confessed, was by
itself rather tempting ; and she fairly sounded, with
this—wound up a little as she was—the note of fun
as the harmless final right of fifty years of mere New
England virtue. Among the things she was afterwards to recall was the indescribable look dropped on
her, at that, by her companion ; she was still seated
there between the candles and before the finished
supper, while Milly moved about, and the look was
long to figure for her as an inscrutable comment on
her notion of freedom. Challenged, at any rate, as for
the last wise word, Milly showed perhaps, musingly,
charmingly, that, though her attention had been
mainly soundless, her friend's story—produced as a
resource unsuspected, a card from up the sleeve—
half-surprised, half-beguiled her. Since the matter,
such as it was, depended on that, she brought out
before she went to bed an easy, a light " Risk everything ! "

This quality in it seemed possibly a little to deny
weight to Maud Lowder's evoked presence—as
Susan Stringham, still sitting up, became, in excited
reflexion, a trifle more conscious. Something determinant, when the girl had left her, took place in her
—nameless but, as soon as she had given way, coercive.
It was as if she knew again, in this fulness of time,
that she had been, after Maud's marriage, just sensibly

outlived or, as people nowadays said, shunted. Mrs. Lowder had left her behind, and on the occasion, subsequently, of the corresponding date in her own life—not the second, the sad one, with its dignity of sadness, but the first, with the meagreness of its supposed felicity—she had been, in the same spirit, almost patronisingly pitied. If that suspicion, even when it had ceased to matter, had never quite died out for her, there was doubtless some oddity in its now offering itself as a link, rather than as another break, in the chain; and indeed there might well have been for her a mood in which the notion of the development of patronage in her quondam schoolmate would have settled her question in another sense. It was actually settled—if the case be worth our analysis— by the happy consummation, the poetic justice, the generous revenge, of her having at last something to show. Maud, on their parting company, had appeared to have so much, and would now—for wasn't it also in general quite the rich law of English life?— have, with accretions, promotions, expansions, ever so much more. Very good; such things might be; she rose to the sense of being ready for them. Whatever Mrs. Lowder might have to show—and one hoped one did the presumptions all justice—she would have nothing like Milly Theale, who constituted the trophy producible by poor Susan. Poor Susan lingered late —till the candles were low, and as soon as the table was cleared she opened her neat portfolio. She hadn't lost the old clue; there were connexions she remembered, addresses she could try; so the thing was to begin. She wrote on the spot.

BOOK FOURTH

I

It had all gone so fast after this that Milly uttered but the truth nearest to hand in saying to the gentleman on her right—who was, by the same token, the gentleman on her hostess's left—that she scarce even then knew where she was : the words marking her first full sense of a situation really romantic. They were already dining, she and her friend, at Lancaster Gate, and surrounded, as it seemed to her, with every English accessory ; though her consciousness of Mrs. Lowder's existence, and still more of her remarkable identity, had been of so recent and so sudden a birth. Susie, as she was apt to call her companion for a lighter change, had only had to wave a neat little wand for the fairy-tale to begin at once ; in consequence of which Susie now glittered—for, with Mrs. Stringham's new sense of success, it came to that— in the character of a fairy godmother. Milly had almost insisted on dressing her, for the present occasion, as one ; and it was no fault of the girl's if the good lady hadn't now appeared in a peaked hat, a short petticoat and diamond shoe-buckles, brandishing the magic crutch. The good lady bore herself in truth not less contentedly than if these insignia had marked her work ; and Milly's observation to Lord Mark had doubtless just been the result of such a light exchange of looks with her as even the great length of the table couldn't baffle. There were twenty persons between them, but this sustained passage was the sharpest sequel yet to that other comparison of views during the pause on the Swiss pass. It almost appeared to Milly that their fortune had been unduly precipitated—as if properly they were in the position of having ventured on a small joke and found the answer out of proportion grave. She couldn't at this moment for instance have said whether, with her quickened perceptions, she were more enlivened or oppressed ; and the case might in fact have been serious hadn't she, by good fortune, from the moment the picture loomed, quickly made up her mind that what finally most concerned her was neither to seek nor to shirk, wasn't even to wonder too much, but was to let things come as they would, since there was little enough doubt of how they would go.

Lord Mark had been brought to her before dinner —not by Mrs. Lowder, but by the handsome girl, that lady's niece, who was now at the other end and on the same side as Susie ; he had taken her in, and she meant presently to ask him about Miss Croy, the handsome girl, actually offered to her sight—though now in a splendid way—but for the second time. The first time had been the occasion—only three days before—of her calling at their hotel with her aunt and then making, for our other two heroines, a great impression of beauty and eminence. This impression had remained so with Milly that at present, and although her attention was aware at the same time of everything else, her eyes were mainly engaged with Kate Croy when not engaged with Susie. That wonderful creature's eyes moreover readily met them —she ranked now as a wonderful creature ; and it seemed part of the swift prosperity of the American visitors that, so little in the original reckoning, she should yet appear conscious, charmingly, frankly conscious, of possibilities of friendship for them.

Milly had easily and, as a guest, gracefully general-
ised : English girls had a special strong beauty which
particularly showed in evening dress—above all
when, as was strikingly the case with this one, the
dress itself was what it should be. That observation
she had all ready for Lord Mark when they should,
after a little, get round to it. She seemed even now to
see that there might be a good deal they would get
round to ; the indication being that, taken up once
for all with her other neighbour, their hostess would
leave them much to themselves. Mrs. Lowder's other
neighbour was the Bishop of Murrum—a real bishop,
such as Milly had never seen, with a complicated
costume, a voice like an old-fashioned wind instrument, and a face all the portrait of a prelate ; while
the gentleman on our young lady's left, a gentleman
thick-necked, large and literal, who looked straight
before him and as if he were not to be diverted by vain
words from that pursuit, clearly counted as an offset
to the possession of Lord Mark. As Milly made out
these things—with a shade of exhilaration at the way
she already fell in—she saw how she was justified of
her plea for people and her love of life. It wasn't
then, as the prospect seemed to show, so difficult to
get into the current, or to stand at any rate on the
bank. It was easy to get near—if they *were* near ;
and yet the elements were different enough from any
of her old elements, and positively rich and strange.

She asked herself if her right-hand neighbour would
understand what she meant by such a description of
them should she throw it off ; but another of the
things to which precisely her sense was awakened was
that no, decidedly, he wouldn't. It was nevertheless
by this time open to her that his line would be to be
clever ; and indeed, evidently, no little of the interest
was going to be in the fresh reference and fresh effect
both of people's cleverness and of their simplicity.

She thrilled, she consciously flushed, and all to turn pale again, with the certitude—it had never been so present—that she should find herself completely involved : the very air of the place, the pitch of the occasion, had for her both so sharp a ring and so deep an undertone. The smallest things, the faces, the hands, the jewels of the women, the sound of words, especially of names, across the table, the shape of the forks, the arrangement of the flowers, the attitude of the servants, the walls of the room, were all touches in a picture and denotements in a play ; and they marked for her moreover her alertness of vision. She had never, she might well believe, been in such a state of vibration ; her sensibility was almost too sharp for her comfort : there were for example more indications than she could reduce to order in the manner of the friendly niece, who struck her as distinguished and interesting, as in fact surprisingly genial. This young woman's type had, visibly, other possibilities ; yet here, of its own free movement, it had already sketched a relation. Were they, Miss Croy and she, to take up the tale where their two elders had left it off so many years before ?—were they to find they liked each other and to try for themselves whether a scheme of constancy on more modern lines could be worked ? She had doubted, as they came to England, of Maud Manningham, had believed her a broken reed and a vague resource, had seen their dependence on her as a state of mind that would have been shamefully silly —so far as it *was* dependence—had they wished to do anything so inane as " get into society." To have made their pilgrimage all for the sake of such society as Mrs. Lowder might have in reserve for them— that didn't bear thinking of at all, and she herself had quite chosen her course for curiosity about other matters. She would have described this curiosity as a desire to see the places she had read about, and *that*

description of her motive she was prepared to give her
neighbour—even though, as a consequence of it, he
should find how little she had read. It was almost
at present as if her poor prevision had been rebuked
by the majesty—she could scarcely call it less—of the
event, or at all events by the commanding character
of the two figures (she could scarcely call *that* less
either) mainly presented. Mrs. Lowder and her niece,
however dissimilar, had at least in common that each
was a great reality. That was true, primarily, of the
aunt—so true that Milly wondered how her own
companion had arrived in other years at so odd an
alliance ; yet she none the less felt Mrs. Lowder as a
person of whom the mind might in two or three days
roughly make the circuit. She would sit there massive
at least while one attempted it ; whereas Miss Croy,
the handsome girl, would indulge in incalculable
movements that might interfere with one's tour. She
was the amusing resisting ominous fact, none the less,
and each other person and thing was just such a fact ;
and it served them right, no doubt, the pair of them,
for having rushed into their adventure.

Lord Mark's intelligence meanwhile, however, had
met her own quite sufficiently to enable him to tell her
how little he could clear up her situation. He explained, for that matter—or at least he hinted—
that there was no such thing to-day in London as
saying where any one was. Every one was everywhere—nobody was anywhere. He should be put
to it—yes, frankly—to give a name of any sort or
kind to their hostess's " set." *Was* it a set at all, or
wasn't it, and were there not really no such things
as sets in the place any more ?—was there anything
but the groping and pawing, that of the vague billows
of some great greasy sea in mid-Channel, of masses of
bewildered people trying to " get " they didn't know
what or where ? He threw out the question, which

seemed large ; Milly felt that at the end of five minutes
he had thrown out a great many, though he followed
none more than a step or two ; perhaps he would prove
suggestive, but he helped her as yet to no discriminations : he spoke as if he had given them up from too
much knowledge. He was thus at the opposite extreme from herself, but, as a consequence of it, also
wandering and lost ; and he was furthermore, for all
his temporary incoherence, to which she guessed there
would be some key, as packed a concretion as either
Mrs. Lowder or Kate. The only light in which he
placed the former of these ladies was that of an extraordinary woman—a most extraordinary woman, and
" the more extraordinary the more one knows her,"
while of the latter he said nothing for the moment
but that she was tremendously, yes, quite tremendously, good-looking. It was some time, she thought,
before his talk showed his cleverness, and yet each
minute she believed in that mystery more, quite
apart from what her hostess had told her on first
naming him. Perhaps he was one of the cases she
had heard of at home—those characteristic cases of
people in England who concealed their play of mind
so much more than they advertised it. Even Mr.
Densher a little did that. And what made Lord
Mark, at any rate, so real either, when this was a
trick he had apparently so mastered ? His type somehow, as by a life, a need, an intention of its own, took
all care for vividness off his hands ; that was enough.
It was difficult to guess his age—whether he were a
young man who looked old or an old man who looked
young ; it seemed to prove nothing, as against other
things, that he was bald and, as might have been said,
slightly stale, or, more delicately perhaps, dry : there
was such a fine little fidget of preoccupied life in him,
and his eyes, at moments—though it was an appearance they could suddenly lose—were as candid and

clear as those of a pleasant boy. Very neat, very light, and so fair that there was little other indication of his moustache than his constantly feeling it—which was again boyish—he would have affected her as the most intellectual person present if he had not affected her as the most frivolous. The latter quality was rather in his look than in anything else, though he constantly wore his double eye-glass, which was, much more, Bostonian and thoughtful.

The idea of his frivolity had, no doubt, to do with his personal designation, which represented—as yet, for our young woman, a little confusedly—a connexion with an historic patriciate, a class that in turn, also confusedly, represented an affinity with a social element she had never heard otherwise described than as " fashion." The supreme social element in New York had never known itself but as reduced to that category, and though Milly was aware that, as applied to a territorial and political aristocracy, the label was probably too simple, she had for the time none other at hand. She presently, it is true, enriched her idea with the perception that her interlocutor was indifferent ; yet this, indifferent as aristocracies notoriously were, saw her but little further, inasmuch as she felt that, in the first place, he would much rather get on with her than not, and in the second was only thinking of too many matters of his own. If he kept her in view on the one hand and kept so much else on the other—the way he crumbed up his bread was a proof—why did he hover before her as a potentially insolent noble ? She couldn't have answered the question, and it was precisely one of those that swarmed. They were complicated, she might fairly have said, by his visibly knowing, having known from afar off, that she was a stranger and an American, and by his none the less making no more of it than if she and her like were the chief of his diet.

He took her, kindly enough, but imperturbably, irre-
claimably, for granted, and it wouldn't in the least
help that she herself knew him, as quickly, for having
been in her country and threshed it out. There would
be nothing for her to explain or attenuate or brag
about ; she could neither escape nor prevail by her
strangeness ; he would have, for that matter, on such
a subject, more to tell her than to learn from her.
She might learn from *him* why she was so different
from the handsome girl—which she didn't know,
being merely able to feel it ; or at any rate might
learn from him why the handsome girl was so different
from her.

On these lines, however, they would move later ;
the lines immediately laid down were, in spite of his
vagueness for his own convenience, definite enough,
She was already, he observed to her, thinking what
she should say on her other side—which was what
Americans were always doing. She needn't in conscience say anything at all ; but Americans never
knew that, nor ever, poor creatures, yes (*she* had interposed the " poor creatures ! ") what not to do. The
burdens they took on—the things, positively, they
made an affair of ! This easy and after all friendly
jibe at her race was really for her, on her new friend's
part, the note of personal recognition so far as she
required it ; and she gave him a prompt and conscious
example of morbid anxiety by insisting that her desire
to be, herself, " lovely " all round was justly founded
on the lovely way Mrs. Lowder had met her. He was
directly interested in that, and it was not till afterwards she fully knew how much more information
about their friend he had taken than given. Here
again for instance was a characteristic note : she had,
on the spot, with her first plunge into the obscure
depths of a society constituted from far back, encountered the interesting phenomenon of complicated,

of possibly sinister motive. However, Maud Manningham (her name, even in her presence, somehow still fed the fancy) *had*, all the same, been lovely, and one was going to meet her now quite as far on as one had one's self been met. She had been with them at their hotel—they were a pair—before even they had supposed she could have got their letter. Of course indeed they had written in advance, but they had followed that up very fast. She had thus engaged them to dine but two days later, and on the morrow again, without waiting for a return visit, without waiting for anything, she had called with her niece. It was as if she really cared for them, and it was magnificent fidelity—fidelity to Mrs. Stringham, her own companion and Mrs. Lowder's former schoolmate, the lady with the charming face and the rather high dress down there at the end.

Lord Mark took in through his nippers these balanced attributes of Susie. " But isn't Mrs. Stringham's fidelity then equally magnificent ? "

" Well, it's a beautiful sentiment ; but it isn't as if she had anything to *give*."

" Hasn't she got you ? " Lord Mark asked without excessive delay.

" Me—to give Mrs. Lowder ? " Milly had clearly not yet seen herself in the light of such an offering. " Oh I'm rather a poor present ; and I don't feel as if, even at that, I had as yet quite been given."

" You've been shown, and if our friend has jumped at you it comes to the same thing." He made his jokes, Lord Mark, without amusement for himself ; yet it wasn't that he was grim. " To be seen, you must recognise, *is*, for you, to be jumped at ; and, if it's a question of being shown, here you are again. Only it has now been taken out of your friend's hands ; it's Mrs. Lowder already who's getting the benefit. Look round the table, and you'll make out, I think, that you're being, from top to bottom, jumped at."

" Well then," said Milly, " I seem also to feel that I like it better than being made fun of."

It was one of the things she afterwards saw— Milly was for ever seeing things afterwards—that her companion had here had some way of his own, quite unlike any one's else, of assuring her of his consideration. She wondered how he had done it, for he had neither apologised nor protested. She said to herself at any rate that he had led her on ; and what was most odd was the question by which he had done so. " Does she know much about you ? "

" No, she just likes us."

Even for this his travelled lordship, seasoned and saturated, had no laugh. " I mean *you* particularly. Has that lady with the charming face, which *is* charming, told her ? "

Milly cast about. " Told her what ? "

" Everything."

This, with the way he dropped it, again considerably moved her—made her feel for a moment that as a matter of course she was a subject for disclosures. But she quickly found her answer. " Oh as for that you must ask *her*."

" Your clever companion ? "

" Mrs. Lowder."

He replied to this that their hostess was a person with whom there were certain liberties one never took, but that he was none the less fairly upheld, inasmuch as she was for the most part kind to him and as, should he be very good for a while, she would probably herself tell him. " And I shall have at any rate in the meantime the interest of seeing what she does with you. That will teach me more or less, you see, how much she knows."

Milly followed this—it was lucid, but it suggested

something apart. " How much does she know about *you* ? "

" Nothing," said Lord Mark serencly. " But that doesn't matter—for what she docs with me." And then as to anticipate Milly's question about the nature of such doing : " This for instance—turning me straight on for *you*."

The girl thought. " And you mean she wouldn't if she did know——? "

He met it as if it were really a point. " No. I believe, to do her justice, she still would. So you can be easy."

Milly had the next instant then acted on the per-mission. " Because you're even at the worst the best thing she has ? "

With this he was at last amused. " I was till you came. You're the best now."

It was strange his words should have given her the sense of his knowing, but it was positive that they did so, and to the extent of making her believe them, though still with wonder. That really from this first of their meetings was what was most to abide with her : she accepted almost helplessly—she surrendered so to the inevitable in it—being the sort of thing, as he might have said, that he at least thoroughly believed he had, in going about, seen enough of for all practical purposes. Her submission was naturally moreover not to be impaired by her learning later on that he had paid at short intervals, though at a time apparently just previous to her own emergence from the obscurity of extreme youth, three separate visits to New York, where his namable friends and his contrasted contacts had been numerous. His impres-sion, his recollection of the whole mixed quantity, was still visibly rich. It had helped him to place her, and she was more and more sharply conscious of having—as with the door sharply slammed upon her

and the guard's hand raised in signal to the train—
been popped into the compartment in which she was
to travel for him. It was a use of her that many a girl
would have been doubtless quick to resent ; and the
kind of mind that thus, in our young lady, made all
for mere seeing and taking is precisely one of the
charms of our subject. Milly had practically just
learned from him, had made out, as it were, from her
rumbling compartment, that he gave her the highest
place among their friend's actual properties. She was
a success, that was what it came to, he presently
assured her, and this was what it was to be a success ;
it always happened before one could know it. One's
ignorance was in fact often the greatest part of it.
"You haven't had time yet," he said; "this is nothing.
But you'll see. You'll see everything. You *can*,
you know—everything you dream of."

He made her more and more wonder ; she almost
felt as if he were showing her visions while he spoke ;
and strangely enough, though it was visions that had
drawn her on, she hadn't had them in connexion—
that is in such preliminary and necessary connexion
—with such a face as Lord Mark's, such eyes and
such a voice, such a tone and such a manner. He had
for an instant the effect of making her ask herself if
she were after all going to be afraid ; so distinct was
it for fifty seconds that a fear passed over her. There
they were again—yes, certainly : Susie's overture to
Mrs. Lowder had been their joke, but they had pressed
in that gaiety an electric bell that continued to sound.
Positively while she sat there she had the loud rattle
in her ears, and she wondered during these moments
why the others didn't hear it. They didn't stare,
they didn't smile, and the fear in her that I speak of
was but her own desire to stop it. That dropped,
however, as if the alarm itself had ceased ; she seemed
to have seen in a quick though tempered glare that

there were two courses for her, one to leave London again the first thing in the morning, the other to do nothing at all. Well, she would do nothing at all; she was already doing it; more than that, she had already done it, and her chance was gone. She gave herself up—she had the strangest sense, on the spot, of so deciding; for she had turned a corner before she went on again with Lord Mark. Inexpressive but intensely significant, he met as no one else could have done the very question she had suddenly put to Mrs. Stringham on the Brünig. Should she have it, whatever she did have, that question had been, for long? "Ah so possibly not," her neighbour appeared to reply; "therefore, don't you see? *I'm* the way." It was vivid that he might be, in spite of his absence of flourish; the way being doubtless just *in* that absence. The handsome girl, whom she didn't lose sight of and who, she felt, kept her also in view— Mrs. Lowder's striking niece would perhaps be the way as well, for in her too was the absence of flourish, though she had little else, so far as one could tell, in common with Lord Mark. Yet how indeed *could* one tell, what did one understand, and of what was one, for that matter, provisionally conscious but of their being somehow together in what they represented? Kate Croy, fine but friendly, looked over at her as really with a guess at Lord Mark's effect on her. If she could guess this effect what then did she know about it and in what degree had she felt it herself? Did that represent, as between them, anything particular, and should she have to count with them as duplicating, as intensifying by a mutual intelligence, the relation into which she was sinking? Nothing was so odd as that she should have to recognise so quickly in each of these glimpses of an instant the various signs of a relation; and this anomaly itself, had she had more time to give to it, might well, might

almost terribly have suggested to her that her doom
was to live fast.   It was queerly a question of the short
run and the consciousness proportionately crowded.

These were immense excursions for the spirit of a
young person at Mrs. Lowder's mere dinner-party ;
but what was so significant and so admonitory as the
fact of their being possible ?   What could they have
been but just a part, already, of the crowded consciousness ?   And it was just a part likewise that while
plates were changed and dishes presented and periods
in the banquet marked ; while appearances insisted
and phenomena multiplied and words reached her
from here and there like plashes of a slow thick tide ;
while Mrs. Lowder grew somehow more stout and
more instituted and Susie, at her distance and in comparison, more thinly improvised and more different
—different, that is, from every one and every thing :
it was just a part that while this process went forward
our young lady alighted, came back, taking up her
destiny again as if she had been able by a wave or
two of her wings to place herself briefly in sight of an
alternative to it.   Whatever it was it had showed in
this brief interval as better than the alternative ; and
it now presented itself altogether in the image and in
the place in which she had left it.   The image was
that of her being, as Lord Mark had declared, a
success.   This depended more or less of course on his
idea of the thing—into which at present, however,
she wouldn't go.   But, renewing soon, she had asked
him what he meant then that Mrs. Lowder would do
with her, and he had replied that this might safely
be left.   " She'll get back," he pleasantly said, " her
money."   He could say it too—which was singular—
without affecting her either as vulgar or as " nasty " ;
and he had soon explained himself by adding :
" Nobody here, you know, does anything for
nothing."

" Ah if you mean that we shall reward her as hard as ever we can, nothing is more certain. But she's an idealist," Milly continued, " and idealists, in the long run, I think, *don't* feel that they lose."

Lord Mark seemed, within the limits of his enthusiasm, to find this charming. " Ah she strikes you as an idealist ? "

" She idealises *us*, my friend and me, absolutely. She sees us in a light," said Milly. " That's all I've got to hold on by. So don't deprive me of it."

" I wouldn't think of such a thing for the world. But do you suppose," he continued as if it were suddenly important for him—" do you suppose she sees *me* in a light ? "

She neglected his question for a little, partly because her attention attached itself more and more to the handsome girl, partly because, placed so near their hostess, she wished not to show as discussing her too freely. Mrs. Lowder, it was true, steering in the other quarter a course in which she called at subjects as if they were islets in an archipelago, continued to allow them their ease, and Kate Croy at the same time steadily revealed herself as interesting. Milly in fact found of a sudden her ease—found it all as she bethought herself that what Mrs. Lowder was really arranging for was a report on her quality and, as perhaps might be said, her value, from Lord Mark. She wished him, the wonderful lady, to have no pretext for not knowing what he thought of Miss Theale. Why his judgement so mattered remained to be seen ; but it was this divination that in any case now determined Milly's rejoinder. " No. She knows you. She has probably reason to. And you all here know each other—I see that—so far as you know anything. You know what you're used to, and it's your being used to it—that, and that only—that makes you. But there are things you don't know."

He took it in as if it might fairly, to do him justice, be a point. " Things that *I* don't—with all the pains I take and the way I've run about the world to leave nothing unlearned ? "

Milly thought, and it was perhaps the very truth of his claim—its not being negligible—that sharpened her impatience and thereby her wit. " You're *blasé*, but you're not enlightened. You're familiar with everything, but conscious really of nothing. What I mean is that you've no imagination."

Lord Mark at this threw back his head, ranging with his eyes the opposite side of the room and showing himself at last so much more flagrantly diverted that it fairly attracted their hostess's notice. Mrs. Lowder, however, only smiled on Milly for a sign that something racy was what she had expected, and resumed, with a splash of her screw, her cruise among the islands. " Oh I've heard that," the young man replied, " before ! "

" There it is then. You've heard everything before. You've heard *me* of course before, in my country, often enough."

" Oh never too often," he protested. "I'm sure I hope I shall still hear you again and again."

" But what good then has it done you ? " the girl went on as if now frankly to amuse him.

" Oh you'll see when you know me."

" But most assuredly I shall never know you."

" Then that will be exactly," he laughed, " the good ! "

If it established thus that they couldn't or wouldn't mix, why did Milly none the less feel through it a perverse quickening of the relation to which she had been in spite of herself appointed ? What queerer consequence of their not mixing than their talking —for it was what they had arrived at—almost intimately ? She wished to get away from him, or indeed, much rather, away from herself so far as she was present to him. She saw already—wonderful creature, after all, herself too—that there would be a good deal more of him to come for her, and that the special sign of their intercourse would be to keep herself out of the question. Everything else might come in—only never that ; and with such an arrangement they would perhaps even go far. This in fact might quite have begun, on the spot, with her returning again to the topic of the handsome girl. If she was to keep herself out she could naturally best do so by putting in somebody else. She accordingly put in Kate Croy, being ready to that extent—as she was not at all afraid for her—to sacrifice her if necessary. Lord Mark himself, for that matter, had made it easy by saying a little while before that no one among them did anything for nothing. " What then "—she was aware of being abrupt—" does Miss Croy, if she's so interested, do it for ? What has she to gain by *her* lovely welcome ? Look at her *now* ! " Milly broke out with characteristic freedom of praise, though pulling herself up also with a compunctious " Oh ! " as the direction thus given to their eyes happened to coincide with a turn of Kate's face to them. All she had meant to do was to insist that this face was fine ; but what she had in fact done was to renew again her effect of showing herself to its possessor as conjoined with Lord Mark for some interested view of it. He had, however, promptly met her question.

" To gain ? Why your acquaintance."

" Well, what's my acquaintance to *her* ? She can care for me—she must feel that—only by being sorry for me ; and that's why she's lovely : to be already willing to take the trouble to be. It's the height of the disinterested."

There were more things in this than one that Lord Mark might have taken up ; but in a minute he had made his choice. " Ah then I'm nowhere, for I'm afraid *I'm* not sorry for you in the least. What do you make then," he asked, " of your success ? "

" Why just the great reason of all. It's just because our friend there sees it that she pities me. She understands," Milly said ; " she's better than any of you. She's beautiful."

He appeared struck with this at last—with the point the girl made of it ; to which she came back even after a diversion created by a dish presented between them. " Beautiful in character, I see. *Is* she so ? You must tell me about her."

Milly wondered. " But haven't you known her longer than I ? Haven't you seen her for yourself ? "

" No—I've failed with her. It's no use. I don't make her out. And I assure you I really should like to." His assurance had in fact for his companion a positive suggestion of sincerity ; he affected her as now saying something he did feel ; and she was the more struck with it as she was still conscious of the failure even of curiosity he had just shown in respect to herself. She had meant something—though indeed for herself almost only—in speaking of their friend's natural pity ; it had doubtless been a note of questionable taste, but it had quavered out in spite of her and he hadn't so much as cared to inquire " Why ' natural ' ? " Not that it wasn't really much better for her that he shouldn't : explanations would in truth have taken her much too far. Only she now perceived that, in comparison, her word about this other person really " drew " him ; and there were things in that probably, many things, as to which she would learn more and which glimmered there already as part and parcel of that larger " real " with which, in her new situation, she was to be beguiled. It was in fact at the very moment, this element, not absent from what Lord Mark was further saying.

THE WINGS OF THE DOVE

" So you're wrong, you see, as to our knowing all
about each other. There are cases where we break
down. I at any rate give *her* up—up, that is, to you.
You must do her for me—tell me, I mean, when you
know more. You'll notice," he pleasantly wound up,
" that I've confidence in you."

" Why shouldn't you have ? " Milly asked, observing in this, as she thought, a fine, though for such a
man a surprisingly artless, fatuity. It was as if there
might have been a question of her falsifying for the
sake of her own show—that is of the failure of her
honesty to be proof against her desire to keep well
with him herself. She didn't, none the less, otherwise protest against his remark ; there was something
else she was occupied in seeing. It was the handsome
girl alone, one of his own species and his own society,
who had made him feel uncertain ; of his certainties
about a mere little American, a cheap exotic, imported
almost wholesale and whose habitat, with its conditions of climate, growth and cultivation, its immense
profusion but its few varieties and thin development,
he was perfectly satisfied. The marvel was too that
Milly understood his satisfaction—feeling she expressed the truth in presently saying : " Of course ; I
make out that she must be difficult ; just as I see that
I myself must be easy." And that was what, for all
the rest of this occasion, remained with her—as the
most interesting thing that *could* remain. She was
more and more content herself to be easy ; she would
have been resigned, even had it been brought
straighter home to her, to passing for a cheap exotic.
Provisionally, at any rate, that protected her wish to
keep herself, with Lord Mark, in abeyance. They
had all affected her as inevitably knowing each other,
and if the handsome girl's place among them was
something even their initiation couldn't deal with—
why then she would indeed be a quantity.

II

THAT sense of quantities, separate or mixed, was
really, no doubt, what most prevailed at first for our
slightly gasping American pair ; it found utterance
for them in their frequent remark to each other that
they had no one but themselves to thank. It dropped
from Milly more than once that if she had ever known
it was so easy———! though her exclamation mostly
ended without completing her idea. This, however,
was a trifle to Mrs. Stringham, who cared little
whether she meant that in this case she would have
come sooner. She couldn't have come sooner, and
she perhaps on the contrary meant—for it would
have been like her—that she wouldn't have come
at all ; why it was so easy being at any rate a matter
as to which her companion had begun quickly to pick
up views. Susie kept some of these lights for the
present to herself, since, freely communicated, they
might have been a little disturbing ; with which,
moreover, the quantities that we speak of as surround-
ing the two ladies were in many cases quantities of
things—and of other things—to talk about. Their
immediate lesson accordingly was that they just had
been caught up by the incalculable strength of a wave
that was actually holding them aloft and that would
naturally dash them wherever it liked. They meanwhile, we hasten to add, made the best of their precarious position, and if Milly had had no other help

148

for it she would have found not a little in the sight of
Susan Shepherd's state. The girl had had nothing to
say to her, for three days, about the " success "
announced by Lord Mark—which they saw, besides,
otherwise established ; she was too taken up, too
touched, by Susie's own exaltation. Susie glowed in
the light of her justified faith ; everything had
happened that she had been acute enough to think
least probable ; she had appealed to a possible
delicacy in Maud Manningham—a delicacy, mind you,
but *barely* possible—and her appeal had been met in a
way that was an honour to human nature. This
proved sensibility of the lady of Lancaster Gate performed verily for both our friends during these first
days the office of a fine floating gold-dust, something
that threw over the prospect a harmonising blur. The
forms, the colours behind it were strong and deep—
we have seen how they already stood out for Milly ;
but nothing, comparatively, had had so much of the
dignity of truth as the fact of Maud's fidelity to a
sentiment. That was what Susie was proud of, much
more than of her great place in the world, which she
was moreover conscious of not as yet wholly measuring. That was what was more vivid even than her
being—in senses more worldly and in fact almost in
the degree of a revelation—English and distinct and
positive, with almost no inward but with the finest
outward resonance.

Susan Shepherd's word for her, again and again,
was that she was " large " ; yet it was not exactly a
case, as to the soul, of echoing chambers : she might
have been likened rather to a capacious receptacle,
originally perhaps loose, but now drawn as tightly as
possible over its accumulated contents—a packed
mass, for her American admirer, of curious detail.
When the latter good lady, at home, had handsomely
figured her friends as not small—which was the way

she mostly figured them—there was a certain implication that they were spacious because they were
empty. Mrs. Lowder, by a different law, was spacious
because she was full, because she had something in
common, even in repose, with a projectile, of great
size, loaded and ready for use. That indeed, to Susie's
romantic mind, announced itself as half the charm of
their renewal—a charm as of sitting in springtime,
during a long peace, on the daisied grassy bank of
some great slumbering fortress. True to her psycho-
logical instincts, certainly, Mrs. Stringham had noted
that the " sentiment " she rejoiced in on her old
schoolmate's part was all a matter of action and
movement, was not, save for the interweaving of a
more frequent plump " dearest " than she would
herself perhaps have used, a matter of much other
embroidery. She brooded with interest on this
further mark of race, feeling in her own spirit a different economy. The joy, for her, was to know *why* she
acted—the reason was half the business ; whereas
with Mrs. Lowder there might have been no reason :
" why " was the trivial seasoning-substance, the
vanilla or the nutmeg, omittable from the nutritive
pudding without spoiling it. Mrs. Lowder's desire
was clearly sharp that their young companions should
also prosper together ; and Mrs. Stringham's account
of it all to Milly, during the first days, was that when,
at Lancaster Gate, she was not occupied in telling, as
it were, about her, she was occupied in hearing much
of the history of her hostess's brilliant niece.

They had plenty, on these lines, the two elder
women, to give and to take, and it was even not quite
clear to the pilgrim from Boston that what she should
mainly have arranged for in London was not a series
of thrills for herself. She had a bad conscience,
indeed almost a sense of immorality, in having to
recognise that she was, as she said, carried away. She

laughed to Milly when she also said that she didn't know where it would end ; and the principle of her uneasiness was that Mrs. Lowder's life bristled for her with elements that she was really having to look at for the first time.   They represented, she believed, the world, the world that, as a consequence of the cold shoulder turned to it by the Pilgrim Fathers, had never yet boldly crossed to Boston—it would surely have sunk the stoutest Cunarder—and she couldn't pretend that she faced the prospect simply because Milly had had a caprice.   She was in the act herself of having one, directed precisely to their present spectacle.   She could but seek strength in the thought that she had never had one—or had never yielded to one, which came to the same thing—before. The sustaining sense of it all moreover as literary material—that quite dropped from her.   She must wait, at any rate, she should see : it struck her, so far as she had got, as vast, obscure, lurid.   She reflected in the watches of the night that she was probably just going to love it for itself—that is for itself and Milly. The odd thing was that she could think of Milly's loving it without dread—or with dread at least not on the score of conscience, only on the score of peace. It was a mercy at all events, for the hour, that their two spirits jumped together.

While, for this first week that followed their dinner, she drank deep at Lancaster Gate, her companion was no less happily, appeared to be indeed on the whole quite as romantically, provided for.   The hand-some English girl from the heavy English house had been as a figure in a picture stepping by magic out of its frame : it was a case in truth for which Mrs. Stringham presently found the perfect image.   She had lost none of her grasp, but quite the contrary, of that other conceit in virtue of which Milly was the wander-ing princess : so what could be more in harmony

now than to see the princess waited upon at the city
gate by the worthiest maiden, the chosen daughter
of the burgesses ?   It was the real again, evidently,
the amusement of the meeting for the princess too ;
princesses living for the most part, in such an appeased
way, on the plane of mere elegant representation.
That was why they pounced, at city gates, on deputed
flower-strewing damsels ; that was why, after effigies,
processions and other stately games, frank human
company was pleasant to them.   Kate Croy really
presented herself to Milly—the latter abounded for
Mrs. Stringham in accounts of it—as the wondrous
London girl in person (by what she had conceived,
from far back, of the London girl ; conceived from
the tales of travellers and the anecdotes of New York,
from old porings over *Punch* and a liberal acquaintance with the fiction of the day).   The only thing was
that she was nicer, since the creature in question had
rather been, to our young woman, an image of dread.
She had thought of her, at her best, as handsome just
as Kate was, with turns of head and tones of voice,
felicities of stature and attitude, things " put on "
and, for that matter, put off, all the marks of the
product of a packed society who should be at the
same time the heroine of a strong story.   She placed
this striking young person from the first in a story,
saw her, by a necessity of the imagination, for a
heroine, felt it the only character in which she wouldn't
be wasted ; and this in spite of the heroine's pleasant
abruptness, her forbearance from gush, her umbrellas
and jackets and shoes—as these things sketched
themselves to Milly—and something rather of a
breezy boy in the carriage of her arms and the
occasional freedom of her slang.

When Milly had settled that the extent of her good
will itself made her shy, she had found for the moment
quite a sufficient key, and they were by that time

thoroughly afloat together. This might well have
been the happiest hour they were to know, attacking
in friendly independence their great London—the
London of shops and streets and suburbs oddly interesting to Milly, as well as of museums, monuments,
" sights " oddly unfamiliar to Kate, while their
elders pursued a separate course ; these two rejoicing
not less in their intimacy and each thinking the
other's young woman a great acquisition for her own.
Milly expressed to Susan Shepherd more than once
that Kate had some secret, some smothered trouble,
besides all the rest of her history ; and that if she had
so good-naturedly helped Mrs. Lowder to meet them
this was exactly to create a diversion, to give herself
something else to think about. But on the case thus
postulated our young American had as yet had no
light : she only felt that when the light should come
it would greatly deepen the colour ; and she liked
to think she was prepared for anything. What she
already knew moreover was full, to her vision, of
English, of eccentric, of Thackerayan character—
Kate Croy having gradually become not a little
explicit on the subject of her situation, her past, her
present, her general predicament, her small success,
up to the present hour, in contenting at the same time
her father, her sister, her aunt and herself. It was
Milly's subtle guess, imparted to her Susie, that the
girl had somebody else as well, as yet unnamed, to
content—it being manifest that such a creature
couldn't help having ; a creature not perhaps, if one
would, exactly formed to inspire passions, since that
always implied a certain silliness, but essentially
seen, by the admiring eye of friendship, under the
clear shadow of some probably eminent male interest.
The clear shadow, from whatever source projected,
hung at any rate over Milly's companion the whole
week, and Kate Croy's handsome face smiled out of

THE WINGS OF THE DOVE

it, under bland skylights, in the presence alike of old
masters passive in their glory and of thoroughly new
ones, the newest, who bristled restlessly with pins
and brandished snipping shears.

It was meanwhile a pretty part of the intercourse
of these young ladies that each thought the other
more remarkable than herself—that each thought
herself, or assured the other she did, a comparatively
dusty object and the other a favourite of nature and
of fortune and covered thereby with the freshness of
the morning. Kate was amused, amazed, at the way
her friend insisted on " taking " her, and Milly wondered if Kate were sincere in finding her the most
extraordinary—quite apart from her being the most
charming—person she had come across. They had
talked, in long drives, and quantities of history had
not been wanting—in the light of which Mrs. Lowder's
niece might superficially seem to have had the best of
the argument. Her visitor's American references,
with their bewildering immensities, their confounding
moneyed New York, their excitements of high pressure,
their opportunities of wild freedom, their record of
used-up relatives, parents, clever eager fair slim
brothers—these the most loved—all engaged, as well
as successive superseded guardians, in a high extravagance of speculation and dissipation that had left
this exquisite being her black dress, her white face
and her vivid hair as the mere last broken link : such
a picture quite threw into the shade the brief bio-
graphy, however sketchily amplified, of a mere
middle-class nobody in Bayswater. And though that
indeed might be but a Bayswater way of putting it,
in addition to which Milly was in the stage of interest
in Bayswater ways, this critic so far prevailed that,
like Mrs. Stringham herself, she fairly got her companion to accept from her that she was quite the
nearest approach to a practical princess Bayswater

could hope ever to know. It was a fact—it became one at the end of three days—that Milly actually began to borrow from the handsome girl a sort of view of her state ; the handsome girl's impression of it was clearly so sincere. This impression was a tribute, a tribute positively to power, power the source of which was the last thing Kate treated as a mystery. There were passages, under all their skylights, the succession of their shops being large, in which the latter's easy yet the least bit dry manner sufficiently gave out that if *she* had had so deep a pocket—— !

It was not moreover by any means with not having the imagination of expenditure that she appeared to charge her friend, but with not having the imagination of terror, of thrift, the imagination or in any degree the habit of a conscious dependence on others. Such moments, when all Wigmore Street, for instance, seemed to rustle about and the pale girl herself to be facing the different rustlers, usually so undiscrimin-ated, as individual Britons too, Britons personal, parties to a relation and perhaps even intrinsically remarkable—such moments in especial determined for Kate a perception of the high happiness of her companion's liberty. Milly's range was thus immense ; she had to ask nobody for anything, to refer nothing to any one ; her freedom, her fortune and her fancy were her law ; an obsequious world surrounded her, she could sniff up at every step its fumes. And Kate, these days, was altogether in the phase of forgiving her so much bliss ; in the phase moreover of believing that, should they continue to go on together, she would abide in that generosity. She had at such a point as this no suspicion of a rift within the lute—by which we mean not only none of anything's coming between them, but none of any definite flaw in so much clearness of quality. Yet, all the same, if Milly, at Mrs. Lowder's banquet, had described herself to Lord Mark as kindly used by the young woman on the other side because of some faintly-felt special propriety in it, so there really did match with this, privately, on the young woman's part, a feeling not analysed but divided, a latent impression that Mildred Theale was not, after all, a person to change places, to change even chances with. Kate, verily, would perhaps not quite have known what she meant by this discrimination, and she came near naming it only when she said to herself that, rich as Milly was, one probably wouldn't—which was singular—ever hate her for it. The handsome girl had, with herself, these felicities and crudities : it wasn't obscure to her that, without some very particular reason to help, it might have proved a test of one's philosophy not to be irritated by a mistress of millions, or whatever they were, who, as a girl, so easily might have been, like herself, only vague and cruelly female. She was by no means sure of liking Aunt Maud as much as *she* deserved, and Aunt Maud's command of funds was obviously inferior to Milly's. There was thus clearly, as pleading for the latter, some influence that would later on become distinct ; and meanwhile, decidedly, it was enough that she was as charming as she was queer and as queer as she was charming—all of which was a rare amusement ; as well, for that matter, as further sufficient that there were objects of value she had already pressed on Kate's acceptance. A week of her society in these conditions—conditions that Milly chose to sum up as ministering immensely, for a blind vague pilgrim, to aid and comfort—announced itself from an early hour as likely to become a week of presents, acknowledgments, mementoes, pledges of gratitude and admiration, that were all on one side. Kate as promptly embraced the propriety of making it clear that she must forswear shops till she should

receive some guarantee that the contents of each one
she entered as a humble companion shouldn't be
placed at her feet ; yet that was in truth not before
she had found herself in possession, under whatever
protests, of several precious ornaments and other
minor conveniences.

Great was the absurdity too that there should have
come a day, by the end of the week, when it appeared
that all Milly would have asked in definite " return,"
as might be said, was to be told a little about Lord
Mark and to be promised the privilege of a visit to
Mrs. Condrip. Far other amusements had been
offered her, but her eagerness was shamelessly human,
and she seemed really to count more on the revelation
of the anxious lady at Chelsea than on the best nights
of the opera. Kate admired, and showed it, such an
absence of fear : to the fear of being bored in such a
connexion she would have been so obviously entitled.
Milly's answer to this was the plea of her curiosities—
which left her friend wondering as to their odd
direction. Some among them, no doubt, were rather
more intelligible, and Kate had heard without wonder
that she was blank about Lord Mark. This young
lady's account of him, at the same time, professed
itself frankly imperfect ; for what they best knew him
by at Lancaster Gate was a thing difficult to explain.
One knew people in general by something they had
to show, something that, either for them or against,
could be touched or named or proved ; and she could
think of no other case of a value taken as so great and
yet flourishing untested. His value was his future,
which had somehow got itself as accepted by Aunt
Maud as if it had been his good cook or his steam-
launch. She, Kate, didn't mean she thought him a
humbug ; he might do great things—but they were
as yet, so to speak, all he had done. On the other
hand, it was of course something of an achievement,

THE WINGS OF THE DOVE

and not open to every one, to have got one's self taken
so seriously by Aunt Maud. The best thing about
him doubtless, on the whole, was that Aunt Maud
believed in him. She was often fantastic, but she
knew a humbug, and—no, Lord Mark wasn't that.
He had been a short time in the House, on the Tory
side, but had lost his seat on the first opportunity,
and this was all he had to point to. However, he
pointed to nothing ; which was very possibly just a
sign of his real cleverness, one of those that the really
clever had in common with the really void. Even
Aunt Maud frequently admitted that there was a
good deal, for her view of him, to bring up the rear.
And he wasn't meanwhile himself indifferent—indifferent to himself—for he was working Lancaster
Gate for all it was worth : just as it was, no doubt,
working *him*, and just as the working and the worked
were in London, as one might explain, the parties to
every relation.

Kate did explain, for her listening friend ; every
one who had anything to give—it was true they were
the fewest—made the sharpest possible bargain for
it, got at least its value in return. The strangest
thing furthermore was that this might be in cases a
happy understanding. The worker in one connexion
was the worked in another ; it was as broad as it was
long—with the wheels of the system, as might be seen,
wonderfully oiled. People could quite like each other
in the midst of it, as Aunt Maud, by every appearance, quite liked Lord Mark, and as Lord Mark, it
was to be hoped, liked Mrs. Lowder, since if he didn't
he was a greater brute than one could believe. She,
Kate, hadn't yet, it was true, made out what he
was doing for her—besides which the dear woman
needed him, even at the most he could do, much less
than she imagined ; so far as all of which went, moreover, there were plenty of things on every side she

hadn't yet made out. She believed, on the whole, in any one Aunt Maud took up ; and she gave it to Milly as worth thinking of that, whatever wonderful people this young lady might meet in the land, she would meet no more extraordinary woman. There were greater celebrities by the million, and of course greater swells, but a bigger *person*, by Kate's view, and a larger natural handful every way, would really be far to seek. When Milly inquired with interest if Kate's belief in *her* was primarily on the lines of what Mrs. Lowder " took up," her interlocutress could handsomely say yes, since by the same principle she believed in herself. Whom but Aunt Maud's niece, pre-eminently, had Aunt Maud taken up, and who was thus more in the current, with her, of working and of being worked ? " You may ask," Kate said, " what in the world *I* have to give ; and that indeed is just what I'm trying to learn. There must be something, for her to think she can get it out of me. She *will* get it—trust her ; and then I shall see what it is ; which I beg you to believe I should never have found out for myself." She declined to treat any question of Milly's own " paying " power as discussable ; that Milly would pay a hundred per cent—and even to the end, doubtless, through the nose—was just the beautiful basis on which they found themselves.

These were fine facilities, pleasantries, ironies, all these luxuries of gossip and philosophies of London and of life, and they became quickly, between the pair, the common form of talk, Milly professing herself delighted to know that something was to be done with her. If the most remarkable woman in England was to do it, so much the better, and if the most remarkable woman in England had them both in hand together why what could be jollier for each ? When she reflected indeed a little on the oddity of her wanting two at once Kate had the natural reply that it was exactly what showed her sincerity. She invariably gave way to feeling, and feeling had distinctly popped up in her on the advent of her girlhood's friend. The way the cat would jump was always, in presence of anything that moved her, interesting to see; visibly enough, moreover, it hadn't for a long time jumped anything like so far. This in fact, as we already know, remained the marvel for Milly Theale, who, on sight of Mrs. Lowder, had found fifty links in respect to Susie absent from the chain of association. She knew so herself what she thought of Susie that she would have expected the lady of Lancaster Gate to think something quite different; the failure of which endlessly mystified her. But her mystification was the cause for her of another fine impression, inasmuch as when she went so far as to observe to Kate that Susan Shepherd—and especially Susan Shepherd emerging so uninvited from an irrelevant past—ought by all the proprieties simply to have bored Aunt Maud, her confidant agreed to this without a protest and abounded in the sense of her wonder. Susan Shepherd at least bored the niece— that was plain; this young woman saw nothing in her—nothing to account for anything, not even for Milly's own indulgence : which little fact became in turn to the latter's mind a fact of significance. It was a light on the handsome girl—representing more than merely showed—that poor Susie was simply as nought to her. This was in a manner too a general admonition to poor Susie's companion, who seemed to see marked by it the direction in which she had best most look out. It just faintly rankled in her that a person who was good enough and to spare for Milly Theale shouldn't be good enough for another girl ; though, oddly enough, she could easily have forgiven Mrs. Lowder herself the impatience. Mrs. Lowder didn't feel it, and Kate Croy felt it with ease ;

yet in the end, be it added, she grasped the reason,
and the reason enriched her mind. Wasn't it sufficiently the reason that the handsome girl was, with
twenty other splendid qualities, the least bit brutal
too, and didn't she suggest, as no one yet had ever
done for her new friend, that there might be a wild
beauty in that, and even a strange grace ? Kate
wasn't brutally brutal—which Milly had hitherto
benightedly supposed the only way ; she wasn't even
aggressively so, but rather indifferently, defensively
and, as might be said, by the habit of anticipation.
She simplified in advance, was beforehand with her
doubts, and knew with singular quickness what she
wasn't, as they said in New York, going to like. In
that way at least people were clearly quicker in
England than at home ; and Milly could quite see
after a little how such instincts might become usual
in a world in which dangers abounded. There were
clearly more dangers roundabout Lancaster Gate
than one suspected in New York or could dream of
in Boston. At all events, with more sense of them,
there were more precautions, and it was a remarkable
world altogether in which there could be precautions,
on whatever ground, against Susie.

III

SHE certainly made up with Susie directly, however, for any allowance she might have had privately to extend to tepid appreciation ; since the late and long talks of these two embraced not only everything offered and suggested by the hours they spent apart, but a good deal more besides. She might be as detached as the occasion required at four o'clock in the afternoon, but she used no such freedom to any one about anything as she habitually used about everything to Susan Shepherd at midnight. All the same, it should with much less delay than this have been mentioned, she hadn't yet—hadn't, that is, at the end of six days—produced any news for her comrade to compare with an announcement made her by the latter as a result of a drive with Mrs. Lowder, for a change, in the remarkable Battersea Park. The elder friends had sociably revolved there while the younger ones followed bolder fancies in the admirable equipage appointed to Milly at the hotel—a heavier, more emblazoned, more amusing chariot than she had ever, with " stables " notoriously mismanaged, known at home ; whereby, in the course of the circuit, more than once repeated, it had " come out," as Mrs. Stringham said, that the couple at Lancaster Gate were, of all people, acquainted with Mildred's other English friend, the gentleman, the one connected with the English newspaper (Susie hung fire a little over his

162

name) who had been with her in New York so shortly
previous to present adventures. He had been named
of course in Battersea Park—else he couldn't have
been identified ; and Susie had naturally, before she
could produce her own share in the matter as a kind
of confession, to make it plain that her allusion was to
Mr. Merton Densher. This was because Milly had at
first a little air of not knowing whom she meant ;
and the girl really kept, as well, a certain control of
herself while she remarked that the case was surprising, the chance one in a thousand. They knew him,
both Maud and Miss Croy knew him, she gathered too,
rather well, though indeed it wasn't on any show of
intimacy that he had happened to be mentioned. It
hadn't been—Susie made the point—she herself who
brought·him in : he had in fact not been brought in
at all, but only referred to as a young journalist known
to Mrs. Lowder and who had lately gone to their
wonderful country—Mrs. Lowder always said " your
wonderful country "—on behalf of his journal. But
Mrs. Stringham had taken it up—with the tips of her
fingers indeed ; and that was the confession : she had,
without meaning any harm, recognised Mr. Densher
as an acquaintance of Milly's, though she had also
pulled herself up before getting in too far. Mrs.
Lowder had been struck, clearly—it wasn't too much
to say ; then she also, it had rather seemed, had pulled
herself up ; and there had been a little moment during
which each might have been keeping something from
the other. " Only," said Milly's informant, " I luckily
remembered in time that I had nothing whatever to
keep—which was much simpler and nicer. I don't know
what Maud has, but there it is. She was interested,
distinctly, in your knowing him—in his having met you
over there with so little loss of time. But I ventured
to tell her it hadn't been so long as to make you as
yet great friends. I don't know if I was right."

Whatever time this explanation might have taken, there had been moments enough in the matter now—before the elder woman's conscience had done itself justice—to enable Milly to reply that although the fact in question doubtless had its importance she imagined they wouldn't find the importance overwhelming. It *was* odd that their one Englishman should so instantly fit ; it wasn't, however, miraculous—they surely all had often seen how extraordinarily " small," as every one said, was the world. Undoubtedly also Susie had done just the plain thing in not letting his name pass. Why in the world should there be a mystery ?—and what an immense one they would appear to have made if he should come back and find they had concealed their knowledge of him ! " I don't know, Susie dear," the girl observed, " what you think I have to conceal."

" It doesn't matter, at a given moment," Mrs. Stringham returned, " what you know or don't know as to what I think ; for you always find out the very next minute, and when you do find out, dearest, you never *really* care. Only," she presently asked, " have you heard of him from Miss Croy ? "

" Heard of Mr. Densher ? Never a word. We haven't mentioned him. Why should we ? "

" That *you* haven't I understand ; but that your friend hasn't," Susie opined, " may mean something."

" May mean what ? "

" Well," Mrs. Stringham presently brought out, " I tell you all when I tell you that Maud asks me to suggest to you that it may perhaps be better for the present not to speak of him : not to speak of him to her niece, that is, unless she herself speaks to you first. But Maud thinks she won't."

Milly was ready to engage for anything ; but in

164

respect to the facts—as they so far possessed them
—it all sounded a little complicated. "Is it because
there's anything between them?"

"No—I gather not; but Maud's state of mind is
precautionary. She's afraid of something. Or perhaps it would be more correct to say she's afraid of
everything."

"She's afraid, you mean," Milly asked, "of their
—a—liking each other?"

Susie had an intense thought and then an effusion.
"My dear child, we move in a labyrinth."

"Of course we do. That's just the fun of it!"
said Milly with a strange gaiety. Then she added:
"Don't tell me that—in this for instance—there are
not abysses. I want abysses."

Her friend looked at her—it was not unfrequently
the case—a little harder than the surface of the occasion seemed to require; and another person present
at such times might have wondered to what inner
thought of her own the good lady was trying to fit
the speech. It was too much her disposition, no
doubt, to treat her young companion's words as
symptoms of an imputed malady. It was none the
less, however, her highest law to be light when the
girl was light. She knew how to be quaint with the
new quaintness—the great Boston gift; it had been
happily her note in the magazines; and Maud Lowder,
to whom it was new indeed and who had never heard
anything remotely like it, quite cherished her, as a
social resource, by reason of it. It shouldn't therefore fail her now; with it in fact one might face most
things. "Ah then let us hope we shall sound the
depths—I'm prepared for the worst—of sorrow and
sin! But she would like her niece—we're not ignorant
of that, are we?—to marry Lord Mark. Hasn't she
told you so?"

"Hasn't Mrs. Lowder told me?"

"No ; hasn't Kate ? It isn't, you know, that she doesn't know it."

Milly had, under her comrade's eyes, a minute of mute detachment. She had lived with Kate Croy for several days in a state of intimacy as deep as it had been sudden, and they had clearly, in talk, in many directions, proceeded to various extremities. Yet it now came over her as in a clear cold wave that there was a possible account of their relations in which the quantity her new friend had told her might have figured as small, as smallest, beside the quantity she hadn't. She couldn't say at any rate whether or no Kate had made the point that her aunt designed her for Lord Mark : it had only sufficiently come out —which had been, moreover, eminently guessable— that she was involved in her aunt's designs. Somehow, for Milly, brush it over nervously as she might and with whatever simplifying hand, this abrupt extrusion of Mr. Densher altered all proportions, had an effect on all values. It was fantastic of her to let it make a difference that she couldn't in the least have defined—and she was at least, even during these instants, rather proud of being able to hide, on the spot, the difference it did make. Yet all the same the effect for her was, almost violently, of that gentleman's having been there—having been where she had stood till now in her simplicity—before her. It would have taken but another free moment to make her see abysses—since abysses were what she wanted— in the mere circumstance of his own silence, in New York, about his English friends. There had really been in New York little time for anything ; but, had she liked, Milly could have made it out for herself that he had avoided the subject of Miss Croy and that Miss Croy was yet a subject it could never be natural to avoid. It was to be added at the same time that even if his silence had been a labyrinth—which was

absurd in view of all the other things too he couldn't
possibly have spoken of—this was exactly what must
suit her, since it fell under the head of the plea she had
just uttered to Susie. These things, however, came
and went, and it set itself up between the companions,
for the occasion, in the oddest way, both that their
happening all to know Mr. Densher—except indeed
that Susie didn't, but probably would—was a fact
attached, in a world of rushing about, to one of the
common orders of chance ; and yet further that it
was amusing—oh awfully amusing !—to be able
fondly to hope that there was " something *in* " its
having been left to crop up with such suddenness.
There seemed somehow a possibility that the ground
or, as it were, the air might in a manner have under-
gone some pleasing preparation ; though the question
of this possibility would probably, after all, have
taken some threshing out. The truth, moreover—
and there they were, already, our pair, talking about
it, the " truth " !—hadn't in fact quite cropped out.
This, obviously, in view of Mrs. Lowder's request to
her old friend.

It was accordingly on Mrs. Lowder's recommenda-
tion that nothing should be said to Kate—it was on
all this might cover in Aunt Maud that the idea of
an interesting complication could best hope to perch ;
and when in fact, after the colloquy we have reported,
Milly saw Kate again without mentioning any name,
her silence succeeded in passing muster with her as the
beginning of a new sort of fun. The sort was all the
newer by its containing measurably a small element of
anxiety : when she had gone in for fun before it had
been with her hands a little more free. Yet it *was*,
none the less, rather exciting to be conscious of a still
sharper reason for interest in the handsome girl, as
Kate continued even now pre-eminently to remain
for her ; and a reason—this was the great point—of

which the young woman herself could have no suspicion. Twice over thus, for two or three hours
together, Milly found herself seeing Kate, quite fixing
her, in the light of the knowledge that it was a face on
which Mr. Densher's eyes had more or less familiarly
rested and which, by the same token, had looked,
rather *more* beautifully than less, into his own. She
pulled herself up indeed with the thought that it had
inevitably looked, as beautifully as one would, into
thousands of faces in which one might oneself never
trace it ; but just the odd result of the thought was to
intensify for the girl that side of her friend which she
had doubtless already been more prepared than she
quite knew to think of as the " other," the not wholly
calculable. It was fantastic, and Milly was aware of
this ; but the other side was what had, of a sudden,
been turned straight toward her by the show of Mr.
Densher's propinquity. She hadn't the excuse of
knowing it for Kate's own, since nothing whatever as
yet proved it particularly to be such. Never mind ;
it was with this other side now fully presented that
Kate came and went, kissed her for greeting and for
parting, talked, as usual, of everything but—as it
had so abruptly become for Milly—*the* thing. Our
young woman, it is true, would doubtless not have
tasted so sharply a difference in this·pair of occasions
hadn't she been tasting so peculiarly her own possible
betrayals. What happened was that afterwards, on
separation, she wondered if the matter hadn't mainly
been that she herself was so " other," so taken up
with the unspoken ; the strangest thing of all being,
still subsequently, that when she asked herself how
Kate could have failed to feel it she became conscious
of being here on the edge of a great darkness. She
should never know how Kate truly felt about anything
such a one as Milly Theale should give her to feel.
Kate would never—and not from ill will nor from

duplicity, but from a sort of failure of common terms —reduce it to such a one's comprehension or put it within her convenience.

It was as such a one, therefore, that, for three or four days more, Milly watched Kate as just such another ; and it was presently as such a one that she threw herself into their promised visit, at last achieved, to Chelsea, the quarter of the famous Carlyle, the field of exercise of his ghost, his votaries, and the residence of " poor Marian," so often referred to and actually a somewhat incongruous spirit there. With our young woman's first view of poor Marian everything gave way but the sense of how in England, apparently, the social situation of sisters could be opposed, how common ground for a place in the world could quite fail them : a state of things sagely perceived to be involved in an hierarchical, an aristocratic order. Just whereabouts in the order Mrs. Lowder had established her niece was a question not wholly void as yet, no doubt, of ambiguity—though Milly was withal sure Lord Mark could exactly have fixed the point if he would, fixing it at the same time for Aunt Maud herself ; but it was clear Mrs. Condrip was, as might have been said, in quite another geography. She wouldn't have been to be found on the same social map, and it was as if her visitors had turned over page after page together before the final relief of their benevolent " Here ! " The interval was bridged of course, but the bridge verily was needed, and the impression left Milly to wonder if, in the general connexion, it were of bridges or of intervals that the spirit not locally disciplined would find itself most conscious. It was as if at home, by contrast, there were neither—neither the difference itself, from position to position, nor, on either side, and particularly on one, the awfully good manner, the conscious sinking of a consciousness, that made up for it. The conscious sinking, at all events, and the awfully good manner, the difference, the bridge, the interval, the skipped leaves of the social atlas—these, it was to be confessed, had a little, for our young lady, in default of stouter stuff, to work themselves into the light literary legend—a mixed wandering echo of Trollope, of Thackeray, perhaps mostly of Dickens—under favour of which her pilgrimage had so much appealed. She could relate to Susie later on, late the same evening, that the legend, before she had done with it, had run clear, that the adored author of *The Newcomes*, in fine, had been on the whole the note : the picture lacking thus more than she had hoped, or rather perhaps showing less than she had feared, a certain possibility of Pickwickian outline. She explained how she meant by this that Mrs. Condrip hadn't altogether proved another Mrs. Nickleby, nor even—for she might have proved almost anything, from the way poor worried Kate had spoken—a widowed and aggravated Mrs. Micawber.

Mrs. Stringham, in the midnight conference, intimated rather yearningly that, however the event might have turned, the side of English life such experiences opened to Milly were just those she herself seemed " booked "—as they were all, roundabout her now, always saying—to miss : she had begun to have a little, for her fellow observer, these moments of fanciful reaction (reaction in which she was once more all Susan Shepherd) against the high sphere of colder conventions into which her overwhelming connexion with Maud Manningham had rapt her. Milly never lost sight for long of the Susan Shepherd side of her, and was always there to meet it when it came up and vaguely, tenderly, impatiently to pat it, abounding in the assurance that they would still provide for it. They had, however, to-night another matter in hand ; which proved to be presently, on the

girl's part, in respect to her hour of Chelsea, the revelation that Mrs. Condrip, taking a few minutes when
Kate was away with one of the children, in bed upstairs for some small complaint, had suddenly (without its being in the least " led up to ") broken ground
on the subject of Mr. Densher, mentioned him with
impatience as a person in love with her sister. " She
wished me, if I cared for Kate, to know," Milly said
—" for it would be quite too dreadful, and one might
do something."

Susie wondered. " Prevent anything coming of
it ? That's easily said. Do what ? "

Milly had a dim smile. " I think that what she
would like is that I should come a good deal to see
her about it."

" And doesn't she suppose you've anything else
to do ? "

The girl had by this time clearly made it out.
" Nothing but to admire and make much of her sister
—whom she doesn't, however, herself in the least
understand—and give up one's time, and everything
else, to it." It struck the elder friend that she spoke
with an almost unprecedented approach to sharpness ;
as if Mrs. Condrip had been rather indescribably
disconcerting. Never yet so much as just of late had
Mrs. Stringham seen her companion exalted, and by
the very play of something within, into a vague
golden air that left irritation below. That was the
great thing with Milly—it was her characteristic
poetry, or at least it was Susan Shepherd's. " But
she made a point," the former continued, " of my
keeping what she says from Kate. I'm not to mention
that she has spoken."

" And why," Mrs. Stringham presently asked, " is
Mr. Densher so dreadful ? "

Milly had, she thought, a delay to answer—something that suggested a fuller talk with Mrs. Condrip

than she inclined perhaps to report. " It isn't so much he himself." Then the girl spoke a little as for the romance of it ; one could never tell, with her, where romance would come in. " It's the state of his fortunes."

" And is that very bad ? "

" He has no ' private means,' and no prospect of any. He has no income, and no ability, according to Mrs. Condrip, to make one. He's as poor, she calls it, as ' poverty,' and she says she knows what that is."

Again Mrs. Stringham considered, and it presently produced something. " But isn't he brilliantly clever ? "

Milly had also then an instant that was not quite fruitless. " I haven't the least idea."

To which, for the time, Susie only replied " Oh ! " —though by the end of a minute she had followed it with a slightly musing " I see " ; and that in turn with : " It's quite what Maud Lowder thinks."

" That he'll never do anything ? "

" No—quite the contrary : that he's exceptionally able."

" Oh yes ; I know "—Milly had again, in reference to what her friend had already told her of this, her little tone of a moment before. " But Mrs. Condrip's own great point is that Aunt Maud herself won't hear of any such person. Mr. Densher, she holds—that's the way, at any rate, it was explained to me—won't ever be either a public man or a rich man. If he were public she'd be willing, as I understand, to help him ; if he were rich—without being anything else—she'd do her best to swallow him. As it is she taboos him."

" In short," said Mrs. Stringham as with a private purpose, " she told you, the sister, all about it. But Mrs. Lowder likes him," she added.

" Mrs. Condrip didn't tell me that."

" Well, she does, all the same, my dear, extremely."

" Then there it is ! " On which, with a drop and one of those sudden slightly sighing surrenders to a vague reflux and a general fatigue that had recently more than once marked themselves for her companion, Milly turned away. Yet the matter wasn't left so, that night, between them, albeit neither perhaps could afterwards have said which had first come back to it. Milly's own nearest approach at least, for a little, to doing so, was to remark that they appeared all—every one they saw—to think tremendously of money. This prompted in Susie a laugh, not untender, the innocent meaning of which was that it came, as a subject for indifference, money did, easier to some people than to others : she made the point in fairness, however, that you couldn't have told, by any too crude transparency of air, what place it held for Maud Manningham. She did her worldliness with grand proper silences—if it mightn't better be put perhaps that she did her detachment with grand occasional pushes. However Susie put it, in truth, she was really, in justice to herself, thinking of the difference, as favourites of fortune, between her old friend and her new. Aunt Maud sat somehow in the midst of her money, founded on it and surrounded by it, even if with a masterful high manner about it, her manner of looking, hard and bright, as if it weren't there. Milly, about hers, had no manner at all— which was possibly, from a point of view, a fault : she was at any rate far away on the edge of it, and you hadn't, as might be said, in order to get at her nature, to traverse, by whatever avenue, any piece of her property. It was clear, on the other hand, that Mrs. Lowder was keeping her wealth as for purposes, imaginations, ambitions, that would figure as large, as honourably unselfish, on the day they should take effect. She would impose her will, but her will would be only that a person or two shouldn't lose a benefit by not submitting if they could be made to submit. To Milly, as so much younger, such far views couldn't be imputed : there was nobody she was supposable as interested for. It was too soon, since she wasn't interested for herself. Even the richest woman, at her age, lacked motive, and Milly's motive doubtless had plenty of time to arrive. She was meanwhile beautiful, simple, sublime without it—whether missing it and vaguely reaching out for it or not ; and with it, for that matter, in the event, would really be these things just as much. Only then she might very well have, like Aunt Maud, a manner. Such were the connexions, at all events, in which the colloquy of our two ladies freshly flickered up—in which it came round that the elder asked the younger if she had herself, in the afternoon, named Mr. Densher as an acquaintance.

"Oh no—I said nothing of having seen him. I remembered," the girl explained, "Mrs. Lowder's wish."

"But that," her friend observed after a moment, "was for silence to Kate."

"Yes—but Mrs. Condrip would immediately have told Kate."

"Why so ?—since she must dislike to talk about him."

"Mrs. Condrip must ? " Milly thought. "What she would like most is that her sister should be brought to think ill of him ; and if anything she can tell her will help that——" But the girl dropped suddenly here, as if her companion would see.

Her companion's interest, however, was all for what she herself saw. "You mean she'll immediately speak ? " Mrs. Stringham gathered that this

THE WINGS OF THE DOVE

was what Milly meant, but it left still a question. " How will it be against him that you know him ? "

" Oh how can I say ? It won't be so much one's knowing him as one's having kept it out of sight."

" Ah," said Mrs. Stringham as for comfort, " *you* haven't kept it out of sight. Isn't it much rather Miss Croy herself who has ? "

" It isn't my acquaintance with him," Milly smiled, " that she has dissimulated."

" She has dissimulated only her own ? Well then the responsibility's hers."

" Ah but," said the girl, not perhaps with marked consequence, " she has a right to do as she likes."

" Then so, my dear, have you ! " smiled Susan Shepherd.

Milly looked at her as if she were almost venerably simple, but also as if this were what one loved her for. " We're not quarrelling about it, Kate and I, *yet*."

" I only meant," Mrs. Stringham explained, " that I don't see what Mrs. Condrip would gain."

" By her being able to tell Kate ? " Milly thought. " I only meant that I don't see what I myself should gain."

" But it will have to come out—that he knows you both—some time."

Milly scarce assented. " Do you mean when he comes back ? "

" He'll find you both here, and he can hardly be looked to, I take it, to ' cut ' either of you for the sake of the other."

This placed the question at last on a basis more distinctly cheerful. " I might get at him somehow beforehand," the girl suggested ; " I might give him what they call here the ' tip '—that he's not to know me when we meet. Or, better still, I mightn't be here at all."

" Do you want to run away from him ? "

It was, oddly enough, an idea Milly seemed half to accept. " I don't know *what* I want to run away from ! "

It dispelled, on the spot—something, to the elder woman's ear, in the sad, sweet sound of it—any ghost of any need of explaining. The sense was constant for her that their relation might have been afloat, like some island of the south, in a great warm sea that represented, for every conceivable chance, a margin, an outer sphere, of general emotion ; and the effect of the occurrence of anything in particular was to make the sea submerge the island, the margin flood the text. The great wave now for a moment swept over. " I'll go anywhere else in the world you 'like."

But Milly came up through it. " Dear old Susie —how I do work you ! "

" Oh this is nothing yet."

" No indeed—to what it will be."

" You're not—and it's vain'to pretend," said dear old Susie, who had been taking her in, " as sound and strong as I insist on having you."

" Insist, insist—the more the better. But the day I *look* as sound and strong as that, you know," Milly went on—" on that day I shall be just sound and strong enough to take leave of you sweetly for ever. That's where one is," she continued thus agreeably to embroider, " when even one's *most* ' beaux moments ' aren't such as to qualify, so far as appearance goes, for anything gayer than a handsome cemetery. Since I've lived all these years as if I were dead, I shall die, no doubt, as if I were alive— which will happen to be as you want me. So, you see," she wound up, " you'll never really know where I am. Except indeed when I'm gone ; and then you'll only know where I'm not."

"I'd die *for* you," said Susan Shepherd after a moment.

"'Thanks awfully'! Then stay here for me."

"But we can't be in London for August, nor for many of all these next weeks."

"Then we'll go back."

Susie blenched. "Back to America?"

"No, abroad—to Switzerland, Italy, anywhere. I mean by your staying 'here' for me," Milly pursued, "your staying with me wherever I may be, even though we may neither of us know at the time where it is. No," she insisted, "I *don't* know where I am, and you never will, and it doesn't matter—and I dare say it's quite true," she broke off, "that everything will have to come out." Her friend would have felt of her that she joked about it now, hadn't her scale from grave to gay been a thing of such unnameable shades that her contrasts were never sharp. She made up for failures of gravity by failures of mirth; if she hadn't, that is, been at times as earnest as might have been liked, so she was certain not to be at other times as easy as she would like herself. "I must face the music. It isn't at any rate its 'coming out,'" she added; "it's that Mrs. Condrip would put the fact before her to his injury."

Her companion wondered. "But how to *his*?"

"Why if he pretends to love her——!"

"And does he only 'pretend'?"

"I mean if, trusted by her in strange countries, he forgets her so far as to make up to other people."

The amendment, however, brought Susie in, as with gaiety, for a comfortable end. "Did he make up, the false creature, to *you*?"

"No—but the question isn't of that. It's of what Kate might be made to believe."

"That, given the fact of his having evidently more or less followed up his acquaintance with you, to say nothing of your obvious weird charm, he must have been all ready if you had a little bit led him on ? "

Milly neither accepted nor qualified this ; she only said after a moment and as with a conscious excess of the pensive : " No, I don't think she'd quite wish to suggest that I made up to *him* ; for that I should have had to do so would only bring out his constancy. All I mean is," she added—and now at last, as with a supreme impatience—" that her being able to make him out a little a person who could give cause for jealousy would evidently help her, since she's afraid of him, to do him in her sister's mind a useful ill turn."

Susan Shepherd perceived in this explanation such signs of an appetite for motive as would have sat gracefully even on one of her own New England heroines. It was seeing round several corners ; but that was what New England heroines did, and it was moreover interesting for the moment to make out how many her young friend had actually undertaken to see round. Finally, too, weren't they braving the deeps ? They got their amusement where they could. " Isn't it only," she asked, " rather probable she'd see that Kate's knowing him as (what's the pretty old word ?) *volage*—— ? "

" Well ? " She hadn't filled out her idea, but neither, it seemed, could Milly.

" Well, might but do what that often does—by all *our* blessed little laws and arrangements at least : excite Kate's own sentiment instead of depressing it."

The idea was bright, yet the girl but beautifully stared. " Kate's own sentiment ? Oh she didn't speak of that. I don't think," she added as if she had been unconsciously giving a wrong impression, " I don't think Mrs. Condrip imagines *she's* in love."

It made Mrs. Stringham stare in turn. " Then what's her fear ? "

" Well, only the fact of Mr. Densher's possibly himself keeping it up—the fear of some final result from *that.*"

" Oh," said Susie, intellectually a little disconcerted—" she looks far ahead ! "

At this, however, Milly threw off another of her sudden vague " sports." " No—it's only we who do."

" Well, don't let us be more interested for them than they are for themselves ! "

" Certainly not "—the girl promptly assented. A certain interest nevertheless remained ; she appeared to wish to be clear. " It wasn't of anything on Kate's own part she spoke."

" You mean she thinks her sister distinctly doesn't care for him ? "

It was still as if, for an instant, Milly had to be sure of what she meant ; but there it presently was. " If she did care Mrs. Condrip would have told me."

What Susan Shepherd seemed thereupon for a little to wonder was why then they had been talking so. " But did you ask her ? "

" Ah no ! "

" Oh ! " said Susan Shepherd.

Milly, however, easily explained that she wouldn't have asked her for the world.

BOOK FIFTH

I

LORD MARK looked at her to-day in particular as if
to wring from her a confession that she had originally
done him injustice ; and he was entitled to whatever
there might be in it of advantage or merit that his
intention really in a manner took effect : he cared
about something, after all, sufficiently to make her
feel absurdly as if she *were* confessing—all the while
it was quite the case that neither justice nor injustice
was what had been in question between them. He
had presented himself at the hotel, had found her
and had found Susan Shepherd at home, had been
" civil " to Susan—it was just that shade, and Susan's
fancy had fondly caught it ; and then had come again
and missed them, and then had come and found them
once more : besides letting them easily see that if it
hadn't by this time been the end of everything—
which they could feel in the exhausted air, that of the
season at its last gasp—the places they might have
liked to go to were such as they would have had only
to mention. Their feeling was—or at any rate their
modest general plea—that there was no place they
would have liked to go to ; there was only the sense
of finding they liked, wherever they were, the place
to which they had been brought. Such was highly
the case as to their current consciousness—which
could be indeed, in an equally eminent degree, but a
matter of course ; impressions this afternoon having

by a happy turn of their wheel been gathered for them into a splendid cluster, an offering like an armful of the rarest flowers. They were in presence of the offering—they had been led up to it ; and if it had been still their habit to look at each other across distances for increase of unanimity his hand would have been silently named between them as the hand applied to the wheel. He had administered the touch that, under light analysis, made the difference—the difference of their not having lost, as Susie on the spot and at the hour phrased it again and again, both for herself and for such others as the question might concern, so beautiful and interesting an experience ; the difference also, in fact, of Mrs. Lowder's not having lost it either, though it was superficially with Mrs. Lowder they had come, and though it was further with that lady that our young woman was directly engaged during the half-hour or so of her most agreeably inward response to the scene.

The great historic house had, for Milly, beyond terrace and garden, as the centre of an almost extravagantly grand Watteau-composition, a tone as of old gold kept " down " by the quality of the air, summer full-flushed but attuned to the general perfect taste. Much, by her measure, for the previous hour, appeared, in connexion with this revelation of it, to have happened to her—a quantity expressed in introductions of charming new people, in walks through halls of armour, of pictures, of cabinets, of tapestry, of tea-tables, in an assault of reminders that this largeness of style was the sign of *appointed* felicity. The largeness of style was the great containing vessel, while everything else, the pleasant personal affluence, the easy murmurous welcome, the honoured age of illustrious host and hostess, all at once so distinguished and so plain, so public and so shy, became but this or that element of the infusion. The elements melted together and seasoned the draught, the essence of which might have struck the girl as distilled into the small cup of iced coffee she had vaguely accepted from somebody, while a fuller flood somehow kept bearing her up—all the freshness of response of her young life, the freshness of the first and only prime. What had perhaps brought on just now a kind of climax was the fact of her appearing to make out, through Aunt Maud, what was really the matter. It couldn't be less than a climax for a poor shaky maiden to find it put to her of a sudden that she herself was the matter—for that was positively what, on Mrs. Lowder's part, it came to. Everything was great, of course, in great pictures, and it was doubtless precisely a part of the brilliant life—since the brilliant life, as one had faintly figured it, just *was* humanly led—that all impressions within its area partook of its brilliancy; still, letting that pass, it fairly stamped an hour as with the official seal for one to be able to take in so comfortably one's companion's broad blandness. " You must stay among us—you must stay ; anything else is impossible and ridiculous ; you don't know yet, no doubt—you can't ; but you will soon enough : you can stay in *any* position." It had been as the murmurous consecration to follow the murmurous welcome ; and even if it were but part of Aunt Maud's own spiritual ebriety—for the dear woman, one could see, was spiritually " keeping " the day—it served to Milly, then and afterwards, as a high-water mark of the imagination.

It was to be the end of the short parenthesis which had begun but the other day at Lancaster Gate with Lord Mark's informing her that she was a " success " —the key thus again struck ; and though no distinct, no numbered revelations had crowded in, there had, as we have seen, been plenty of incident for the space and the time. There had been thrice as much, and all

gratuitous and genial—if, in portions, not exactly
hitherto *the* revelation—as three unprepared weeks
could have been expected to produce. Mrs. Lowder
had improvised a " rush " for them, but out of elements, as Milly was now a little more freely aware,
somewhat roughly combined. Therefore if at this
very instant she had her reasons for thinking of the
parenthesis as about to close—reasons completely
personal—she had on behalf of her companion a
divination almost as deep. The parenthesis would
close with this admirable picture, but the admirable
picture still would show Aunt Maud as not absolutely
sure either if she herself were destined to remain in it.
What she was doing, Milly might even not have
escaped seeming to see, was to talk herself into a sub-
limer serenity while she ostensibly talked Milly. It
was fine, the girl fully felt, the way she did talk *her*,
little as, at bottom, our young woman needed it or
found other persuasions at fault. It was in particular
during the minutes of her grateful absorption of iced
coffee—qualified by a sharp doubt of her wisdom—
that she most had in view Lord Mark's relation to her
being there, or at least to the question of her being
amused at it. It wouldn't have taken much by the
end of five minutes quite to make her feel that this
relation was charming. It might, once more, simply
have been that everything, anything, was charming
when one was so justly and completely charmed ; but,
frankly, she hadn't supposed anything so serenely
sociable could settle itself between them as the
friendly understanding that was at present somehow
in the air. They were, many of them together, near
the marquee that had been erected on a stretch of
sward as a temple of refreshment and that happened
to have the property—which was all to the good—of
making Milly think of a " durbar " ; her iced coffee
had been a consequence of this connexion, through

which, further, the bright company scattered about
fell thoroughly into place. Certain of its members
might have represented the contingent of " native
princes "—familiar, but scarce the less grandly gre-
garious term !—and Lord Mark would have done
for one of these even though for choice he but presented himself as a supervisory friend of the family.
The Lancaster Gate family, he clearly intended, in
which he included its American recruits, and included
above all Kate Croy—a young person blessedly easy
to take care of. She knew people, and people knew
her, and she was the handsomest thing there—this
last a declaration made by Milly, in a sort of soft
midsummer madness, a straight skylark - flight of
charity, to Aunt Maud.

Kate had for her new friend's eyes the extraordinary and attaching property of appearing at a given
moment to show as a beautiful stranger, to cut her
connexions and lose her identity, letting the imagination for the time make what it would of them—make
her merely a person striking from afar, more and
more pleasing as one watched, but who was above all
a subject for curiosity. Nothing could have given her,
as a party to a relation, a greater freshness than this
sense, which sprang up at its own hours, of one's
being as curious about her as if one hadn't known her.
It had sprung up, we have gathered, as soon as Milly
had seen her after hearing from Mrs. Stringham of
her knowledge of Merton Densher ; she had *looked*
then other and, as Milly knew the real critical mind
would call it, more objective ; and our young woman
had foreseen it of her on the spot that she would often
look so again. It was exactly what she was doing this
afternoon ; and Milly, who had amusements of
thought that were like the secrecies of a little girl
playing with dolls when conventionally " too big,"
could almost settle to the game of what one would

THE WINGS OF THE DOVE

suppose her, how one would place her, if one didn't
know her. She became thus, intermittently, a figure
conditioned only by the great facts of aspect, a figure
to be waited for, named and fitted. This was doubtless but a way of feeling that it was of her essence to
be peculiarly what the occasion, whatever it might be,
demanded when its demand was highest. There were
probably ways enough, on these lines, for such a consciousness; another of them would be for instance
to say that she was made for great social uses. Milly
wasn't wholly sure she herself knew what great
social uses might be—unless, as a good example,
to exert just that sort of glamour in just that sort of
frame were one of them : she would have fallen back
on knowing sufficiently that they existed at all events
for her friend. It imputed a primness, all round, to be
reduced but to saying, by way of a translation of one's
amusement, that she was always so *right*—since
that, too often, was what the *insupportables* themselves were ; yet it was, in overflow to Aunt Maud,
what she had to content herself withal—save for the
lame enhancement of saying she was lovely. It
served, despite everything, the purpose, strengthened
the bond that for the time held the two ladies together,
distilled in short its drop of rose-colour for Mrs.
Lowder's own view. That was really the view Milly
had, for most of the rest of the occasion, to give herself to immediately taking in ; but it didn't prevent
the continued play of those swift cross-lights, odd
beguilements of the mind, at which we have already
glanced.

Mrs. Lowder herself found it enough simply to
reply, in respect to Kate, that she was indeed a luxury
to take about the world : she expressed no more surprise than that at her " rightness " to-day. Didn't it
by this time sufficiently shine out that it was precisely
as the very luxury she was proving that she had, from

far back, been appraised and waited for ? Crude elation, however, might be kept at bay, and the circumstance none the less made clear that they were all swimming together in the blue. It came back to Lord Mark again, as he seemed slowly to pass and repass and conveniently to linger before them ; he was personally the note of the blue—like a suspended skein of silk within reach of the broiderer's hand. Aunt Maud's free-moving shuttle took a length of him at rhythmic intervals ; and one of the accessory truths that flickered across to Milly was that he ever so consentingly knew he was being worked in. This was almost like an understanding with her at Mrs. Lowder's expense, which she would have none of ; she wouldn't for the world have had him make any such point as that he wouldn't have launched them at Matcham—or whatever it was he *had* done—only for Aunt Maud's *beaux yeux*. What he had done, it would have been guessable, was something he had for some time been desired in vain to do ; and what they were all now profiting by was a change comparatively sudden, the cessation of hope delayed. What had caused the cessation easily showed itself as none of Milly's business ; and she was luckily, for that matter, in no real danger of hearing from him directly that her individual weight had been felt in the scale. Why then indeed was it an effect of his diffused but subdued participation that he might absolutely have been saying to her " Yes, let the dear woman take her own tone " ? " Since she's here she may stay," he might have been adding—" for whatever she can make of it. But you and I are different." Milly knew *she* was different in truth—his own difference was his own affair ; but also she knew that after all, even at their distinctest, Lord Mark's " tips " in this line would be tacit. He practically placed her—it came round again to that—under no obligation whatever. It was a matter of equal ease, moreover, her letting Mrs. Lowder take a tone. She might have taken twenty—they would have spoiled nothing.

" You must stay on with us ; you *can*, you know, in any position you like ; any, any, *any*, my dear child "—and her emphasis went deep. " You must make your home with us ; and it's really open to you to make the most beautiful one in the world. You mustn't be under a mistake—under any of any sort ; and you must let us all think for you a little, take care of you and watch over you. Above all you must help me with Kate, and you must stay a little *for* her ; nothing for a long time has happened to me so good as that you and she should have become friends. It's beautiful ; it's great ; it's everything. What makes it perfect is that it should have come about through our dear delightful Susie, restored to me, after so many years, by such a miracle. No—that's more charming to me than even your hitting it off with Kate. God has been good to one—positively ; for I couldn't, at my age, have made a new friend—undertaken, I mean, out of whole cloth, the real thing. It's like changing one's bankers—after fifty : one doesn't do that. That's why Susie has been kept for me, as you seem to keep people in your wonderful country, in lavender and pink paper—coming back at last as straight as out of a fairy-tale and with you as an attendant fairy." Milly hereupon replied appreciatively that such a description of herself made her feel as if pink paper were her dress and lavender its trimming ; but Aunt Maud wasn't to be deterred by a weak joke from keeping it up. The young person under her protection could feel besides that she kept it up in perfect sincerity. She was somehow at this hour a very happy woman, and a part of her happiness might precisely have been that her affections and her views were moving as never before in concert.

Unquestionably she loved Susie ; but she also loved Kate and loved Lord Mark, loved their funny old host and hostess, loved every one within range, down to the very servant who came to receive Milly's empty ice-plate—down, for that matter, to Milly herself, who was, while she talked, really conscious of the enveloping flap of a protective mantle, a shelter with the weight of an Eastern carpet. An Eastern carpet, for wishing-purposes of one's own, was a thing to be on rather than under ; still, however, if the girl should fail of breath it wouldn't be, she could feel, by Mrs. Lowder's fault. One of the last things she was afterwards to recall of this was Aunt Maud's going on to say that she and Kate must stand together because together they could do anything. It was for Kate of course she was essentially planning ; but the plan, enlarged and uplifted now, somehow required Milly's prosperity too for its full operation, just as Milly's prosperity at the same time involved Kate's. It was nebulous yet, it was slightly confused, but it was comprehensive and genial, and it made our young woman understand things Kate had said of her aunt's possibilities, as well as characterisations that had ̓ ''
from Susan Shepherd. One of the most freque
the lips of the latter had been that dear Maud ˑ
grand natural force.

II

A PRIME reason, we must add, why sundry impressions were not to be fully present to the girl till later on was that they yielded at this stage, with an effect of sharp supersession, to a detached quarter of an hour—her only one—with Lord Mark. " Have you seen the picture in the house, the beautiful one that's so like you ? "—he was asking that as he stood before her ; having come up at last with his smooth intimation that any wire he had pulled and yet wanted not to remind her of wasn't quite a reason for his having no joy at all.

" I've been through rooms and I've seen pictures. But if I'm ' like ' anything so beautiful as most of them seemed to me—— ! " It needed in short for Milly some evidence which he only wanted to supply. She was the image of the wonderful Bronzino, which she must have a look at on every ground. He had thus called her off and led her away ; the more easily that the house within was above all what had already drawn round her its mystic circle. Their progress meanwhile was not of the straightest ; it was an advance, without haste, through innumerable natural pauses and soft concussions, determined for the most part by the appearance before them of ladies and gentlemen, singly, in couples, in clusters, who brought them to a stand with an inveterate " I say, Mark." What they said she never quite made out ; it was their all so domestically knowing him, and his knowing them, that mainly struck her, while her impression, for the rest, was but of fellow strollers more vaguely afloat than themselves, supernumeraries mostly a little battered, whether as jaunty males or as ostensibly elegant women. They might have been moving a good deal by a momentum that had begun far back, but they were still brave and personable, still warranted for continuance as long again, and they gave her, in especial collectively, a sense of pleasant voices, pleasanter than those of actors, of friendly empty words and kind lingering eyes that took somehow pardonable liberties. The lingering eyes looked her over, the lingering eyes were what went, in almost confessed simplicity, with the pointless " I say, Mark " ; and what was really most flagrant of all was that, as a pleasant matter of course, if she didn't mind, he seemed to suggest their letting people, poor dear things, have the benefit of her.

The odd part was that he made her herself believe, for amusement, in the benefit, measured by him in mere manner—for wonderful, of a truth, was, as a means of expression, his slightness of emphasis— that her present good nature conferred. It was, as she could easily see, a mild common carnival of good nature—a mass of London people together, of sorts and sorts, but who mainly knew each other and who, in their way, did, no doubt, confess to curiosity. It had gone round that she was there ; questions about her would be passing ; the easiest thing was to run the gauntlet with *him*—just as the easiest thing was in fact to trust him generally. Couldn't she know for herself, passively, how little harm they meant her ?— to that extent that it made no difference whether or not he introduced them. The strangest thing of all for Milly was perhaps the uplifted assurance and indifference with which she could simply give back the particular bland stare that appeared in such cases to mark civilisation at its highest. It was so little her fault, this oddity of what had " gone round " about her, that to accept it without question might be as good a way as another of feeling life. It was inevitable to supply the probable description—that of the awfully rich young American who was so queer to behold, but nice, by all accounts, to know ; and she had really but one instant of speculation as to fables or fantasies perchance originally launched. She asked herself once only if Susie could, inconceivably, have been blatant about her ; for the question, on the spot, was really blown away for ever. She knew in fact on the spot and with sharpness just why she had " elected " Susan Shepherd : she had had from the first hour the conviction of her being precisely the person in the world least possibly a trumpeter. So it wasn't their fault, it wasn't their fault, and anything might happen that would, and everything now again melted together, and kind eyes were always kind eyes —if it were never to be worse than that ! She got with her companion into the house ; they brushed, beneficently, past all their accidents. The Bronzino was, it appeared, deep within, and the long afternoon light lingered for them on patches of old colour and waylaid them, as they went, in nooks and opening vistas.

It was all the while for Milly as if Lord Mark had really had something other than this spoken pretext in view ; as if there were something he wanted to say to her and were only—consciously yet not awkwardly, just delicately—hanging fire. At the same time it was as if the thing had practically been said by the moment they came in sight of the picture ; since what it appeared to amount to was " Do let a fellow who isn't a fool take care of you a little." The thing somehow, with the aid of the Bronzino, was done ; it hadn't seemed to matter to her before if he were a fool or no ; but now, just where they were, she liked his not being ; and it was all moreover none the worse for coming back to something of the same sound as Mrs. Lowder's so recent reminder. She too wished to take care of her—and wasn't it, *à peu près*, what all the people with the kind eyes were wishing ? Once more things melted together—the beauty and the history and the facility and the splendid midsummer glow : it was a sort of magnificent maximum, the pink dawn of an apotheosis coming so curiously soon. What in fact befell was that, as she afterwards made out, it was Lord Mark who said nothing in particular —it was she herself who said all. She couldn't help that—it came ; and the reason it came was that she found herself, for the first moment, looking at the mysterious portrait through tears. Perhaps it was her tears that made it just then so strange and fair—as wonderful as he had said : the face of a young woman, all splendidly drawn, down to the hands, and splendidly dressed ; a face almost livid in hue, yet handsome in sadness and crowned with a mass of hair, rolled back and high, that must, before fading with time, have had a family resemblance to her own. The lady in question, at all events, with her slightly Michael-angelesque squareness, her eyes of other days, her full lips, her long neck, her recorded jewels, her brocaded and wasted reds, was a very great personage—only unaccompanied by a joy. And she was dead, dead, dead. Milly recognised her exactly in words that had nothing to do with her. " I shall never be better than this."

He smiled for her at the portrait. " Than she ? You'd scarce need to be better, for surely that's well enough. But you *are*, one feels, as it happens, better ; because, splendid as she is, one doubts if she was good."

195

He hadn't understood. She was before the picture, but she had turned to him, and she didn't care if for the minute he noticed her tears. It was probably as good a moment as she should ever have with him. It was perhaps as good a moment as she should have with any one, or have in any connexion whatever. " I mean that everything this afternoon has been too beautiful, and that perhaps everything together will never be so right again. I'm very glad therefore you've been a part of it."

Though he still didn't understand her he was as nice as if he had ; he didn't ask for insistence, and that was just a part of his looking after her. He simply protected her now from herself, and there was a world of practice in it. " Oh we must talk about these things ! "

Ah they had already done that, she knew, as much as she ever would ; and she was shaking her head at her pale sister the next moment with a world, on her side, of slowness. " I wish I could see the resemblance. Of course her complexion's green," she laughed ; " but mine's several shades greener."

" It's down to the very hands," said Lord Mark.

" Her hands are large," Milly went on. " but mine are larger. Mine are huge."

" Oh you go her, all round, ' one better '—which is just what I said. But you're a pair. You must surely catch it," he added as if it were important to his character as a serious man not to appear to have invented his plea.

" I don't know—one never knows one's self. It's a funny fancy, and I don't imagine it would have occurred——"

" I see it *has* occurred "—he had already taken her up. She had her back, as she faced the picture, to one of the doors of the room, which was open, and on her turning as he spoke she saw that they were in the presence of three other persons, also, as appeared, interested inquirers. Kate Croy was one of these ; Lord Mark had just become aware of her, and she, all arrested, had immediately seen, and made the best of it, that she was far from being first in the field. She had brought a lady and a gentleman to whom she wished to show what Lord Mark was showing Milly, and he took her straightway as a re-enforcement. Kate herself had spoken, however, before he had had time to tell her so.

" *You* had noticed too ? "—she smiled at him without looking at Milly. " Then I'm not original— which one always hopes one has been. But the likeness is so great." And now she looked at Milly— for whom again it was, all round indeed, kind, kind eyes. " Yes, there you are, my dear, if you want to know. And you're superb." She took now but a glance at the picture, though it was enough to make her question to her friends not too straight. " Isn't she superb ? "

" I brought Miss Theale," Lord Mark explained to the latter, " quite off my own bat."

" I wanted Lady Aldershaw," Kate continued to Milly, " to see for herself."

" Les grands esprits se rencontrent ! " laughed her attendant gentleman, a high but slightly stooping, shambling and wavering person who represented urbanity by the liberal aid of certain prominent front teeth and whom Milly vaguely took for some sort of great man.

Lady Aldershaw meanwhile looked at Milly quite as if Milly had been the Bronzino and the Bronzino only Milly. " Superb, superb. Of course I had noticed you. It *is* wonderful," she went on with her back to the picture, but with some other eagerness which Milly felt gathering, felt directing her motions now. It was enough—they were introduced, and

she was saying " I wonder if you could give us the
pleasure of coming——" She wasn't fresh, for she
wasn't young, even though she denied at every pore
that she was old ; but she was vivid and much
bejewelled for the midsummer daylight ; and she was
all in the palest pinks and blues. She didn't think, at
this pass, that she could " come " anywhere—Milly
didn't ; and she already knew that somehow Lord
Mark was saving her from the question. He had interposed, taking the words out of the lady's mouth
and not caring at all if the lady minded. That was
clearly the right way to treat her—at least for him ;
as she had only dropped, smiling, and then turned
away with him. She had been dealt with—it would
have done an enemy good. The gentleman still stood,
a little helpless, addressing himself to the intention of
urbanity as if it were a large loud whistle ; he had been
sighing sympathy, in his way, while the lady made
her overture ; and Milly had in this light soon
arrived at their identity. They were Lord and Lady
Aldershaw, and the wife was the clever one. A
minute or two later the situation had changed, and
she knew it afterwards to have been by the subtle
operation of Kate. She was herself saying that she
was afraid she must go now if Susie could be found ;
but she was sitting down on the nearest seat to say it.
The prospect, through opened doors, stretched before
her into other rooms, down the vista of which Lord
Mark was strolling with Lady Aldershaw, who, close
to him and much intent, seemed to show from behind
as peculiarly expert. Lord Aldershaw, for his part,
had been left in the middle of the room, while Kate,
with her back to him, was standing before her with
much sweetness of manner. The sweetness was all
for *her* ; she had the sense of the poor gentleman's
having somehow been handled as Lord Mark had
handled his wife. He dangled there, he shambled a
198

little ; then he bethought himself of the Bronzino, before which, with his eye-glass, he hovered. It drew from him an odd vague sound, not wholly distinct from a grunt, and a " Humph—most remarkable ! " which lighted Kate's face with amusement. The next moment he had creaked away over polished floors after the others and Milly was feeling as if *she* had been rude. But Lord Aldershaw was in every way a detail and Kate was saying to her that she hoped she wasn't ill.

Thus it was that, aloft there in the great gilded historic chamber and the presence of the pale personage on the wall, whose eyes all the while seemed engaged with her own, she found herself suddenly sunk in something quite intimate and humble and to which these grandeurs were strange enough witnesses. It had come up, in the form in which she had had to accept it, all suddenly, and nothing about it, at the same time, was more marked than that she had in a manner plunged into it to escape from something else. Something else, from her first vision of her friend's appearance three minutes before, had been present to her even through the call made by the others on her attention ; something that was perversely *there*, she was more and more uncomfortably finding, at least for the first moments and by some spring of its own, with every renewal of their meeting. " Is it the way she looks to *him* ? " she asked herself —the perversity being how she kept in remembrance that Kate was known to him. It wasn't a fault in Kate—nor in him assuredly ; and she had a horror, being generous and tender, of treating either of them as if it had been. To Densher himself she couldn't make it up—he was too far away ; but her secondary impulse was to make it up to Kate. She did so now with a strange soft energy—the impulse immediately acting. " Will you render me to-morrow a great service ? "

" Any service, dear child, in the world."

" But it's a secret one—nobody must know. I must be wicked and false about it."

" Then I'm your woman," Kate smiled, " for that's the kind of thing I love. *Do* let us do something bad. You're impossibly without sin, you know."

Milly's eyes, on this, remained a little with their companion's. " Ah I shan't perhaps come up to your idea. It's only to deceive Susan Shepherd."

" Oh ! " said Kate as if this were indeed mild.

" But thoroughly—as thoroughly as I can."

" And for cheating," Kate asked, " my powers will contribute ? Well, I'll do my best for you." In accordance with which it was presently settled between them that Milly should have the aid and comfort of her presence for a visit to Sir Luke Strett. Kate had needed a minute for enlightenment, and it was quite grand for her comrade that this name should have said nothing to her. To Milly herself it had for some days been secretly saying much. The personage in question was, as she explained, the greatest of medical lights—if she had got hold, as she believed (and she had used to this end the wisdom of the serpent) of the right, the special man. She had written to him three days before, and he had named her an hour, eleven-twenty ; only it had come to her on the eve that she couldn't go alone. Her maid on the other hand wasn't good enough, and Susie was too good. Kate had listened above all with high indulgence. " And I'm betwixt and between, happy thought ! Too good for what ? "

Milly thought. " Why to be worried if it's nothing. And to be still more worried—I mean before she need be—if it isn't."

Kate fixed her with deep eyes. " What in the world is the matter with you ? " It had inevitably a sound of impatience, as if it had been a challenge really to produce something ; so that Milly felt her for the moment only as a much older person, standing above her a little, doubting the imagined ailments; suspecting the easy complaints, of ignorant youth. It somewhat checked her, further, that the matter with her was what exactly as yet she wanted knowledge about ; and she immediately declared, for conciliation, that if she were merely fanciful Kate would see her put to shame. Kate vividly uttered, in return, the hope that, since she could come out and be so charming, could so universally dazzle and interest, she wasn't all the while in distress or in anxiety—didn't believe herself to be in any degree seriously menaced. " Well, I want to make out—to make out ! " was all that this consistently produced. To which Kate made clear answer : " Ah then let us by all means ! "

" I thought," Milly said, " you'd like to help me. But I must ask you, please, for the promise of absolute silence."

" And how, if you *are* ill, can your friends remain in ignorance ? "

" Well, if I am it must of course finally come out. But I can go for a long time." Milly spoke with her eyes again on her painted sister's—almost as if under their suggestion. She still sat there before Kate, yet not without a light in her face. " That will be one of my advantages. I think I could die without its being noticed."

" You're an extraordinary young woman," her friend, visibly held by her, declared at last. " What a remarkable time to talk of such things ! "

" Well, we won't talk, precisely "—Milly got herself together again. " I only wanted to make sure of you."

" Here in the midst of—— ! " But Kate could only sigh for wonder—almost visibly too for pity.

It made a moment during which her companion waited on her word ; partly as if from a yearning, shy but deep, to have her case put to her just as Kate was struck by it ; partly as if the hint of pity were already giving a sense to her whimsical " shot," with Lord Mark, at Mrs. Lowder's first dinner. Exactly this—the handsome girl's compassionate manner, her friendly descent from her own strength—was what she had then foretold. She took Kate up as if positively for the deeper taste of it. " Here in the midst of what ? "

" Of everything. There's nothing you can't have. There's nothing you can't do."

" So Mrs. Lowder tells me."

It just kept Kate's eyes fixed as possibly for more of that ; then, however, without waiting, she went on. " We all adore you."

" You're wonderful—you dear things ! " Milly laughed.

" No, it's *you*." And Kate seemed struck with the real interest of it. " In three weeks ! "

Milly kept it up. " Never were people on such terms ! All the more reason," she added, " that I shouldn't needlessly torment you."

" But me ? what becomes of *me* ? " said Kate.

" Well, you "—Milly thought—" if there's anything to bear you'll bear it."

" But I *won't* bear it ! " said Kate Croy.

" Oh yes you will : all the same ! You'll pity me awfully, but you'll help me very much. And I absolutely trust you. So there we are." There they were then, since Kate had so to take it ; but there, Milly felt, she herself in particular was ; for it was just the point at which she had wished to arrive. She had wanted to prove to herself that she didn't horribly blame her friend for any reserve ; and what better proof could there be than this quite special confidence ? If she desired to show Kate that she really believed Kate liked her, how could she show it more than by asking her help ?

III

WHAT it really came to, on the morrow, this first time
—the time Kate went with her—was that the great
man had, a little, to excuse himself ; had, by a rare
accident—for he kept his consulting-hours in general
rigorously free—but ten minutes to give her ; ten
mere minutes which he yet placed at her service in a
manner that she admired still more than she could
meet it : so crystal-clean the great empty cup of
attention that he set between them on the table. He
was presently to jump into his carriage, but he
promptly made the point that he must see her again,
see her within a day or two ; and he named for her
at once another hour—easing her off beautifully too
even then in respect to her possibly failing of justice
to her errand. The minutes affected her in fact as
ebbing more swiftly than her little army of items
could muster, and they would probably have gone
without her doing much more than secure another
hearing, hadn't it been for her sense, at the last, that
she had gained above all an impression. The impression—all the sharp growth of the final few moments—
was neither more nor less than that she might make,
of a sudden, in quite another world, another straight
friend, and a friend who would moreover be, wonderfully, the most appointed, the most thoroughly
adjusted of the whole collection, inasmuch as he
would somehow wear the character scientifically,

203

ponderably, provably—not just loosely and sociably.
Literally, furthermore, it wouldn't really depend on
herself, Sir Luke Strett's friendship, in the least :
perhaps what made her most stammer and pant was
its thus queerly coming over her that she might find
she had interested him even beyond her intention,
find she was in fact launched in some current that
would lose itself in the sea of science. At the same
time that she struggled, however, she also surrendered ;
there was a moment at which she almost dropped
the form of stating, of explaining, and threw herself,
without violence, only with a supreme pointless
quaver that had turned the next instant to an intensity of interrogative stillness, upon his general good-
will. His large settled face, though firm, was not, as
she had thought at first, hard ; he looked, in the oddest
manner, to her fancy, half like a general and half like
a bishop, and she was soon sure that, within some such
handsome range, what it would show her would be
what was good, what was best for her. She had
established, in other words, in this time-saving way,
a relation with it ; and the relation was the special
trophy that, for the hour, she bore off. It was like an
absolute possession, a new resource altogether, something done up in the softest silk and tucked away
under the arm of memory. She hadn't had it when
she went in, and she had it when she came out ; she
had it there under her cloak, but dissimulated,
invisibly carried, when smiling, smiling, she again
faced Kate Croy. That young lady had of course
awaited her in another room, where, as the great man
was to absent himself, no one else was in attendance ;
and she rose for her with such a face of sympathy as
might have graced the vestibule of a dentist. " Is it
out ? " she seemed to ask as if it had been a question
of a tooth ; and Milly indeed kept her in no suspense
at all.

" He's a dear.   I'm to come again."

" But what does he say ? "

Milly was almost gay.   " That I'm not to worry
about anything in the world, and that if I'll be a good
girl and do exactly what he tells me he'll take care of
me for ever and ever."

Kate wondered as if things scarce fitted.   " But
does he allow then that you're ill ? "

" I don't know what he allows, and I don't care.
I *shall* know, and whatever it is it will be enough.
He knows all about me, and I like it.   I don't hate it
a bit."

Still, however, Kate stared.   " But could he, in so
few minutes, ask you enough——— ? "

" He asked me scarcely anything—he doesn't need
to do anything so stupid," Milly said.   " He can
tell.   He knows," she repeated ;   " and when I go
back—for he'll have thought me over a little—it will
be all right."

Kate after a moment made the best of this.   " Then
when are we to come ? "

It just pulled her friend up, for even while they
talked—at least it was one of the reasons—she stood
there suddenly, irrelevantly, in the light of her *other*
identity, the identity she would have for Mr. Densher.
This was always, from one instant to another, an
incalculable light, which, though it might go off faster
than it came on, necessarily disturbed.   It sprang,
with a perversity all its own, from the fact that, with
the lapse of hours and days, the chances themselves
that made for his being named continued so oddly to
fail.   There were twenty, there were fifty, but none of
them turned up.   This in particular was of course not
a juncture at which the least of them would naturally
be present ;   but it would make, none the less, Milly
saw, another day practically all stamped with avoidance.   She saw in a quick glimmer, and with it all

Kate's unconsciousness ; and then she shook off the
obsession. But it had lasted long enough to qualify
her response. No, she had shown Kate how she
trusted her ; and that, for loyalty, would somehow do.
" Oh, dear thing, now that the ice is broken I shan't
trouble *you* again."

" You'll come alone ? "

" Without a scruple. Only I shall ask you, please,
for your absolute discretion still."

Outside, at a distance from the door, on the wide
pavement of the great contiguous square, they had to
wait again while their carriage, which Milly had kept,
completed a further turn of exercise, engaged in by
the coachman for reasons of his own. The footman
was there and had indicated that he was making the
circuit ; so Kate went on while they stood. " But
don't you ask a good deal, darling, in proportion to
what you give ? "

This pulled Milly up still shorter—so short in fact
that she yielded as soon as she had taken it in. But
she continued to smile. " I see. Then you *can* tell."

" I don't want to ' tell,' " said Kate. " I'll be as
silent as the tomb if I can only have the truth from
you. All I want is that you shouldn't keep from me
how you find out that you really are."

" Well then I won't ever. But you see for yourself," Milly went on, " how I really am. I'm satisfied.
I'm happy."

Kate looked at her long. " I believe you like it.
The way things turn out for you——! "

Milly met her look now without a thought of anything but the spoken. She had ceased to be Mr.
Densher's image ; she stood for nothing but herself,
and she was none the less fine. Still, still, what had
passed was a fair bargain and it would do. " Of
course I like it. I feel—I can't otherwise describe
it—as if I had been on my knees to the priest. I've

confessed and I've been absolved. It has been lifted off."

Kate's eyes never quitted her. " He must have liked *you*."

" Oh—doctors ! " Milly said. " But I hope," she added, " he didn't like me too much." Then as if to escape a little from her friend's deeper sounding, or as impatient for the carriage, not yet in sight, her eyes, turning away, took in the great stale square. As its staleness, however, was but that of London fairly fatigued, the late hot London with its dance all danced and its story all told, the air seemed a thing of blurred pictures and mixed echoes, and an impression met the sense—an impression that broke the next moment through the girl's tightened lips. " Oh it's a beautiful big world, and every one, yes, every one—— ! " It presently brought her back to Kate, and she hoped she didn't actually look as much as if she were crying as she must have looked to Lord Mark among the portraits at Matcham.

Kate at all events understood. " Every one wants to be so nice ? "

" So nice," said the grateful Milly.

" Oh," Kate laughed, " we'll pull you through ! And won't you now bring Mrs. Stringham ? "

But Milly after an instant was again clear about that. " Not till I've seen him once more."

She was to have found this preference, two days later, abundantly justified ; and yet when, in prompt accordance with what had passed between them, she reappeared before her distinguished friend—that character having for him in the interval built itself up still higher—the first thing he asked her was whether she had been accompanied. She told him, on this, straightway, everything ; completely free at present from her first embarrassment, disposed even —as she felt she might become—to undue volubility,

and conscious moreover of no alarm from his thus
perhaps wishing she had not come alone. It was
exactly as if, in the forty-eight hours that had passed,
her acquaintance with him had somehow increased
and his own knowledge in particular received mysterious additions. They had been together, before,
scarce ten minutes ; but the relation, the one the ten
minutes had so beautifully created, was there to take
straight up : and this not, on his own part, from mere
professional heartiness, mere bedside manner, which
she would have disliked—much rather from a quiet
pleasant air in him of having positively asked about
her, asked here and asked there and found out. Of
course he couldn't in the least have asked, or have
wanted to ; there was no source of information to his
hånd, and he had really needed none : he had found
out simply by his genius—and found out, she meant,
literally everything. Now she knew not only that she
didn't dislike this—the state of being found out about ;
but that on the contrary it was truly what she had
come for, and that for the time at least it would give
her something firm to stand on. She struck herself
as aware, aware as she had never been, of really not
having had from the beginning anything firm. It
would be strange for the firmness to come, after all,
from her learning in these agreeable conditions that
she was in some way doomed ; but above all it would
prove how little she had hitherto had to hold her up.
If she was now to be held up by the mere process—
since that was perhaps on the cards—of being let
down, this would only testify in turn to her queer
little history. *That* sense of loosely rattling had been
no process at all ; and it was ridiculously true that her
thus sitting there to see her life put into the scales
represented her first approach to the taste of orderly
living. Such was Milly's romantic version—that her
life, especially by the fact of this second interview,

was put into the scales ; and just the best part of the
relation established might have been, for that matter,
that the great grave charming man knew, had known
at once, that it was romantic, and in that measure
allowed for it. Her only doubt, her only fear, was
whether he perhaps wouldn't even take advantage of
her being a little romantic to treat her as romantic
altogether. This doubtless was her danger with him ;
but she should see, and dangers in general meanwhile
dropped and dropped.

The very place, at the end of a few minutes, the
commodious " handsome " room, far back in the fine
old house, soundless from position, somewhat sallow
with years of celebrity, somewhat sombre even at
midsummer—the very place put on for her a look of
custom and use, squared itself solidly round her as
with promises and certainties. She had come forth
to see the world, and this then was to be the world's
light, the rich dusk of a London " back," these the
world's walls, those the world's curtains and carpet.
She should be intimate with the great bronze clock
and mantel-ornaments, conspicuously presented in
gratitude and long ago ; she should be as one of
the circle of eminent contemporaries, photographed,
engraved, signatured, and in particular framed and
glazed, who made up the rest of the decoration, and
made up as well so much of the human comfort ; and
while she thought of all the clean truths, unfringed,
unfingered, that the listening stillness, strained into
pauses and waits, would again and again, for years,
have kept distinct, she also wondered what *she* would
eventually decide upon to present in gratitude. She
would give something better at least than the brawny
Victorian bronzes. This was precisely an instance of
what she felt he knew of her before he had done with
her : that she was secretly romancing at that rate, in
the midst of so much else that was more urgent, all

over the place. So much for her secrets with him,
none of which really required to be phrased. It would
have been thoroughly a secret for her from any one
else that without a dear lady she had picked up just
before coming over she wouldn't have a decently
near connexion of any sort, for such an appeal as she
was making, to put forward : no one in the least, as it
were, to produce for respectability. But *his* seeing it
she didn't mind a scrap, and not a scrap either his
knowing how she had left the dear lady in the dark.
She had come alone, putting her friend off with a
fraud : giving a pretext of shops, of a whim, of she
didn't know what—the amusement of being for once
in the streets by herself. The streets by herself
were new to her—she had always had in them a
companion or a maid ; and he was never to believe
moreover that she couldn't take full in the face anything he might have to say. He was softly amused at
her account of her courage ; though he yet showed it
somehow without soothing her too grossly. Still, he
did want to know whom she had. Hadn't there been
a lady with her on Wednesday ?

"Yes—a different one. Not the one who's travel-
ling with me. I've told *her*."

Distinctly he was amused, and it added to his air—
the greatest charm of all—of giving her lots of time.
" You've told her what ? "

" Well," said Milly, " that I visit you in secret."

" And how many persons will she tell ? "

" Oh she's devoted. Not one."

" Well, if she's devoted doesn't that make another
friend for you ? "

It didn't take much computation, but she nevertheless had to think a moment, conscious as she was
that he distinctly *would* want to fill out his notion of
her—even a little, as it were, to warm the air for her.
That however—and better early than late—he must

accept as of no use ; and she herself felt for an
instant quite a competent certainty on the subject of
any such warming. The air, for Milly Theale, was,
from the very nature of the case, destined never to
rid itself of a considerable chill. This she could tell
him with authority, if she could tell him nothing else ;
and she seemed to see now, in short, that it would
importantly simplify. " Yes, it makes another ; but
they all together wouldn't make—well, I don't know
what to call it but the difference. I mean when one
is—really alone. I've never seen anything like the
kindness." She pulled up a minute while he waited
—waited again as if with his reasons for letting her,
for almost making her, talk. What she herself
wanted was not, for the third time, to cry, as it were,
in public. She *had* never seen anything like the kindness, and she wished to do it justice ; but she knew
what she was about, and justice was not wronged by
her being able presently to stick to her point. " Only
one's situation is what it is. It's *me* it concerns.
The rest is delightful and useless. Nobody can really
help. That's why I'm by myself to-day. I *want* to
be—in spite of Miss Croy, who came with me last. If
you can help, so much the better—and also of course
if one can a little oneself. Except for that—you and
me doing our best—I like you to see me just as I am.
Yes, I like it—and I don't exaggerate. Shouldn't
one, at the start, show the worst—so that anything
after that may be better ? It wouldn't make any
real difference—it *won't* make any, anything that may
happen won't—to any one. Therefore I feel myself,
this way, with you, just as I am ; and—if you do in
the least care to know—it quite positively bears me
up."

She put it as to his caring to know, because his
manner seemed to give her all her chance, and the
impression was there for her to take. It was strange

and deep for her, this impression, and she did accordingly take it straight home. It showed him—showed him in spite of himself—as allowing, somewhere far within, things comparatively remote, things in fact quite, as she would have said, outside, delicately to weigh with him; showed him as interested on her behalf in other questions beside the question of what was the matter with her. She accepted such an interest as regular in the highest type of scientific mind—his own *being* the highest, magnificently— because otherwise obviously it wouldn't be there; but she could at the same time take it as a direct source of light upon herself, even though that might present her a little as pretending to equal him. Wanting to know more about a patient than how a patient was constructed or deranged couldn't be, even on the part of the greatest of doctors, anything but some form or other of the desire to let the patient down easily. When that was the case the reason, in turn, could only be, too manifestly, pity; and when pity held up its tell-tale face like a head on a pike, in a French revolution, bobbing before a window, what was the inference but that the patient was bad? He might say what he would now—she would always have seen the head at the window; and in fact from this moment she only wanted him to say what he would. He might say it too with the greater ease to himself as there wasn't one of her divinations that— *as* her own—he would in any way put himself out for. Finally, if he was making her talk she *was* talking, and what it could at any rate come to for him was that she wasn't afraid. If he wanted to do the dearest thing in the world for her he would show her he believed she wasn't; which undertaking of hers—. not to have misled him—was what she counted at the moment as her presumptuous little hint to him that she was as good as himself. It put forward the bold idea that he could really *be* misled ; and there actually passed between them for some seconds a sign, a sign of the eyes only, that they knew together where they were This made, in their brown old temple of truth, its momentary flicker ; then what followed it was that he had her, all the same, in his pocket ; and the whole thing wound up for that consummation with his kind dim smile. Such kindness was wonderful with such dimness ; but brightness—that even of sharp steel—was of course for the other side of the business, and it would all come in for her to one tune or another. " Do you mean," he asked, " that you've no relations at all ?—not a parent, not a sister, not even a cousin nor an aunt ? "

She shook her head as with the easy habit of an interviewed heroine or a freak of nature at a show. " Nobody whatever "—but the last thing she had come for was to be dreary about it. " I'm a survivor —a survivor of a general wreck. You see," she added, " how that's to be taken into account—that every one else *has* gone. When I was ten years old there were, with my father and my mother, six of us. I'm all that's left. But they died," she went on, to be fair all round, " of different things. Still, there it is. And, as I told you before, I'm American. Not that I mean that makes me worse. However, you'll probably know what it makes me."

" Yes "—he even showed amusement for it. " I know perfectly what it makes you. It makes you, to begin with; a capital case."

She sighed, though gratefully, as if again before the social scene. " Ah there you are ! "

" Oh no ; there ' we ' aren't at all ! There I am only—but as much as you like. I've no end of American friends : there *they* are, if you please, and it's a fact that you couldn't very well be in a better place than in their company. It puts you with

213

plenty of others — and that isn't pure solitude."
Then he pursued: " I'm sure you've an excellent
spirit ; but don't try to bear more things than you
need." Which after an instant he further explained.
" Hard things have come to you in youth, but you
mustn't think life will be for you all hard things.
You've the right to be happy. You must make up
your mind to it. You must accept any form in which
happiness may come."

" Oh I'll accept any whatever ! " she almost gaily
returned. " And it seems to me, for that matter, that
I'm accepting a new one every day. Now *this* ! " she
smiled.

" This is very well so far as it goes. You can
depend on me," the great man said, " for unlimited
interest. But I'm only, after all, one element in fifty.
We must gather in plenty of others. Don't mind who
knows. Knows, I mean, that you and I are friends."

" Ah you do want to see some one ! " she broke out.
" You want to get at some one who cares for me."
With which, however, as he simply met this spontaneity in a manner to show that he had often had it
from young persons of her race, and that he was
familiar even with the possibilities of *their* familiarity,
she felt her freedom rendered vain by his silence, and
she immediately tried to think of the most reasonable
thing she could say. This would be, precisely, on the
subject of that freedom, which she now quickly spoke
of as complete. " That's of course by itself a great
boon ; so please don't think I don't know it. I can
do exactly what I like—anything in all the wide world.
I haven't a creature to ask—there's not a finger to
stop me. I can shake about till I'm black and blue.
That perhaps isn't *all* joy ; but lots of people, I know,
would like to try it." He had appeared about to put
a question, but then had let her go on, which she
promptly did, for she understood him the next

THE WINGS OF THE DOVE

moment as having thus taken it from her that her
means were as great as might be. She had simply
given it to him so, and this was all that would ever
pass between them on the odious head. Yet she
couldn't help also knowing that an important effect,
for his judgement, or at least for his amusement—
which was his feeling, since marvellously, he did have
feeling—was produced by it. All her little pieces had
now then fallen together for him like the morsels of
coloured glass that used to make combinations, under
the hand, in the depths of one of the polygonal
peep-shows of childhood. " So that if it's a question of my doing anything under the sun that will
help—— ! "

" You'll *do* anything under the sun ? Good." He
took that beautifully, ever so pleasantly, for what it
was worth ; but time was needed—the minutes or
so were needed on the spot—to deal even provisionally with the substantive question. It was convenient, in its degree, that there was nothing she
wouldn't do ; but it seemed also highly and agreeably
vague that she should have to do anything. They
thus appeared to be taking her, together, for the
moment, and almost for sociability, as prepared to
proceed to gratuitous extremities ; the upshot of
which was in turn that after much interrogation,
auscultation, exploration, much noting of his own
sequences and neglecting of hers, had duly kept up the
vagueness, they might have struck themselves, or may
at least strike us, as coming back from an undeterred
but useless voyage to the North Pole. Milly was
ready, under orders, for the North Pole ; which fact
was doubtless what made a blinding anticlimax of her
friend's actual abstention from orders. " No," she
heard him again distinctly repeat it, " I don't want
you for the present to do anything at all ; anything,
that is, but obey a small prescription or two that will

be made clear to you, and let me within a few days come to see you at home."

It was at first heavenly. " Then you'll see Mrs. Stringham." But she didn't mind a bit now.

" Well, I shan't be afraid of Mrs. Stringham." And he said it once more as she asked once more : " Absolutely not ; I ' send ' you nowhere. England's all right—anywhere that's pleasant, convenient, decent, will be all right. You say you can do exactly as you like. Oblige me therefore by being so good as to do it. There's only one thing : you ought of course, now, as soon as I've seen you again, to get out of London."

Milly thought. " May I then go back to the Continent ? "

• " By all means back to the Continent. Do go back to the Continent."

" Then how will you keep seeing me ? But perhaps," she quickly added, " you won't want to keep seeing me."

He had it all ready ; he had really everything all ready. " I shall follow you up ; though if you mean that I don't want you to keep seeing *me*——"

" Well ? " she asked.

It was only just here that he struck her the least bit as stumbling. " Well, see all you can. That's what it comes to. Worry about nothing. You *have* at least no worries. It's a great rare chance."

She had got up, for she had had from him both that he would send her something and would advise her promptly of the date of his coming to her, by which she was virtually dismissed. Yet for herself one or two things kept her. " May I come back to England too ? "

" Rather ! Whenever you like. But always, when you do come, immediately let me know."

" Ah," said Milly, " it won't be a great going to and fro."

" Then if you'll stay with us so much the better."

It touched her, the way he controlled his impatience of her ; and the fact itself affected her as so precious that she yielded to the wish to get more from it. " So you don't think I'm out of my mind ? "

" Perhaps that *is*," he smiled, " all that's the matter."

She looked at him longer. " No, that's too good. Shall I at any rate suffer ? "

" Not a bit."

" And yet then live ? "

" My dear young lady," said her distinguished friend, " isn't to ' live ' exactly what I'm trying to persuade you to take the trouble to do ? "

IV

SHE had gone out with these last words so in her ears that when once she was well away—back this time in the great square alone—it was as if some instant application of them had opened out there before her. It was positively, that effect, an excitement that carried her on ; she went forward into space under the sense of an impulse received—an impulse simple and direct, easy above all to act upon. She was borne up for the hour, and now she knew why she had wanted to come by herself. No one in the world could have sufficiently entered into her state ; no tie would have been close enough to enable a companion to walk beside her without some disparity. She literally felt, in this first flush, that her only company must be the human race at large, present all round her, but inspiringly impersonal, and that her only field must be, then and there, the grey immensity of London. Grey immensity had somehow of a sudden become her element ; grey immensity was what her distinguished friend had, for the moment, furnished her world with and what the question of "living," as he put it to her, living by option, by volition, inevitably took on for its immediate face. She went straight before her, without weakness, altogether with strength ; and still as she went she was more glad to be alone, for nobody—not Kate Croy, not Susan Shepherd either—would have wished to rush with her as she rushed. She had asked him at the last whether, being on foot, she might go home so, or elsewhere, and he had replied as if almost amused again at her extravagance : " You're active, luckily, by nature—it's beautiful : therefore rejoice in it. *Be* active, without folly—for you're not foolish : be as active as you can and as you like." That had been in fact the final push, as well as the touch that most made a mixture of her consciousness—à strange mixture that tasted at one and the same time of what she had lost and what had been given her. It was wonderful to her, while she took her random course, that these quantities felt so equal : she had been treated—hadn't she ?—as if it were in her power to live ; and yet one wasn't treated so—was one ?—unless it had come up, quite as much, that one might die. The beauty of the bloom had gone from the small old sense of safety—that was distinct : she had left it behind her there for ever. But the beauty of the idea of a great adventure, a big dim experiment or struggle in which she might more responsibly than ever before take a hand, had been offered her instead. It was as if she had had to pluck off her breast, to throw away, some friendly ornament, a familiar flower, a little old jewel, that was part of her daily dress ; and to take up and shoulder as a substitute some queer defensive weapon, a musket, a spear, a battle-axe—conducive possibly in a higher degree to a striking appearance, but demanding all the effort of the military posture.

She felt this instrument, for that matter, already on her back, so that she proceeded now in very truth after the fashion of a soldier on a march—proceeded as if, for her initiation, the first charge had been sounded. She passed along unknown streets, over dusty littery ways, between long rows of fronts not enhanced by the August light ; she felt good for miles

and only wanted to get lost ; there were moments at
corners, where she stopped and chose her direction,
in which she quite lived up to his injunction to rejoice
that she was active. It was like a new pleasure to
have so new a reason ; she would affirm without
delay her option, her volition ; taking this personal
possession of what surrounded her was a fair affirmation to start with ; and she really didn't care if she
made it at the cost of alarms for Susie. Susie would
wonder in due course " whatever," as they said at the
hotel, had become of her ; yet this would be nothing
either, probably, to wonderments still in store.
Wonderments in truth, Milly felt, even now attended
her steps : it was quite as if she saw in people's eyes
the reflexion of her appearance and pace. She found
herself moving at times in regions visibly not haunted
by odd-looking girls from New York, duskily draped,
sable-plumed, all but incongruously shod and gazing
about them with extravagance ; she might, from the
curiosity she clearly excited in by-ways, in side-
streets peopled with grimy children and costermongers'
carts, which she hoped were slums, literally have had
her musket on her shoulder, have announced herself as
freshly on the war-path. But for the fear of over-
doing the character she would here and there have
begun conversation, have asked her way ; in spite of
the fact that, as this would help the requirements of
adventure, her way was exactly what she wanted not
to know. The difficulty was that she at last accident-
ally found it ; she had come out, she presently saw, at
the Regent's Park, round which on two or three
occasions with Kate Croy her public chariot had
solemnly rolled. But she went into it further now ;
this was the real thing ; the real thing was to be quite
away from the pompous roads, well within the centre
and on the stretches of shabby grass. Here were
benches and smutty sheep ; here were idle lads at

games of ball, with their cries mild in the thick air ; here were wanderers anxious and tired like herself ; here doubtless were hundreds of others just in the same box. Their box, their great common anxiety, what was it, in this grim breathing-space, but the practical question of life ? They could live if they would ; that is, like herself, they had been told so : she saw them all about her, on seats, digesting the information, recognising it again as something in a slightly different shape familiar enough, the blessed old truth that they would live if they could. All she thus shared with them made her wish to sit in their company ; which she so far did that she looked for a bench that was empty, eschewing a still emptier chair that she saw hard by, and for which she would have paid, with superiority, a fee.

The last scrap of superiority had soon enough left her, if only because she before long knew herself for more tired than she had proposed. This and the charm, after a fashion, of the situation in itself made her linger and rest ; there was an accepted spell in the sense that nobody in the world knew where she was. It was the first time in her life that this had happened ; somebody, everybody appeared to have known before, at every instant of it, where she was ; so that she was now suddenly able to put it to herself that that hadn't been a life. This present kind of thing therefore might be—which was where precisely her distinguished friend seemed to be wishing her to come out. He wished her also, it was true, not to make, as she was perhaps doing now, too much of her isolation ; at the same time, however, as he clearly desired to deny her no decent source of interest. He was interested—she arrived at that—in her appealing to as many sources as possible ; and it fairly filtered into her, as she sat and sat, that he was essentially propping her up. Had she been doing it herself she would

have called it bolstering—the bolstering that was
simply for the weak ; and she thought and thought as
she put together the proofs that it was as one of the
weak he was treating her.   It was of course as one of
the weak that she had gone to him—but oh with how
sneaking a hope that he might pronounce her, as to
all indispensables, a veritable young lioness !   What
indeed she was really confronted with was the consciousness that he hadn't after all pronounced her
anything : she nursed herself into the sense that he
had beautifully got out of it.   Did he think, however,
she wondered, that he could keep out of it to the end ?
—though as she weighed the question she yet felt it
a little unjust.   Milly weighed, in this extraordinary
hour, questions numerous and strange ; but she had
happily, before she moved, worked round to a simplification.   Stranger than anything for instance was the
effect of its rolling over her that, when one considered
it, he might perhaps have " got out " by one door but
to come in with a beautiful beneficent dishonesty by
another.   It kept her more intensely motionless there
that what he might fundamentally be " up to " was
some disguised intention of standing by her as a
friend.   Wasn't that what women always said they
wanted to do when they deprecated the addresses of
gentlemen they couldn't more intimately go on with ?
It was what they, no doubt, sincerely fancied they
could make of men of whom they couldn't make
husbands.   And she didn't even reason that it was
by a similar law the expedient of doctors in general
for the invalids of whom they couldn't make patients :
she was somehow so sufficiently aware that *her* doctor
was—however fatuous it might sound—exceptionally
moved   This was the damning little fact—if she
could talk of damnation : that she could believe
herself to have caught him in the act of irrelevantly
liking her.   She hadn't gone to him to be liked, she

had gone to him to be judged ; and he was quite a great enough man to be in the habit, as a rule, of observing the difference. She could like *him*, as she distinctly did—that was another matter ; all the more that her doing so was now, so obviously for herself, compatible with judgement. Yet it would have been all portentously mixed had not, as we say, a final and merciful wave, chilling rather, but washing clear, come to her assistance.

It came of a sudden when all other thought was spent. She had been asking herself why, if her case was grave—and she knew what she meant by that— he should have talked to her at all about what she might with futility " do " ; or why on the other hand, if it were light, he should attach an importance to the office of friendship. She had him, with her little lonely acuteness—as acuteness went during the dog-days in the Regent's Park—in a cleft stick : she either mattered, and then she was ill ; or she didn't matter, and then she was well enough. Now he was " acting," as they said at home, as if she did matter—until he should prove the contrary. It was too evident that a person at his high pressure must keep his inconsist-encies, which were probably his highest amusements, only for the very greatest occasions. Her prevision, in fine, of just where she should catch him furnished the light of that judgement in which we describe her as daring to indulge. And the judgement it was that made her sensation simple. He *had* distinguished her —that was the chill. He hadn't known—how could he ?—that she was devilishly subtle, subtle exactly in the manner of the suspected, the suspicious, the condemned. He in fact confessed to it, in his way, as to an interest in her combinations, her funny race, her funny losses, her funny gains, her funny freedom, and, no doubt, above all, her funny manners—funny, like those of Americans at their best, without being vulgar, legitimating amiability and helping to pass it off. In his appreciation of these redundancies he dressed out for her the compassion he so signally permitted himself to waste ; but its operation for herself was as directly divesting, denuding, exposing. It reduced her to her ultimate state, which was that of a poor girl—with her rent to pay for example—staring before her in a great city. Milly had her rent to pay, her rent for her future ; everything else but how to meet it fell away from her in pieces, in tatters. This was the sensation the great man had doubtless not purposed. Well, she must go home, like the poor girl, and see. There might after all be ways ; the poor girl too would be thinking. It came back for that matter perhaps to views already presented. She looked about her again, on her feet, at her scattered melancholy comrades—some of them so melancholy as to be down on their stomachs in the grass, turned away, ignoring, burrowing ; she saw once more, with them, those two faces of the question between which there was so little to choose for inspiration. It was perhaps superficially more striking that one could live if one would ; but it was more appealing, insinuating, irresistible in short, that one would live if one could.

She found after this, for the day or two, more amusement than she had ventured to count on in the fact, if it were not a mere fancy, of deceiving Susie ; and she presently felt that what made the difference was the mere fancy—as this *was* one—of a countermove to her great man. His taking on himself— should he do so—to get at her companion made her suddenly, she held, irresponsible, made any notion of her own all right for her ; though indeed at the very moment she invited herself to enjoy this impunity she became aware of new matter for surprise, or at least for speculation. Her idea would rather have been that Mrs. Stringham would have looked at her hard

—her sketch of the grounds of her independent long
excursion showing, she could feel, as almost cynically
superficial. Yet the dear woman so failed, in the
event, to avail herself of any right of criticism that it
was sensibly tempting to wonder for an hour if Kate
Croy had been playing perfectly fair. Hadn't she
possibly, from motives of the highest benevolence,
promptings of the finest anxiety, just given poor Susie
what she would have called the straight tip ? It must
immediately be mentioned, however, that, quite apart
from a remembrance of the distinctness of Kate's
promise, Milly, the next thing, found her explanation
in a truth that had the merit of being general. If
Susie at this crisis suspiciously spared her, it was really
that Susie was always suspiciously sparing her—yet
occasionally too with portentous and exceptional
mercies. The girl was conscious of how she dropped
at times into inscrutable impenetrable deferences—
attitudes that, though without at all intending it,
made a difference for familiarity, for the ease of
intimacy. It was as if she recalled herself to manners,
to the law of court-etiquette—which last note above
all helped our young woman to a just appreciation.
It was definite for her, even if not quite solid, that
to treat her as a princess was a positive need of her
companion's mind ; wherefore she couldn't help it if
this lady had her transcendent view of the way the
class in question were treated. Susan had read
history, had read Gibbon and Froude and Saint-
Simon ; she had high lights as to the special allowances
made for the class, and, since she saw them, when
young, as effete and overtutored, inevitably ironic and
infinitely refined, one must take it for amusing if she
inclined to an indulgence verily Byzantine. If one
could only be Byzantine !—wasn't *that* what she insidiously led one on to sigh ? Milly tried to oblige
her—for it really placed Susan herself so handsomely

to be Byzantine now. The great ladies of that race
—it would be somewhere in Gibbon—were apparently
not questioned about their mysteries. But oh poor
Milly and hers ! Susan at all events proved scarce
more inquisitive than if she had been a mosaic at
Ravenna. Susan was a porcelain monument to the
odd moral that consideration might, like cynicism,
have abysses. Besides, the Puritan finally disencum-
bered——! What starved generations wasn't Mrs.
Stringham, in fancy, going to make up for ?

Kate Croy came straight to the hotel—came
that evening shortly before dinner ; specifically
and publicly moreover, in a hansom that, driven
apparently very fast, pulled up beneath their windows
almost with the clatter of an accident, a " smash."
Milly, alone, as happened, in the great garnished void
of their sitting-room, where, a little, really, like a caged
Byzantine, she had been pacing through the queer
long-drawn almost sinister delay of night, an effect
she yet liked—Milly, at the sound, one of the French
windows standing open, passed out to the balcony
that overhung, with pretensions, the general entrance,
and so was in time for the look that Kate, alighting,
paying her cabman, happened to send up to the front.
The visitor moreover had a shilling back to wait for,
during which Milly, from the balcony, looked down at
her, and a mute exchange, but with smiles and nods,
took place between them on what had occurred in the
morning. It was what Kate had called for, and the
tone was thus almost by accident determined for
Milly before her friend came up. What was also,
however, determined for her was, again, yet irre-
pressibly again, that the image presented to her, the
splendid young woman who looked so particularly
handsome in impatience, with the fine freedom of her
signal, was the peculiar property of somebody else's
vision, that this fine freedom in short was the fine

freedom she showed Mr. Densher. Just so was how she looked to him, and just so was how Milly was held by her—held as by the strange sense of seeing through that distant person's eyes. It lasted, as usual, the strange sense, but fifty seconds; yet in so lasting it produced an effect. It produced in fact more than one, and we take them in their order. The first was that it struck our young woman as absurd to say that a girl's looking so to a man could possibly be without connexions; and the second was that by the time Kate had got into the room Milly was in mental possession of the main connexion it must have for herself.

She produced this commodity on the spot—produced it in straight response to Kate's frank " Well, what ? " The inquiry bore of course, with Kate's eagerness, on the issue of the morning's scene, the great man's latest wisdom, and it doubtless affected Milly a little as the cheerful demand for news is apt to affect troubled spirits when news is not, in one of the neater forms, prepared for delivery. She couldn't have said what it was exactly that on the instant determined her; the nearest description of it would perhaps have been as the more vivid impression of all her friend took for granted. The contrast between this free quantity and the maze of possibilities through which, for hours, she had herself been picking her way, put on, in short, for the moment, a grossness that even friendly forms scarce lightened : it helped forward in fact the revelation to herself that she absolutely had nothing to tell. Besides which, certainly, there was something else—an influence at the particular juncture still more obscure. Kate had lost, on the way upstairs, the look—*the* look—that made her young hostess so subtly think and one of the signs of which was that she never kept it for many moments at once; yet she stood there, none the less, so in her

bloom and in her strength, so completely again the
" handsome girl " beyond all others, the " handsome
girl " for whom Milly had at first gratefully taken
her, that to meet her now with the note of the plaintive would amount somehow to a surrender, to a confession. *She* would never in her life be ill ; the
greatest doctor would keep her, at the worst, the fewest minutes ; and it was as if she had asked just *with*
all this practical impeccability for all that was most
mortal in her friend. These things, for Milly, in-
wardly danced their dance ; but the vibration produced and the dust kicked up had lasted less than our
account of them. Almost before she knew it she was
answering, and answering beautifully, with no consciousness of fraud, only as with a sudden flare of the
famous " will-power " she had heard about, read
about, and which was what her medical adviser had
mainly thrown her back on. " Oh it's all right. He's
lovely."

Kate was splendid, and it would have been clear
for Milly now, had the further presumption been
needed, that she had said no word to Mrs. Stringham.
" You mean you've been absurd ? "

" Absurd." It was a simple word to say, but the
consequence of it, for our young woman, was that
she felt it, as soon as spoken, to have done something
for her safety.

And Kate really hung on her lips. " There's
nothing at all the matter ? "

" Nothing to worry about. I shall need a little
watching, but I shan't have to do anything dreadful,
or even in the least inconvenient. I can do in fact as
I like." It was wonderful for Milly how just to put it
so made all its pieces fall at present quite properly into
their places.

Yet even before the full effect came Kate had
seized, kissed, blessed her. " My love, you're too

sweet! It's too dear! But it's as I was sure."
Then she grasped the full beauty. "You can do as
you like?"

"Quite. Isn't it charming?"

"Ah but catch you," Kate triumphed with gaiety,
"*not* doing——! And what *shall* you do?"

"For the moment simply enjoy it. Enjoy"—
Milly was completely luminous—"having got out of
my scrape."

"Learning, you mean, so easily, that you *are*
well?"

It was as if Kate had but too conveniently put the
words into her mouth. "Learning, I mean, so easily,
that I *am* well."

"Only no one's of course well enough to stay in
London now. He can't," Kate went on, "want this
of you."

"Mercy no—I'm to knock about. I'm to go to
places."

"But not beastly 'climates'—Engadines, Rivi-
eras, boredoms?"

"No; just, as I say, where I prefer. I'm to go in
for pleasure."

"Oh the duck!"—Kate, with her own shades of
familiarity, abounded. "But what kind of pleasure?"

"The highest," Milly smiled.

Her friend met it as nobly. "Which *is* the
highest?"

"Well, it's just our chance to find out. You must
help me."

"What have I wanted to do but help you," Kate
asked, "from the moment I first laid eyes on you?"
Yet with this too Kate had her wonder. "I like your
talking, though, about that. What help, with your
luck all round, do you need?"

V

Milly indeed at last couldn't say ; so that she had really for the time brought it along to the point so oddly marked for her by her visitor's arrival, the truth that she was enviably strong. She carried this out, from that evening, for each hour still left her, and the more easily perhaps that the hours were now narrowly numbered. All she actually waited for was Sir Luke Strett's promised visit ; as to her proceeding on which, however, her mind was quite made up. Since he wanted to get at Susie he should have the freest access, and then perhaps he would see how he liked it. What was between *them* they might settle as between them, and any pressure it should lift from her own spirit they were at liberty to convert to their use. If the dear man wished to fire Susan Shepherd with a still higher ideal, he would only after all, at the worst, have Susan on his hands. If devotion, in a word, was what it would come up for the interested pair to organise, she was herself ready to consume it as the dressed and served dish. He had talked to her of her "appetite," her account of which, she felt, must have been vague. But for devotion, she could now see, this appetite would be of the best. Gross, greedy, ravenous—these were doubtless the proper names for her : she was at all events resigned in advance to the machinations of sympathy. The day that followed her lonely excursion was to be the last

230

but two or three of their stay in London ; and the evening of that day practically ranked for them as, in the matter of outside relations, the last of all. People were by this time quite scattered, and many of those who had so liberally manifested in calls, in cards, in evident sincerity about visits, later on, over the land, had positively passed in music out of sight ; whether as members, these latter, more especially, of Mrs. Lowder's immediate circle or as members of Lord Mark's—our friends being by this time able to make the distinction. The general pitch had thus decidedly dropped, and the occasions still to be dealt with were special and few. One of these, for Milly, announced itself as the doctor's call already mentioned, as to which she had now had a note from him : the single other, of importance, was their appointed leave-taking—for the shortest separation—in respect to Mrs. Lowder and Kate. The aunt and the niece were to dine with them alone, intimately and easily —as easily as should be consistent with the question of their afterwards going on together to some absurdly belated party, at which they had had it from Aunt Maud that they would do well to show. Sir Luke was to make his appearance on the morrow of this, and in respect to that complication Milly had already her plan.

The night was at all events hot and stale, and it was late enough by the time the four ladies had been gathered in, for their small session, at the hotel, where the windows were still open to the high balconies and the flames of the candles, behind the pink shades— disposed as for the vigil of watchers—were motionless in the air in which the season lay dead. What was presently settled among them was that Milly, who betrayed on this occasion a preference more marked than usual, shouldn't hold herself obliged to climb that evening the social stair, however it

might stretch to meet her, and that, Mrs. Lowder and
Mrs. Stringham facing the ordeal together, Kate Croy
should remain with her and await their return. It
was a pleasure to Milly, ever, to send Susan Shepherd
forth ; she saw her go with complacency, liked, as
it were, to put people off with her, and noted with
satisfaction, when she so moved to the carriage, the
further denudation—a markedly ebbing tide—of her
little benevolent back. If it wasn't quite Aunt
Maud's ideal, moreover, to take out the new American girl's funny friend instead of the new American
girl herself, nothing could better indicate the range of
that lady's merit than the spirit in which—as at the
present hour for instance—she made the best of the
minor advantage. And she did this with a broad
cheerful absence of illusion ; she did it—confessing
even as much to poor Susie—because, frankly, she
was good-natured. When Mrs. Stringham observed
that her own light was too abjectly borrowed and that
it was as a link alone, fortunately not missing, that
she was valued, Aunt Maud concurred to the extent
of the remark : " Well, my dear, you're better than
nothing." To-night furthermore it came up for Milly
that Aunt Maud had something particular in mind.
Mrs. Stringham, before adjourning with her, had
gone off for some shawl or other accessory, and Kate,
as if a little impatient for their withdrawal, had wandered out to the balcony, where she hovered for the
time unseen, though with scarce more to look at than
the dim London stars and the cruder glow, up the
street, on a corner, of a small public-house in front of
which a fagged cab-horse was thrown into relief.
Mrs. Lowder made use of the moment ; Milly felt as
soon as she had spoken that what she was doing was
somehow for use.

" Dear Susan tells me that you saw in America Mr.
Densher—whom I've never till now, as you may

have noticed, asked you about. But do you mind at
last, in connexion with him, doing something for
me ? " She had lowered her fine voice to a depth,
though speaking with all her rich glibness ; and Milly,
after a small sharpness of surprise, was already guess-
ing the sense of her appeal. " Will you name him, in
any way you like, to *her* "—and Aunt Maud gave a
nod at the window ; " so that you may perhaps find
out whether he's back ? "

Ever so many things, for Milly, fell into line at
this ; it was a wonder, she afterwards thought, that
she could be conscious of so many at once. She smiled
hard, however, for them all. " But I don't know that
it's important to me to ' find out.' " The array of
things was further swollen, however, even as she said
this, by its striking her as too much to say. She therefore tried as quickly to say less. " Except you mean
of course that it's important to *you*." She fancied
Aunt Maud was looking at her almost as hard as she
was herself smiling, and that gave her another impulse. " You know I never *have* yet named him to
her ; so that if I should break out now——"

" Well ? "—Mrs. Lowder waited.

" Why she may wonder what I've been making
a mystery of. She hasn't mentioned him, you know,"
Milly went on, " herself."

" No "—her friend a little heavily weighed it—
" she wouldn't. So it's she, you see then, who has
made the mystery."

Yes, Milly but wanted to see ; only there was so
much. " There has been of course no particular
reason." Yet that indeed was neither here nor there.
" Do you think," she asked, " he *is* back ? "

" It will be about his time, I gather, and rather a
comfort to me definitely to know."

" Then can't you ask her yourself ? "

" Ah we never speak of him ! "

It helped Milly for the moment to the convenience of a puzzled pause. " Do you mean he's an acquaintance of whom you disapprove for her ? "

Aunt Maud, as well, just hung fire. " I disapprove of *her* for the poor young man. She doesn't care for him."

" And *he* cares so much——? "

" Too much, too much. And my fear is," said Mrs. Lowder, " that he privately besets her. She keeps it to herself, but I don't want her worried. Neither, in truth," she both generously and confidentially concluded, " do I want *him*."

Milly showed all her own effort to meet the case. " But what can *I* do ? "

" You can find out where they are. If I myself try," Mrs. Lowder explained, " I shall appear to treat them as if I supposed them deceiving me."

" And you don't. You don't," Milly mused for her, " suppose them deceiving you."

" Well," said Aunt Maud, whose fine onyx eyes failed to blink even though Milly's questions might have been taken as drawing her rather further than she had originally meant to · go—" well, Kate's thoroughly aware of my views for her, and that I take her being with me at present, in the way she *is* with me, if you know what I mean, for a loyal assent to them. Therefore as my views don't happen to provide a place at all for Mr. Densher, much, in a manner, as I like him "—therefore in short she had been prompted to this step, though she completed her sense, but sketchily, with the rattle of her large fan.

It assisted them for the moment perhaps, however, that Milly was able to pick out of her sense what might serve as the clearest part of it. " You do like him then ? "

" Oh dear yes. Don't you ? "

Milly waited, for the question was somehow as the sudden point of something sharp on a nerve that winced. She just caught her breath, but she had ground for joy afterwards, she felt, in not really having failed to choose with quickness sufficient, out of fifteen possible answers, the one that would best serve her. She was then almost proud, as well, that she had cheerfully smiled. "I did—three times—in New York." So came and went, in these simple words, the speech that was to figure for her, later on, that night, as the one she had ever uttered that cost her most. She was to lie awake for the gladness of not having taken any line so really inferior as the denial of a happy impression.

For Mrs. Lowder also moreover her simple words were the right ones ; they were at any rate, that lady's laugh showed, in the natural note of the racy. "You dear American thing ! But people may be very good and yet not good for what one wants."

"Yes," the girl assented, "even I suppose when what one wants is something very good."

"Oh my child, it would take too long just now to tell you all *I* want ! I want everything at once and together—and ever so much for you too, you know. But you've seen us," Aunt Maud continued ; "you'll have made out."

"Ah," said Milly, "I *don't* make out" ; for again —it came that way in rushes—she felt an obscurity in things. "Why, if our friend here doesn't like him—— "

"Should I conceive her interested in keeping things from me ? " Mrs. Lowder did justice to the question. "My dear, how can you ask ? Put yourself in her place. She meets me, but on *her* terms. Proud young women are proud young women. And proud old ones are—well, what *I* am. Fond of you as we both are, you can help us."

Milly tried to be inspired. " Does it come back then to my asking her straight ? "

At this, however, finally, Aunt Maud threw her up. " Oh if you've so many reasons not—— ! "

" I've not so many," Milly smiled—" but I've one. If I break out so suddenly on my knowing him, what will she make of my not having spoken before ? "

Mrs. Lowder looked blank at it. " Why should you care what she makes ? You may have only been decently discreet."

" Ah I *have* been," the girl made haste to say.

" Besides," her friend went on, " I suggested to you, through Susan, your line."

" Yes, that reason's a reason for *me*."

" And for *me*," Mrs. Lowder insisted. " She's not therefore so stupid as not to do justice to grounds so marked. You can tell her perfectly that I had asked you to say nothing."

" And may I tell her that you've asked me now to speak ? "

Mrs. Lowder might well have thought, yet, oddly, this pulled her up. " You can't do it without—— ? "

Milly was almost ashamed to be raising so many difficulties. " I'll do what I can if you'll kindly tell me one thing more." She faltered a little—it was so prying ; but she brought it out. " Will he have been writing to her ? "

" It's exactly, my dear, what I should like to know ! " Mrs. Lowder was at last impatient. " Push in for yourself and I daresay she'll tell you."

Even now, all the same, Milly had not quite fallen back. " It will be pushing in," she continued to smile, " for *you*." She allowed her companion, however, no time to take this up. " The point will be that if he *has* been writing she may have answered."

" But what point, you subtle thing, is that ? "

" It isn't subtle, it seems to me, but quite simple,"

236

Milly said, " that if she has answered she has very possibly spoken of me."

" Very certainly indeed. But what difference will it make ? "

The girl had a moment, at this, of thinking it natural Mrs. Lowder herself should so fail of subtlety. " It will make the difference that he'll have written her in reply that he knows me. And that, in turn," our young woman explained, " will give an oddity to my own silence."

" How so, if she's perfectly aware of having given you no opening ? The only oddity," Aunt Maud lucidly professed, " is for yourself. It's in *her* not having spoken."

" Ah there we are ! " said Milly.

And she had uttered it, evidently, in a tone that struck her friend. " Then it *has* troubled you ? "

But the inquiry had only to be made to bring the rare colour with fine inconsequence to her face. " Not really the least little bit ! " And, quickly feeling the need to abound in this sense, she was on the point, to cut short, of declaring that she cared, after all, no scrap how much she obliged. Only she felt at this instant too the intervention of still other things. Mrs. Lowder was in the first place already beforehand, already affected as by the sudden vision of her having herself pushed too far. Milly could never judge from her face of her uppermost motive—it was so little, in its hard smooth sheen, that kind of human countenance. She looked hard when she spoke fair ; the only thing was that when she spoke hard she didn't likewise look soft. Something, none the less, had arisen in her now—a full appreciable tide, entering by the rupture of some bar. She announced that if what she had asked was to prove in the least a bore her young friend was not to dream of it ; making her young friend at the same time, by the change in her tone,

recoiling on herself. Directness, however evaded, would be, fully, for *her*; nothing in fact would ever have been for her so direct as the evasion. Kate had remained in the window, very handsome and upright, the outer dark framing in a highly favourable way her summery simplicities and lightnesses of dress. Milly had, given the relation of space, no real fear she had heard their talk; only she hovered there as with conscious eyes and some added advantage. Then indeed, with small delay, her friend sufficiently saw. The conscious eyes, the added advantage were but those she had now always at command—those proper to the person Milly knew as known to Merton Densher. It was for several seconds again as if the *total* of her identity had been that of the person known to him—a determination having for result another sharpness of its own. Kate had positively but to be there just as she was to tell her he had come back. It seemed to pass between them in fine without a word that he was in London, that he was perhaps only round the corner; and surely therefore no dealing of Milly's with her would yet have been so direct.

VI

It was doubtless because this queer form of directness had in itself, for the hour, seemed so sufficient
that Milly was afterwards aware of having really, all
the while—during the strange indescribable session
before the return of their companions—done nothing
to intensify it. If she was most aware only afterwards, under the long and discurtained ordeal of the
morrow's dawn, that was because she had really, till
their evening's end came, ceased after a little to miss
anything from their ostensible comfort. What was
behind showed but in gleams and glimpses ; what was
in front never at all confessed to not holding the stage.
Three minutes hadn't passed before Milly quite knew
she should have done nothing Aunt Maud had just
asked her. She knew it moreover by much the same
light that had acted for her with that lady and with
Sir Luke Strett. It pressed upon her then and there
that she was still in a current determined, through
her indifference, timidity, bravery, generosity—she
scarce could say which—by others ; that not she
but the current acted, and that somebody else always
was the keeper of the lock or the dam. Kate for
example had but to open the flood-gate : the current
moved in its mass—the current, as it had been, of her
doing as Kate wanted. What, somehow, in the most
extraordinary way in the world, *had* Kate wanted
but to be, of a sudden, more interesting than she had

THE WINGS OF THE DOVE

ever been ?   Milly, for their evening then, quite held
her breath with the appreciation of it.   If she hadn't
been sure her companion would have had nothing,
from her moments with Mrs. Lowder, to go by, she
would almost have seen the admirable creature
" cutting in " to anticipate a danger.   This fantasy
indeed, while they sat together, dropped after a little ;
even if only because other fantasies multiplied and
clustered, making fairly, for our young woman, the
buoyant medium in which her friend talked and
moved.   They sat together, I say, but Kate moved as
much as she talked ; she figured there, restless and
charming, just perhaps a shade perfunctory, repeatedly
quitting her place, taking slowly, to and fro, in the
trailing folds of her light dress, the length of the room
—almost avowedly performing for the pleasure of
her hostess.

Mrs. Lowder had said to Milly at Matcham that
she and her niece, as allies, could practically conquer
the world ; but though it was a speech about which
there had even then been a vague grand glamour the
girl read into it at present more of an approach to a
meaning.   Kate, for that matter, by herself, could
conquer anything, and *she*, Milly Theale, was probably concerned with the " world " only as the small
scrap of it that most impinged on her and that was
therefore first to be dealt with.   On this basis of being
dealt with she would doubtless herself do her share of
the conquering : she would have something to supply,
Kate something to take—each of them thus, to that
tune, something for squaring with Aunt Maud's ideal.
This in short was what it came to now—that the
occasion, in the quiet late lamplight, had the quality
of a rough rehearsal of the possible big drama.   Milly
knew herself dealt with—handsomely, completely :
she surrendered to the knowledge, for so it was, she
felt, that she supplied her helpful force.   And what

242

Kate had to take Kate took as freely and to all appearance as gratefully ; accepting afresh, with each of her long, slow walks, the relation between them so established and consecrating her companion's surrender simply by the interest she gave it. The interest to Milly herself we naturally mean ; the interest to Kate Milly felt as probably inferior. It easily and largely came for their present talk, for the quick flight of the hour before the breach of the spell—it all came, when considered, from the circumstance, not in the least abnormal, that the handsome girl was in extraordinary " form." Milly remembered her having said that she was at her best late at night ; remembered it by its having, with its fine assurance, made her wonder when *she* was at her best and how happy people must be who had such a fixed time. She had no time at all ; she was never at her best—unless indeed it were exactly, as now, in listening, watching, admiring, collapsing. If Kate moreover, quite mercilessly, had never been so good, the beauty and the marvel of it was that she had never really been so frank : being a person of such a calibre, as Milly would have said, that, even while " dealing " with you and thereby, as it were, picking her steps, she could let herself go, could, in irony, in confidence, in extravagance, tell you things she had never told before. That was the impression—that she was telling things, and quite conceivably for her own relief as well ; almost as if the errors of vision, the mistakes of proportion, the residuary innocence of spirit still to be remedied on the part of her auditor, had their moments of proving too much for her nerves. She went at them just now, these sources of irritation, with an amused energy that it would have been open to Milly to regard as cynical and that was nevertheless called for—as to this the other was distinct—by the way that in certain connexions the

American mind broke down. It seemed at least—the American mind as sitting there thrilled and dazzled in Milly—not to understand English society without a separate confrontation with *all* the cases. It couldn't proceed by—there was some technical term she lacked until Milly suggested both analogy and induction, and then, differently, instinct, none of which were right : it had to be led up and introduced to each aspect of the monster, enabled to walk all round it, whether for the consequent exaggerated ecstasy or for the still more (as appeared to this critic) disproportionate shock. It might, the monster, Kate conceded, loom large for those born amid forms less developed and therefore no doubt less amusing ; it might on some sides be a strange and dreadful monster, calculated to devour the unwary, to abase the proud, to scandalise the good ; but if one had to live with it one must, not to be for ever sitting up, learn how : which was virtually in short to-night what the handsome girl showed herself as teaching.

She gave away publicly, in this process, Lancaster Gate and everything it contained ; she gave away, hand over hand, Milly's thrill continued to note, Aunt Maud and Aunt Maud's glories and Aunt Maud's complacencies ; she gave herself away most of all, and it was naturally what most contributed to her candour. She didn't speak to her friend once more, in Aunt Maud's strain, of how they could scale the skies ; she spoke, by her bright perverse preference on this occasion, of the need, in the first place, of being neither stupid nor vulgar. It might have been a lesson, for our young American, in the art of seeing things as they were—a lesson so various and so sustained that the pupil had, as we have shown, but receptively to gape. The odd thing furthermore was that it could serve its purpose while explicitly disavowing every personal bias. It wasn't that she disliked Aunt Maud, who was everything she had on other occasions declared ; but the dear woman, ineffaceably stamped by inscrutable nature and a dreadful art, wasn't—how *could* she be ?—what she wasn't. She wasn't any one. She wasn't anything. She wasn't anywhere. Milly mustn't think it—one couldn't, as a good friend, let her. Those hours at Matcham were *inespérées*, were pure manna from heaven ; or if not wholly that perhaps, with humbugging old Lord Mark as a backer, were vain as a ground for hopes and calculations. Lord Mark was very well, but he wasn't *the* cleverest creature in England, and even if he had been he still wouldn't have been the most obliging. He weighed it out in ounces, and indeed each of the pair was really waiting for what the other would put down.

" She has put down *you*," said Milly, attached to the subject still ; " and I think what you mean is that, on the counter, she still keeps hold of you."

" Lest "—Kate took it up—" he should suddenly grab me and run ? Oh as he isn't ready to run he's much less ready, naturally, to grab. I *am*—you're so far right as that—on the counter, when I'm not in the shop-window ; in and out of which I'm thus conveniently, commercially whisked : the essence, all of it, of my position, and the price, as properly, of my aunt's protection." Lord Mark was substantially what she had begun with as soon as they were alone ; the impression was even yet with Milly of her having sounded his name, having imposed it, as a topic, in direct opposition to the other name that Mrs. Lowder had left in the air and that all her own look, as we have seen, kept there at first for her companion. The immediate strange effect had been that of her consciously needing, as it were, an *alibi*—which, successfully, she so found. She had worked it to the end, ridden it to and fro across the course marked for

Milly by Aunt Maud, and now she had quite, so to speak, broken it in. "The bore is that if she wants him so much—wants him, heaven forgive her! for *me*—he has put us all out, since your arrival, by wanting somebody else. I don't mean somebody else than you."

Milly threw off the charm sufficiently to shake her head. "Then I haven't made out who it is. If I'm any part of his alternative he had better stop where he is."

"Truly, truly?—always, always?"

Milly tried to insist with an equal gaiety. "Would you like me to swear?"

Kate appeared for a moment—though that was doubtless but gaiety too—to think. "Haven't we been swearing enough?"

"You have perhaps, but I haven't, and I ought to give you the equivalent. At any rate there it is. 'Truly, truly' as you say—'always, always.' So I'm not in the way."

"Thanks," said Kate—"but that doesn't help me."

"Oh it's as simplifying for *him* that I speak of it."

"The difficulty really is that he's a person with so many ideas that it's particularly hard to simplify for him. That's exactly of course what Aunt Maud has been trying. He won't," Kate firmly continued, "make up his mind about me."

"Well," Milly smiled, "give him time."

Her friend met it in perfection. "One's *doing* that—one *is*. But one remains all the same but one of his ideas."

"There's no harm in that," Milly returned, "if you come out in the end as the best of them. What's a man," she pursued, "especially an ambitious one, without a variety of ideas?"

"No doubt. The more the merrier." And Kate

looked at her grandly. "One can but hope to come out, and do nothing to prevent it."

All of which made for the impression, fantastic or not, of the *alibi*. The splendour, the grandeur were for Milly the bold ironic spirit behind it, so interesting too in itself. What, further, was not less interesting was the fact, as our young woman noted it, that Kate confined her point to the difficulties, so far as *she* was concerned, raised only by Lord Mark. She referred now to none that her own taste might present ; which circumstance again played its little part. She was doing what she liked in respect to another person, but she was in no way committed to the other person, and her moreover talking of Lord Mark as not young and not true were only the signs of her clear self-consciousness, were all in the line of her slightly hard but scarce the less graceful extravagance. She didn't wish to show too much her consent to be arranged for, but that was a different thing from not wishing sufficiently to give it. There was something on it all, as well, that Milly still found occasion to say. " If your aunt has been, as you tell me, put out by me, I feel she has remained remarkably kind."

" Oh but she has—whatever might have happened in that respect—plenty of use for you ! You put her in, my dear, more than you put her out. You don't half see it, but she has clutched your petticoat. You can do anything—you can do, I mean, lots that *we* can't. You're an outsider, independent and standing by yourself ; you're not hideously relative to tiers and tiers of others." And Kate, facing in that direction, went further and further ; wound up, while Milly gaped, with extraordinary words. " We're of no use to you—it's decent to tell you. You'd be of use to us, but that's a different matter. My honest advice to you would be "— she went indeed all lengths—" to drop us while you can. It would be funny if you didn't soon see how awfully better you can do. We've not really done for you the least thing worth speaking of—nothing you mightn't easily have had in some other way. Therefore you're under no obligation. You won't want us next year ; we shall only continue to want *you*. But that's no reason for you, and you mustn't pay too dreadfully for poor Mrs. Stringham's having let you in. She has the best conscience in the world ; she's enchanted with what she has done ; but you shouldn't take your people from *her*. It has been quite awful to see you do it."

Milly tried to be amused, so as not—it was too absurd—to be fairly frightened. Strange enough indeed—if not natural enough—that, late at night thus, in a mere mercenary house, with Susie away, a want of confidence should possess her. She recalled, with all the rest of it, the next day, piecing things together in the dawn, that she had felt herself alone with a creature who paced like a panther. That was a violent image, but it made her a little less ashamed of having been scared. For all her scare, none the less, she had now the sense to find words. " And yet without Susie I shouldn't have had *you*."

It had been at this point, however, that Kate flickered highest. " Oh you may very well loathe me yet ! "

Really at last, thus, it had been too much ; as, with her own least feeble flare, after a wondering watch, Milly had shown. She hadn't cared ; she had too much wanted to know ; and, though a small solemnity of remonstrance, a sombre strain, had broken into her tone, it was to figure as her nearest approach to serving Mrs. Lowder. " Why do you say such things to me ? "

This unexpectedly had acted, by a sudden turn of Kate's attitude, as a happy speech. She had risen as she spoke, and Kate had stopped before her, shining

at her instantly with a softer brightness. Poor Milly
hereby enjoyed one of her views of how people, winc-
ing oddly, were often touched by her. "Because
you're a dove." With which she felt herself ever
so delicately, so considerately, embraced; not with
familiarity or as a liberty taken, but almost ceremoni-
ally and in the manner of an *accolade*; partly as if,
though a dove who could perch on a finger, one were
also a princess with whom forms were to be observed.
It even came to her, through the touch of her companion's lips, that this form, this cool pressure, fairly
sealed the sense of what Kate had just said. It was
moreover, for the girl, like an inspiration : she found
herself accepting as the right one, while she caught her
breath with relief, the name so given her. She met it
on the instant as she would have met revealed truth ;
it lighted up the strange dusk in which she lately had
walked. *That* was what was the matter with her.
She was a dove. Oh *wasn't* she ?—it echoed within
her as she became aware of the sound, outside, of the
return of their friends. There was, the next thing,
little enough doubt about it after Aunt Maud had been
two minutes in the room. She had come up, Mrs.
Lowder, with Susan—which she needn't have done,
at that hour, instead of letting Kate come down to
her ; so that Milly could be quite sure it was to catch
hold, in some way, of the loose end they had left.
Well, the way she did catch was simply to make the
point that it didn't now in the least matter. She had
mounted the stairs for this, and she had her moment
again with her younger hostess while Kate, on the
spot, as the latter at the time noted, gave Susan Shepherd unwonted opportunities. Kate was in other
words, as Aunt Maud engaged her friend, listening
with the handsomest response to Mrs. Stringham's
impression of the scene they had just quitted. It was
in the tone of the fondest indulgence—almost, really,

that of dove cooing to dove — that Mrs. Lowder expressed to Milly the hope that it had all gone beautifully. Her " all " had an ample benevolence ; it soothed and simplified ; she spoke as if it were the two young women, not she and her comrade, who had been facing the town together. But Milly's answer had prepared itself while Aunt Maud was on the stair ; she had felt in a rush all the reasons that would make it the most dovelike ; and she gave it, while she was about it, as earnest, as candid. " I don't *think*, dear lady, he's here."

It gave her straightway the measure of the success she could have as a dove : that was recorded in the long look of deep criticism, a look without a word, that Mrs. Lowder poured forth. And the word, presently, bettered it still. " Oh you exquisite thing ! " The luscious innuendo of it, almost startling, lingered in the room, after the visitors had gone, like an oversweet fragrance. But left alone with Mrs. Stringham Milly continued to breathe it : she studied again the dovelike and so set her companion to mere rich reporting that she averted all inquiry into her own case.

That, with the new day, was once more her law— though she saw before her, of course, as something of a complication, her need, each time, to decide. She should have to be 'clear as to how a dove *would* act. She settled it, she thought, well enough this morning by quite readopting her plan in respect to Sir Luke Strett. That, she was pleased to reflect, had originally been pitched in the key of a merely iridescent drab ; and although Mrs. Stringham, after breakfast, began by staring at it as if it had been a priceless Persian carpet suddenly unrolled at her feet, she had no scruple, at the end of five minutes, in leaving her to make the best of it. " Sir Luke Strett comes, by appointment, to see me at eleven, but I'm going out on purpose. He's to be told, please, deceptively, that

I'm at home, and you, as my representative, when he comes up, are to see him instead. He'll like that, this time, better. So do be nice to him." It had taken, naturally, more explanation, and the mention, above all, of the fact that the visitor was the greatest of doctors ; yet when once the key had been offered Susie slipped it on her bunch, and her young friend could again feel her lovely imagination operate. It operated in truth very much as Mrs. Lowder's, at the last, had done the night before : it made the air heavy once more with the extravagance of assent. It might, afresh, almost have frightened our young woman to see how people rushed to meet her : *had* she then so little time to live that the road must always be spared her ? It was as if they were helping her to take it out on the spot. Susie—she couldn't deny, and didn't pretend to—might, of a truth, on *her* side, have treated such news as a flash merely lurid ; as to which, to do Susie justice, the pain of it was all there. But, none the less, the margin always allowed her young friend was all there as well ; and the proposal now made her—what was it in short but Byzantine ? The vision of Milly's perception of the propriety of the matter had, at any rate, quickly engulfed, so far as her attitude was concerned, any surprise and any shock ; so that she only desired, the next thing, perfectly to possess the facts. Milly could easily speak, on this, as if there were only one : she made nothing of such another as that she had felt herself menaced. The great fact, in fine, was that she *knew* him to desire just now, more than anything else, to meet, quite apart, some one interested in her. Who therefore so interested as her faithful Susan ? The only other circumstance that, by the time she had quitted her friend, she had treated as worth mentioning was the circumstance of her having at first intended to keep quiet. She had originally best seen herself as sweetly secretive. As to that she had changed, and her present request was the result. She didn't say why she had changed, but she trusted her faithful Susan. Their visitor would trust her not less, and she herself would adore their visitor. Moreover he wouldn't—the girl felt sure—tell her anything dreadful. The worst would be that he was in love and that he needed a confidant to work it. And now she was going to the National Gallery.

VII

THE idea of the National Gallery had been with her from the moment of her hearing from Sir Luke Strett about his hour of coming. It had been in her mind as a place so meagrely visited, as one of the places that had seemed at home one of the attractions of Europe and one of its highest aids to culture, but that —the old story—the typical frivolous always ended by sacrificing to vulgar pleasures. She had had perfectly, at those whimsical moments on the Brünig, the half-shamed sense of turning her back on such opportunities for real improvement as had figured to her, from of old, in connexion with the continental tour, under the general head of " pictures and things " ; and at last she knew for what she had done so. The plea had been explicit—she had done so for life as opposed to learning ; the upshot of which had been that life was now beautifully provided for. In spite of those few dips and dashes into the many-coloured stream of history for which of late Kate Croy had helped her to find time, there were possible great chances she had neglected, possible great moments she should, save for to-day, have all but missed. She might still, she had felt, overtake one or two of them among the Titians and the Turners ; she had been honestly nursing the hour, and, once she was in the benignant halls, her faith knew itself justified. It was the air she wanted and the world she would now

exclusively choose ; the quiet chambers, nobly overwhelming, rich but slightly veiled, opened out round
her and made her presently say " If I could lose
myself *here* ! " There were people, people in plenty,
but, admirably, no personal question. It was immense, outside, the personal question ; but she had
blissfully left it outside, and the nearest it came, for
a quarter of an hour, to glimmering again into view
was when she watched for a little one of the more
earnest of the lady-copyists. Two or three in particular, spectacled, aproned, absorbed, engaged her
sympathy to an absurd extent, seemed to show her
for the time the right way to live. She should
have been a lady-copyist—it met so the case. The
case was the case of escape, of living under water, of
being at once impersonal and firm. There it was
before one—one had only to stick and stick.

Milly yielded to this charm till she was almost
ashamed ; she watched the lady-copyists till she found
herself wondering what would be thought by others
of a young woman, of adequate aspect, who should
appear to regard them as the pride of the place. She
would have liked to talk to them, to get, as it figured
to her, into their lives, and was deterred but by the
fact that she didn't quite see herself as purchasing
imitations and yet feared she might excite the expecta-
tion of purchase. She really knew before long that
what held her was the mere refuge, that something
within her was after all too weak for the Turners and
Titians. They joined hands about her in a circle too
vast, though a circle that a year before she would only
have desired to trace. They were truly for the larger,
not for the smaller life, the life of which the actual
pitch, for example, was an interest, the interest of
compassion, in misguided efforts. She marked
absurdly her little stations, blinking, in her shrinkage
of curiosity, at the glorious walls, yet keeping an eye

on vistas and approaches, so that she shouldn't be flagrantly caught. The vistas and approaches drew her in this way from room to room, and she had been through many parts of the show, as she supposed, when she sat down to rest. There were chairs in scant clusters, places from which one could gaze. Milly indeed at present fixed her eyes more than elsewhere on the appearance, first, that she couldn't quite, after all, have accounted to an examiner for the order of her " schools," and then on that of her being more tired than she had meant, in spite of her having been so much less intelligent. They found, her eyes, it should be added, other occupation as well, which she let them freely follow : they rested largely, in her vagueness, on the vagueness of other visitors ; they attached themselves in especial, with mixed results, to the surprising stream of her compatriots. She was struck with the circumstance that the great museum, early in August, was haunted with these pilgrims, as also with that of her knowing them from afar, marking them easily, each and all, and recognising not less promptly that they had ever new lights for her—new lights on their own darkness. She gave herself up at last, and it was a consummation like another : what she should have come to the National Gallery for to-day would be to watch the copyists and reckon the Baedekers. That perhaps was the moral of a menaced state of health—that one would sit in public places and count the Americans. It passed the time in a manner ; but it seemed already the second line of defence, and this notwithstanding the pattern, so unmistakable, of her country-folk. They were cut out as by scissors, coloured, labelled, mounted ; but their relation to her failed to act—they somehow did nothing for her. Partly, no doubt, they didn't so much as notice or know her, didn't even recognise their community of collapse with her, the sign on her, as

she sat there, that for her too Europe was " tough."
It came to her idly thus—for her humour could still
play—that she didn't seem then the same success
with them as with the inhabitants of London, who
had taken her up on scarce more of an acquaintance.
She could wonder if they would be different should
she go back with this glamour attached ; and she
could also wonder, if it came to that, whether she
should ever go back. Her friends straggled past, at
any rate, in all the vividness of their absent criticism,
and she had even at last the sense of taking a mean
advantage.

There was a finer instant, however, at which three
ladies, clearly a mother and daughters, had paused
before her under compulsion of a comment apparently
just uttered by one of them and referring to some
object on the other side of the room. Milly had her
back to the object, but her face very much to her
young compatriot, the one who had spoken and in
whose look she perceived a certain gloom of recognition. Recognition, for that matter, sat confessedly
in her own eyes : she *knew* the three, generically, as
easily as a school-boy with a crib in his lap would know
the answer in class ; she felt, like the school-boy,
guilty enough—questioned, as honour went, as to her
right so to possess, to dispossess, people who hadn't
consciously provoked her. She would have been able
to say where they lived, and also how, had the place
and the way been but amenable to the positive ; she
bent tenderly, in imagination, over marital, paternal
Mr. Whatever-he-was, at home, eternally named, with
all the honours and placidities, but eternally unseen •
and existing only as some one who could be financially
heard from. The mother, the puffed and composed
whiteness of whose hair had no relation to her apparent age, showed a countenance almost chemically
clean and dry ; her companions wore an air of vague

resentment humanised by fatigue ; and the three were equally adorned with short cloaks of coloured cloth surmounted by little tartan hoods. The tartans were doubtless conceivable as different, but the cloaks, curiously, only thinkable as one. " Handsome ? Well, if you choose to say so." It was the mother who had spoken, who herself added, after a pause during which Milly took the reference as to a picture : " In the English style." The three pair of eyes had converged, and their possessors had for an instant rested, with the effect of a drop of the subject, on this last characterisation—with that, too, of a gloom not less mute in one of the daughters than murmured in the other. Milly's heart went out to them while they turned their backs ; she said to herself that they ought to have known her, that there was something between them they might have beautifully put together. But she had lost *them* also—they were cold ; they left her in her weak wonder as to what they had been looking at. The " handsome " disposed her to turn—all the more that the " English style " would be the English school, which she liked ; only she saw, before moving, by the array on the side facing her, that she was in fact among small Dutch pictures. The action of this was again appreciable — the dim surmise that it wouldn't then be by a picture that the spring in the three ladies had been pressed. It was at all events time she should go, and she turned as she got on her feet. She had had behind her one of the entrances and various visitors who had come in while she sat, visitors single and in pairs—by one of the former of whom she felt her eyes suddenly held.

This was a gentleman in the middle of the place, a gentleman who had removed his hat and was for a moment, while he glanced, absently, as she could see, at the top tier of the collection, tapping his forehead with his pocket-handkerchief. The occupation held

him long enough to give Milly time to take for granted
—and a few seconds sufficed—that his face was the
object just observed by her friends. This could only
have been because she concurred in their tribute,
even qualified ; and indeed " the English style " of
the gentleman—perhaps by instant contrast to the
American—was what had had the arresting power.
This arresting power, at the same time—and that
was the marvel—had already sharpened almost to
pain, for in the very act of judging the bared head
with detachment she felt herself shaken by a knowledge of it. It was Merton Densher's own, and he
was standing there, standing long enough unconscious for her to fix him and then hesitate. These
successions were swift, so that she could still ask herself in freedom if she had best let him see her. She
could still reply to this that she shouldn't like him to
catch her in the effort to prevent it ; and she might
further have decided that he was too preoccupied to
see anything had not a perception intervened that
surpassed the first in violence. She was unable to
think afterwards how long she had looked at him
before knowing herself as otherwise looked at ; all she
was coherently to put together was that she had had
a second recognition without his having noticed her.
The source of this latter shock was nobody less than
Kate Croy—Kate Croy who was suddenly also in
the line of vision and whose eyes met her eyes at their
next movement. Kate was but two yards off—Mr.
Densher wasn't alone. Kate's face specifically said
so, for after a stare as blank at first as Milly's it broke
into a far smile. That was what, wonderfully—in
addition to the marvel of their meeting—passed from
her for Milly ; the instant reduction to easy terms
of the fact of their being there, the two young women,
together. It was perhaps only afterwards that the
girl fully felt the connexion between this touch and

her already established conviction that Kate was a prodigious person ; yet on the spot she none the less, in a degree, knew herself handled and again, as she had been the night before, dealt with—absolutely even dealt with for her greater pleasure. A minute in fine hadn't elapsed before Kate had somehow made her provisionally take everything as natural. The provisional was just the charm—acquiring that character from one moment to the other ; it represented happily so much that Kate would explain on the very first chance. This left moreover—and that was the greatest wonder—all due margin for amusement at the way things happened, the monstrous oddity of their turning up in such a place on the very heels of their having separated without allusion to it. The handsome girl was thus literally in control of the scene by the time Merton Densher was ready to exclaim with a high flush or a vivid blush—one didn't distinguish the embarrassment from the joy—" Why Miss Theale : fancy ! " and " Why Miss Theale : what luck ! "

Miss Theale had meanwhile the sense that for him too, on Kate's part, something wonderful and unspoken was determinant ; and this although, distinctly, his companion had no more looked at him with a hint than he had looked at her with a question. He had looked and was looking only at Milly herself, ever so pleasantly and considerately—she scarce knew what to call it ; but without prejudice to her consciousness, all the same, that women got out of predicaments better than men. The predicament of course wasn't definite nor phraseable—and the way they let all phrasing pass was presently to recur to our young woman as a characteristic triumph of the civilised state ; but she took it for granted, insistently, with a small private flare of passion, because the one thing she could think of to do for him was to show him how she eased him off. She would really, tired and nervous, have been much disconcerted if the opportunity in question hadn't saved her. It was what had saved her most, what had made her, after the first few seconds, almost as brave for Kate as Kate was for her, had made her only ask herself what their friend would like of her. That he was at the end of three minutes, without the least complicated refer- ence, so smoothly "their" friend was just the effect of their all being sublimely civilised. The flash in which he saw this was, for Milly, fairly inspiring—to that degree in fact that she was even now, on such a plane, yearning to be supreme. It took, no doubt, a big dose of inspiration to treat as not funny—or at least as not unpleasant—the anomaly, for Kate, that *she* knew their gentleman, and for herself, that Kate was spending the morning with him ; but everything continued to make for this after Milly had tasted of her draught. She was to wonder in subsequent reflexion what in the world they had actually said, since they had made such a success of what they didn't say ; the sweetness of the draught for the time, at any rate, was to feel success assured. What depended on this for Mr. Densher was all obscurity to her, and she perhaps but invented the image of his need as a short cut to accommodation. Whatever the facts, their perfect manners, all round, saw them through. The finest part of Milly's own inspiration, it may further be mentioned, was the quick perception that what would be of most service was, so to speak, her own native wood-note. She had long been con- scious with shame for her thin blood, or at least for her poor economy, of her unused margin as an Ameri- can girl—closely indeed as in English air the text might appear to cover the page. She still had reserves of spontaneity, if not of comicality ; so that all this cash in hand could now find employment. She became as spontaneous as possible and as American as it might conveniently appeal to Mr. Densher, after his travels, to find her. She said things in the air, and yet flattered herself that she struck him as saying them not in the tone of agitation but in the tone of New York. In the tone of New York agitation was beautifully discounted, and she had now a sufficient view of how much it might accordingly help her.

The help was fairly rendered before they left the place ; when her friends presently accepted her invitation to adjourn with her to luncheon at her hotel it was in Fifth Avenue that the meal might have waited. Kate had never been there so straight, but Milly was at present taking her ; and if Mr. Densher had been he had at least never had to come so fast. She proposed it as the natural thing—proposed it as the American girl ; and she saw herself quickly justified by the pace at which she was followed. The beauty of the case was that to do it all she had only to appear to take Kate's hint. This had said in its fine first smile " Oh yes, our look's queer—but give me time " ; and the American girl could give time as nobody else could. What Milly thus gave she therefore made them take—even if, as they might surmise, it was rather more than they wanted. In the porch of the museum she expressed her preference for a four-wheeler ; they would take their course in that guise precisely to multiply the minutes. She was more than ever justified by the positive charm that her spirit imparted even to their use of this conveyance ; and she touched her highest point—that is certainly for herself—as she ushered her companions into the presence of Susie. Susie was there with luncheon as well as with her return in prospect ; and nothing could now have filled her own consciousness more to the brim than to see this good friend take in how little she was abjectly anxious. The cup itself actually offered

THE WINGS OF THE DOVE

to this good friend might in truth well be startling, for it was composed beyond question of ingredients oddly mixed. She caught Susie fairly looking at her as if to know whether she had brought in guests to hear Sir Luke Strett's report. Well, it was better her companion should have too much than too little to wonder about ; she had come out " anyway," as they said at home, for the interest of the thing ; and interest truly sat in her eyes. Milly was none the less, at the sharpest crisis, a little sorry for her ; she could of necessity extract from the odd scene so comparatively little of a soothing secret. She saw Mr. Densher suddenly popping up, but she saw nothing else that had happened. She saw in the same way her young friend indifferent to her young friend's doom, and she lacked what would explain it. The only thing to keep her in patience was the way, after luncheon, Kate almost, as might be said, made up to her. This was actually perhaps as well what most kept Milly herself in patience. It had in fact for our young woman a positive beauty—was so marked as a deviation from the handsome girl's previous courses. Susie had been a bore to the handsome girl, and the change was now suggestive. The two sat together, after they had risen from table, in the apartment in which they had lunched, making it thus easy for the other guest and his entertainer to sit in the room adjacent. This, for the latter personage, was the beauty ; it was almost, on Kate's part, like a prayer to be relieved. If she honestly liked better to be " thrown with " Susan Shepherd than with their other friend, why that said practically everything. It didn't perhaps altogether say why she had gone out with him for the morning, but it said, as one thought, about as much as she could say to his face.

Little by little indeed, under the vividness of Kate's behaviour, the probabilities fell back into their order.

Merton Densher was in love and Kate couldn't help it—could only be sorry and kind : wouldn't that, without wild flurries, cover everything ?   Milly at all events tried it as a cover, tried it hard, for the time ; pulled it over her, in the front, the larger room, drew it up to her chin with energy.   If it didn't, so treated, do everything for her, it did so much that she could herself supply the rest.   She made that up by the interest of her great question, the question of whether, seeing him once more, with all that, as she called it to herself, had come and gone, her impression of him would be different from the impression received in New York.   That had held her from the moment of their leaving the museum ; it kept her company through their drive and during luncheon ; and now that she was a quarter of an hour alone with him it became acute.   She was to feel at this crisis that no clear, no common answer, no direct satisfaction on this point, was to reach her ; she was to see her question itself simply go to pieces.   She couldn't tell if he were different or not, and she didn't know nor care if *she* were : these things had ceased to matter in the light of the only thing she did know.   This was that she liked him, as she put it to herself, as much as ever ; and if that were to amount to liking a new person the amusement would be but the greater.   She had thought him at first very quiet, in spite of his recovery from his original confusion ; though even the shade of bewilderment, she yet perceived, had not been due to such vagueness on the subject of her reintensified identity as the probable sight, over there, of many thousands of her kind would sufficiently have justified. No, he was quiet, inevitably, for the first half of the time, because Milly's own lively line—the line of spontaneity—made everything else relative ; and because too, so far as Kate was spontaneous, it was ever so finely in the air among them that the normal

263

pitch must be kept. Afterwards, when they had got a little more used, as it were, to each other's separate felicity, he had begun to talk more, clearly bethinking himself at a given moment of what *his* natural lively line would be. It would be to take for granted she must wish to hear of the States, and to give her in its order everything he had seen and done there. He abounded, of a sudden—he almost insisted ; he returned, after breaks, to the charge ; and the effect was perhaps the more odd as he gave no clue whatever to what he had admired, as he went, or to what he hadn't. He simply drenched her with his sociable story—especially during the time they were away from the others. She had stopped then being American—all to let him be English ; a permission of which he, took, she could feel, both immense and unconscious advantage. She had really never cared less for the States than at this moment ; but that had nothing to do with the matter. It would have been the occasion of her life to learn about them, for nothing could put him off, and he ventured on no reference to what had happened for herself. It might have been almost as if he had known that the greatest of all these adventures was her doing just what she did then.

It was at this point that she saw the smash of her great question complete, saw that all she had to do with was the sense of being there with him. And there was no chill for this in what she also presently saw—that, however he had begun, he was now acting from a particular desire, determined either by new facts or new fancies, to be like every one else, simplifyingly " kind " to her. He had caught on already as to manner—fallen into line with every one else ; and if his spirits verily *had* gone up it might well be that he had thus felt himself lighting on the remedy for all awkwardness. Whatever he did or he didn't Milly knew she should still like him—there was no alternative to that ; but her heart could none the less sink a little on feeling how much his view of her was destined to have in common with—as she now sighed over it—*the* view. She could have dreamed of his not having *the* view, of his having something or other, if need be quite viewless, of his own ; but he might have what he could with least trouble, and *the* view wouldn't be after all a positive bar to her seeing him. The defect of it in general—if she might so ungraciously criticise—was that, by its sweet universality, it made relations rather prosaically a matter of course. It anticipated and superseded the—likewise sweet—operation of real affinities. It was this that was doubtless marked in her power to keep him now —this and her glassy lustre of attention to his pleasantness about the scenery in the Rockies. She was in truth a little measuring her success in detaining him by Kate's success in " standing " Susan. It wouldn't be, if she could help it, Mr. Densher who should first break down. Such at least was one of the forms of the girl's inward tension ; but beneath even this deep reason was a motive still finer. What she had left at home on going out to give it a chance was meanwhile still, was more sharply and actively, there. What had been at the top of her mind about it and then been violently pushed down—this quantity was again working up. As soon as their friends should go Susie would break out, and what she would break out upon wouldn't be—interested in that gentleman as she had more than once shown herself—the personal fact of Mr. Densher. Milly had found in her face at luncheon a feverish glitter, and it told what she was full of. She didn't care now for Mr. Densher's personal facts. Mr. Densher had risen before her only to find his proper place in her imagination already of a sudden occupied. His personal fact failed, so far as she was concerned, to *be* personal, and her companion noticed the failure. This could only mean that she was full to the brim of Sir Luke Strett and of what she had had from him. What *had* she had from him ? It was indeed now working upward again that Milly would do well to know, though knowledge looked stiff in the light of Susie's glitter. It was therefore on the whole because Densher's young hostess was divided from it by so thin a partition that she continued to cling to the Rockies.

END OF VOL. I

Printed in Great Britain by R. & R. Clark, Limited, *Edinburgh.*

Художественное издание

Henry James

The Wings Of The Dove

Редактор: *А. Корелина*
Ведущий редактор: *В. Алимурадова*
Выпускающий редактор: *Д. Серегина*
Компьютерная верстка: *Д. Пермяков*
Корректор: *О. Лебедева*
Художественное оформление: *П. Воронина*

В оформлении использованы материалы
по лицензии агентства *Shutterstock.com*

Проект осуществлён с помощью технологий
print on demand

*Знак информационной продукции согласно
Федеральному закону от 29.12.2010 г. № 436-ФЗ*

Подписано в печать 10.01.2017.
Формат 60x90/16
Усл. печ. л. 18.25

Отпечатано: АО «Т8 Издательские Технологии»
109548, г. Москва, Волгоградский проспект, дом 42, корпус 5
www.t8print.ru; info@t8print.ru
Тел.: +7 (499) 322-38-30

Lightning Source UK Ltd.
Milton Keynes UK
UKHW010755090221
378486UK00001B/62